Lycan Secrets

Laura Prior

Laura Prior

The Falling series

Falling for an Angel

Beware the Wolf

Death by Demon

Valkyrie in Training

Lycan Secrets

Laura Prior

Laura Prior

Laura Prior

Laura Prior

Dedication

Dedicated to my wonderful Simon, for putting up with my craziness while writing the fifth book in the *Falling* series.

I'd like to thank my editor Lauren McKellar for working your magic over my writing and for the hilarious comments that keep me going. To Sheree and Tanya for your unwavering support and enthusiasm for planning plot twists late at night. Thanks to Kyle for making the beautiful covers for the *Falling* books.

I'd like to say a huge thank you to all of my fans and readers of the *Falling* series. I am only able to continue writing because you are buying my books. I hope you have fallen in love with the characters as much as I have. Please continue to show your support by buying the books and recommending them to everyone you know who could use a bit of love and lust in their life.

Laura Prior

Laura Prior

1

"Good girls do bad things sometimes."

Unknown.

The air was unseasonably warm, despite the damp. I could feel the heat emanating from somewhere up ahead. Beads of sweat formed on my skin and began to trickle down my body, clinging on to every hair, pooling in every hollow. I shifted uncomfortably. Sweat had made my T-shirt cling to my body and I plucked it away from my skin, earnestly seeking some relief. There was none to be had. Instead, I gained an odd feeling, the feeling of intense eyes resting on me. Was someone watching me?

I swung around to face to bushes behind. I heard only the whispering of the leaves, the sighing of the branches as they swayed high above me. The shadows stayed still, pensive, as if holding their breath.

Not realizing I had already gone into defense mode, I unclenched my fists and let my frown ease. I was being paranoid; there was nothing there. There was no one watching.

Turning back around, I continued to march in the direction that pulled at me. There was something calling me with intensity; no, an urgency. The need within me to follow it had blossomed into an ache that couldn't be denied. The strange thing was that I didn't even care. Apparently, I didn't mind in the slightest that someone or something was pulling me in an unknown direction, towards another unknown destiny. And wasn't that ironic? The plot lines of my already peculiar life were changing as quickly as I could figure them out. As soon as I thought I knew which way was up, an unseen hand came along and turned it upside-down. .

Right now, I couldn't seem to drag up enough care factor to be bothered about the obvious compulsion I was feeling. I guess I had learned how to land on my feet; I'd figured out that nothing was under my control. I could do nothing by fighting my fate. I would just have to accept whatever was thrown in my path. Going to sleep in my bed beside my lover, then waking up and walking through an unknown forest with not a care in the world was just the latest in a long line of odd things to happen to me.

I marched steadily onwards only to freeze in my tracks. A high-pitched scream rang out, echoing again and again, each time more pitiful and agonizing than the last. When my heart finally began to beat again, I ran. With terror and anguish at the forefront of my mind, I sprinted through the trees towards what I thought was the origin of the scream. My mind was blank, no plans yet formed. The list of enemies that usually clicked through my brain was nowhere to be found. Anyone could be ahead, and today I didn't care.

I regained my common sense after a few minutes. I would be of no help to anyone if I ran straight into danger. I slowed to a jog and cautiously made my way closer to what every fiber in my body told me was my destination.

I inched closer, ducking behind a thick tree trunk when I heard a low rumble of voices. I placed my palms on the trunk before me and leaned close, trying to hear what was being said. I shook my head, thinking to clear my ears as the voices reached me low, guttural and completely muffled. I couldn't understand any of it. I knew what the cries meant though. I recognized the pained bellow, the scream for help, then the anguished sob when none came.

I peered around the tree, clinging so tightly the bark abraded my cheek and arms. I focused intently on the figures, trying to make them out. A group of maybe four or five tall males stood with their back to me. They spoke and laughed with each other, and every now and again one would step forward then retreat. What were they doing? Who were they?

I had to wait longer than I cared to before I found out. Just as I intended to creep across to the right, in the hopes I would get a better view point, they separated, leaving a clear visual path, showing rock rising up from the ground ahead of them.

A man was strung up before them against the rock-face. His arms and legs were spread wide, swords anchoring his flesh to the rock. Blood poured down the wall, leaving a red trail behind him as one at a time, his tormentors reached forward to slash at him. I could make out his shape, I could even tell that he was male but his features were smooth—he had no face. There was no way to identify him. Had his attackers somehow melted his face? My stomach heaved at the thought and I had to hold my abdomen, swallowing the bile that rolled up my throat.

I took a deep breath when I could, filling my lungs to bursting point. Hoping my courage wouldn't fail, I took a step away from the tree. They could see me any second; all it would take was one more step and any one of them could turn around and spot me.

My breath was wrenched away as I was brutally knocked to my back, a heavy weight pinning me to the uneven ground. My head spun and I tried to scream against the hand covering my mouth as loud beeping filled my ears. I bucked my hips, needing to dislodge the weight from my thighs. I scowled and roared out all my anger, however I remained flat against the ground. I rolled to my front and tried to crawl away, anger stirring at the lengths that I had to resort to to get this hulking great brute off of me.

I managed to scramble forward a few feet before I was flipped roughly onto my back. I grunted as my head smacked against the stones beneath me. I began to channel my power, my rage finally beginning to flare into a startlingly ball of heat. It was comforting to be able to feel the flames licking at my skin, singeing my hair and burning my clothes. The heat was delicious and I felt laughter bubble up inside me as red-hot euphoria began to take over, transforming me from a young, innocent Nephilim to an ancient valkyrie. The heat was so scorching it was . . . icy. Icy? I felt shivers running up my arms, cold, frosty trails inching their way towards my heart. My heat was failing, my flames receding. I was *losing*! A scream ripped through my throat but no sound emerged.

The beast straddling me leaned closer. "Be quiet and stop struggling and I'll release your body and your voice," a voice hissed.

I froze as I stared up at the mouth inches away from my own. The one that hadn't moved despite the words I heard whispered in my head.

I stopped struggling and was rewarded when he released one of my hands. Slowly, I lit a flame in the palm of my hand and held it up to light his face so I could see him in the darkness.

Expressive brown eyes gazed down at me, a look of bewilderment and anxiety on his face. Brown hair fell forward across his forehead, following the line of a scar that ran through his eyebrow and continued on through his cheek.

"Get off me!" I hissed through clenched teeth. Panic poured through me as I realized I still hadn't uttered a sound.

He shook his head emphatically. *I saw what you were about to do! You were going to run straight for them.* His voice rumbled through my head accusingly.

He must be talking telepathically, I thought. I was still infuriated and I began to wonder how to form the words in my mind before realizing he had already demonstrated he could hear what I was trying to say.

Someone is being tortured. I gasped silently. *You're just going to hide back here when that person is in agony? When they're screaming for help?*

He frowned fiercely. *And what would you have done exactly? You can't save him!*

I can try, I whispered angrily, *which is more than you're doing.*

How can you . . . you don't understand. He pulled back with a dawning comprehension.

I scrambled back, leaning up on my arms. *I don't understand what?*

He reached forward and grasped my chin between his thumb and fingers. *You're not here. They'll trap you here like us. You need to go back.*

"I am here," I replied. I reached up to touch my throat, relief coursing through me; he had released my voice. I knocked his hand aside. "I can touch you."

He shook his head. "You can't be. This is wrong. You're not meant to be here. You can't do anything to help because you're not meant to be here yet, but they will still be able to sense you. You're not here." He leaped back away from me and stood, towering over me. "If they notice you, there's nothing I can do to help you. Go."

I dragged myself to me feet and looked up at him. I began to understand what he was saying. This reality wasn't mine. It was a vision, like those I'd had of Zach. The same thick air surrounded me, the almost foggy atmosphere soothed my skin just as before. I wasn't here. It was a dream, a vision.

I took a few steps away from him reluctantly, letting the shadows take me.

"Wait," I hissed sharply. "Who are they?"

I heard a sigh. "The horsemen of the apocalypse. Now go!"

2

"Everyone sees what you appear to be, few experience what you really are."

Unknown.

With a gasp I shot upright in bed. I was shaking like a leaf. The hair on my arm stood up on end, tense and prickly nerves shooting through my scalp to run down my spine.

"What's wrong?" a gravelly voice murmured beside me.

I whipped my head around to narrow my eyes at the well-built, jaw-droppingly, heart-meltingly gorgeous man lying on my bed. Too hot, he had pushed the sheets off and was stretched out, completely naked.

My heart fluttered as a slow burn began to simmer low in my abdomen, my attention pulled away from the vision.

Zach . . . my Guardian angel, known as one of the most ferocious warriors of the Heavenly Realm was in my bed. He was mine, my soul mate, and trust me, if I could tattoo my name onto him right beside the thick swirling tattoos that ran down his body, I would.

He was a man made up of contradictions. He was an angry, raging soldier, a merciless killer, yet he had a wounded, tired soul that ached to be at peace. We could have the hottest most furious of rows, and then he would melt my heart with his soft, quiet words and actions. Despite the fact that his protectiveness could sometimes feel like smothering, he had proven he was worth every irritatingly arrogant look he gave me by saving my life countless times.

Besides his oddly endearing personality, my Zach was a lot of man to handle. Towering over me at six-and-a-half feet, his shaved head, eyebrow piercing and thickly-built body complete with muscle ropes *everywhere* sometimes made me think I was dreaming. It wasn't that I thought I was ugly; on the contrary! I had long, blonde hair and a flawless, if a little pale complexion, and gray-green eyes that only seemed to be getting greener. I was five foot six, with a pleasing hourglass figure. I was strong, a fierce fighter and talented at killing. No, it wasn't my looks that made me disbelieve my luck.

When I had thought I was a nephilim—half angel and half human, I could see the link between us, though even an angel and a nephilim together would raise a few eyebrows. However, as it turned out, I wasn't a nephilim at all. No, I was partly made up of the most reviled of beings and an absolute enemy of the angels—I was half fallen angel.

Thankfully the other half of my gene pool came from a valkyrie warrior. As the tale goes, the valkyrie were the Norse God, Odin's, soldiers. They collected the souls of warriors who died in glorious battle and delivered them to the Hall of the Gods where they dined with the Norse Gods until Ragnarok: the final battle . . . the apocalypse.

Everyone I knew seemed to describe it as *harvesting* the human souls, and that was just one of the reasons why the angels and valkyrie didn't get along. Angels preferred for all souls to be judged then taken to the Heavenly realm. They managed to take just about all of the human souls there... except the ones that the valkyrie *collected*.

Either way, my half fallen angel and half valkyrie self wasn't exactly loved in the nephilim safe house. Zach was firmly on my side of course, as were Sam and Gwen—both nephilim, and Trev—now some sort of vampire-nephilim. Haamiah led the angels, being the most senior angel class in the safe house, Elijah tolerated me, and Maion and his newly recovered soul mate, Zanaria, despised me. Seeing as how Zanaria had been decapitated by a nephilim, I used to be able to kind of see their point but *hello*—no longer a nephilim! Their hatred of me made life a little awkward. Maion was Zach's best friend and Zanaria was his sister.

I was still waiting for Zach to take off his rose-colored glasses and see me for what I was: a creature that shouldn't exist, formally a drug-addicted loser, who no one in his life particularly liked. He could definitely do better than me.

"Jasmine, what's up? Are you dreaming?"

My thoughts snapped right back on track. "Yes. No, it wasn't a dream. I think I had a vision."

Zach sat up immediately, his black eyes focused on me, his expression serious.

"Tell me," he demanded.

I shrugged. "It didn't really make a lot of sense. I was in this place . . . a wood, or a forest, I think. I could hear screaming, I could hear someone being tortured so I crept closer."

"Of course you did," he muttered.

I glared at him. "I hid behind a tree and watched; it wasn't as if I ran out into the open!" He didn't need to know that I'd almost done exactly that. "And remember, I'm seriously bad-ass now. I can handle myself."

He rolled his eyes in response and gestured impatiently for me to continue my story.

"Well, there were a bunch of creatures surrounding this person."

"Fallen?"

"I don't know."

"Demons?"

I glared again. "I don't know!" I thought for a second. "Actually, this guy was there and *he* said—"

Zach leaped out of bed and scowled at me. "Someone *saw* you?"

I slipped out of bed and fisted my hands against my hips. "It's not as if I planned to have a vision!"

"Yet you go talking to strangers when someone's being tortured?" he hissed. "Don't you realize you could have been hurt? Visions aren't to be played with Jasmine!"

Rage, blindingly hot poured through my veins, my fallen side flaring to life. I tapered it down, reasoning that he was only worried for my safety.

"The horsemen of the apocalypse," I answered blithely, sick of the argument already.

Zach froze, his face becoming an unreadable mask. "What did you just say?"

I bit my lip anxiously and pushed my messy hair back over my shoulder. "That's what the guy called them. I was going to try to stop them but the guy told me they were the horsemen of the apocalypse. He told me to run." I lifted my hands and shrugged. "Then I woke up."

I blinked and Zach was no longer across the room but just inches away, clasping my shoulders, a blank mask covering his face.

"You're lucky you didn't try to interfere. You wouldn't have survived it," he said sternly.

I frowned. "They wouldn't have been able to tell I was there. I was in a vision, remember?"

Zach shook his head slightly. "The horsemen are different. They can see and reach between dimensions. They would be able to see you and they'd be able to kill you."

"What about the guy I saw? He could see and touch me too."

Zach scowled at that. "I don't know. We need to know about him. Maybe he's affiliated with them."

I shrugged. "He didn't feel evil."

Zach rolled his eyes and grabbed my hand, pulling me towards the bedroom door. I struggled against his hold and pulled back.

"Where are we going?" I hissed.

"We need to confer with Haamiah. I need to know if this might happen to you again and how I can protect you."

I scowled. "I can protect myself."

Zach groaned in frustration. "Enough with your girl-power trip! I know you're strong! I *know* you have faced many evil beings."

"Including the Queen of the Damned," I added angrily.

"Even so, you're no match for them." He reached out to take hold of my arm again.

"Jesus, Zach!" I exclaimed, spinning away. "At least let me put clothes on! And you certainly can't go down looking like...*that*."

I almost smiled at his shocked look, his eyes taking in my nightie and then looking down at himself in all of his nude glory. He growled low in his throat, pulled on a pair of black trousers and snagged a T-shirt from the floor. He left the room, pulling the door closed with a bang.

I sighed and headed for the bathroom. It didn't take long to clean up and dress, so within a few minutes I was following Zach out the door and down the stairs.

The safe house we lived in was beautiful, not just in looks but in its whole purpose for being. A number of them existed across the world, run by angels and lived in by their half-angel half-human offspring. This one was nestled in a quiet suburban area along the coastline, set back near the wetlands. The other houses nearby were equally private, hiding behind luscious gardens and thick vegetation. Ours was a two-story building with a wrap-around porch and a long garden at the front and back of the house. Downstairs, at one end an open-plan kitchen-dining room was large enough to sit the vast amount of nephilim who called this place home. From then onwards, offices and school rooms were used for angelic lessons and were decorated accordingly. Upstairs, thirty bedrooms, some single and some double, ran from one end to the other, with larger dorm rooms in the middle.

The angels didn't need to sleep unless they had expended a large amount of energy or were injured, in which case they usually rested in the medical room where Elijah was stationed, also upstairs. Otherwise, nephilim were the only occupants of the second floor.

I could hear voices downstairs so I quietly quickened my pace, skidding to a halt as Zach and Haamiah turned to look at me. Haamiah looked bedraggled, his thick, black dreadlocks in disarray, his white shirt wrinkled and untucked. I was sure I could even see grass stains on his trousers. He yawned and ran his hand down his face, looking beyond stressed and tired.

Zach scowled at me before beckoning me over. Together we followed Haamiah as he turned away, shuffling towards his office.

It was three in the morning. Why did Haamiah look so exhausted? Where had he been? Had he been fighting?

I glanced up at Zach as he held the door open for me. I passed by him and stood before the desk. Haamiah had thrown himself into his chair, sinking back into the cushion.

"What's going on?" I asked.

Zach and Haamiah glanced at each other, sharing an undecipherable look.

"Seriously, I want to know what's happening," I persisted.

"Haamiah was patrolling. He ran into some . . . complications."

"Complications?" I echoed. "Humans?"

We hadn't yet discovered who was behind the worldwide attack on the humans, but the news channels continued to show coverage of human cities being attacked and demolished by supernatural creatures. Fallen angels had attacked the White House, and simultaneously the Houses of Parliament in London had been blown sky-high by vampires and winged demons.

The world was in turmoil, the mystical world uncovered. In the first few weeks that had followed the attack, the human world fell apart, arrests were made, people were murdered, witch-hunts were led and innocent people burned alive. The human army had been unleashed to try to restore order but the demonic beasts continued to appear all over the world, destroying and killing, torturing the victims and leaving carnage in their wake.

Previously the mythical world had been veiled in mystery and secrets. Our existence was now well known. Some supernatural beings didn't really care about the shift in dynamics; they continued as they always had. Some reveled in their newfound supremacy.

The Angels seemed to have taken it the hardest. Before they had protected and guided humans through life and death, keeping the monsters at bay and preserving their souls, however their job had taken on a more difficult role. The humans were rebelling; factions forming to destroy any unhuman creature, some turning to witchcraft and others worshipping vampires. The Angels had the difficult job of protecting the humans while protecting themselves at the same time.

The safe house hadn't been discovered yet, due to the vigilance of the Angels. Any actions that could appear different were strictly prohibited and the Nephilim were in lockdown until further notice.

Zach sighed loudly, bringing my attention back to him. I had a habit of drifting off into my own thoughts; post Star Mist much worse than pre.

"Sorry." I shrugged. "You were saying there were complications."

Zach and Haamiah exchanged a glance.

"Haamiah found humans surveying the area."

"Surveying the . . ." I paused, my eyes flashing in shock. "Surveying *us*? They were watching *us*?"

Haamiah nodded grimly.

"Do they suspect something?" I gasped. If so we were all in danger. News reports were flying in fast and thick of demon hideouts being attacked, vampire nests being set alight and grenades launched into werewolf dens. Just last night a witch had been captured and burned alive, though whether she was actually a witch or just a horribly mistaken human was anyone's bet.

"Not any more," Zach said darkly.

I turned to him in surprise. Surely the angels wouldn't have killed them? That was against every rule I knew! I whipped my head around to watch Haamiah's expression.

He sighed heavily. "No, we didn't kill them. Mnemosyne assisted us."

I frowned. "Mnemo who?"

A trace of a smirk appeared on Zach's face before being wiped clean. I frowned and raised my eyebrows at Haamiah, demanding an answer.

He splayed his hands across the desk before answering, all the while refusing to meet my gaze. "A friend."

I snorted. "Yeah, try again! Who is . . . that person?" I refused to attempt to pronounce the name again. It wasn't my fault that up until the angels had come crashing into my life, most of the people I knew had normal names.

When Haamiah didn't answer, I glared at Zach. He shrugged and gave in.

"Mnemosyne is the Goddess of memory."

3

"Love comes to those who still hope after disappointment, who still believe after betrayal, and who still love after they've been hurt."

Unknown.

My mouth dropped open as I stared at Zach and then Haamiah. *Goddess?* My mind was screeching at me for so many reasons. The angels only believed in one God so wasn't even admitting another God or Goddess existed blasphemy? Never mind being friends with one.

"You're *friends* with a Goddess?" I scowled, pointing my finger at Haamiah. "*You* have a Goddess friend?"

Haamiah briefly scowled back at me before leaning back in his chair with a groan, refusing to answer.

"You realize I should be outraged, right?" I wondered out loud. "All this, 'there is only one God' stuff . . . what? That's all bullshit?"

Zach loomed over me angrily. "There *is* only one true God. Just because others name themselves so doesn't mean it is true."

"*They* didn't." I glared, not intimidated in the slightest. "*You* just did."

Laura Prior

"We do not recognize them as such. They are merely supernatural creatures, much like others in existence," Haamiah said weakly.

"Whatever! You just named her a Goddess." I rolled my eyes when the two of them simply glared. I could see I wasn't going to get anywhere with these stubborn angels so it wouldn't work pestering . . . for now. I wanted the full story of what had happened tonight. "Leaving that aside for now," I frowned at Zach, promising questioning later, "what did she do?"

"Wiped the memories of the humans, of course," Haamiah answered.

"And replaced them with different ones," Zach finished.

"She can do that?" I asked, shivers running up my spine. I couldn't imagine having my memory tampered with. It seemed sinister somehow, definitely creepy. ""Why was she even here? Or did you summon her?"

Haamiah and Zach paused just a second too long, my addled brain supplying the answer before they could make one up. I gasped as I took in Haamiah's rumpled appearance, clapping a hand to my mouth.

I stood and began to back out of the room. "I should go . . ." I said weakly, my imagination working overtime. Grass stains, rumpled hair, mud . . . ew!

A hand grasped my shoulder and forced me back into the chair. Haamiah glanced up in surprise.

"Jasmine had a vision," Zach began.

Haamiah immediately perked up, leaning forward to rest his elbows on the desk. "A vision?"

"Well, I don't know for certain it was a vision," I amended. At his silence, I relented. I relayed what had happened; the young man and what he had said about the horsemen of the apocalypse, the screams, and the fact that I was touchable unlike the other visions I'd had. Afterwards, his demeanor was even more solemn than before. He actually looked distressed, which was certainly a new expression for Haamiah. Being a Principality angel, he was never surprised by anything that happened; predicting was his game.

"It really has begun," he muttered.

I bit my lip. "Ragnarok?"

Haamiah frowned and stared at me as though trying to decipher something.

"Judgment day, the apocalypse, whatever you want to call it." He clearly didn't like the valkyrie terminology.

"Which is another name for Ragnarok," I supplied, irritated by his superiority.

"Only if you believe in the Norse Gods," he said. He spoke softly, quietly. Was he testing me? Testing my loyalty? I couldn't move. I didn't know what he wanted from me. I could only tell him the truth.

"Haamiah . . . I don't know about any of this. Sometimes I wake up and still get stuck on the fact that angels exist. Who would have thought that vampires and werewolves walk this planet? I don't know about Gods. I don't know which Gods are real, let alone which ones I want to support. I'll never be the type of girl to pray to one. I wouldn't even know what to pray for." I shook my head. "I thought I was human. Then I thought I was crazy, then I was Nephilim and now I'm some kind of weird valkyrie-fallen angel hybrid! I'm still undecided if I'm hallucinating or if this whole thing is actually real, so don't ask me which God I believe in, Haamiah, because even one hundred years from now I imagine I still won't be able to answer you." I took a deep breath and stood up to face Zach while still addressing Haamiah. "That being said, my loyalty will always lie with Zach, my soul mate and my Guardian. Wherever he leads I will go."

I stared into Zach's black eyes for a long minute, the silence comforting, his eyes seeming to absorb my essence. I felt as though in that moment, we were one. Slowly I turned my head to see what Haamiah made of my speech.

He appraised me for a while before a smile spread across his lips. He nodded and grinned at Zach who looked just as confused as I had confessed to being.

"So what is your plan then?" Haamiah asked.

I turned to Zach, waiting for him to answer. When he remained silent, stubbornly looking in Haamiah's direction, I turned and froze as Haamiah gave me a bemused look.

"*My* plan?" I croaked.

He nodded, trying to hold back a laugh.

Now I was really confused. Why was he asking me to come up with a plan? He was the angel and the leader of the house; surely he would be telling us what to do?

"Umm . . . well . . ." I coughed to clear the lump in my throat. "I guess we need to save that person . . . or creature."

Haamiah crooked his eyebrow.

"Okay, so that's not really a plan, but you have just put me on the spot," I hissed.

Haamiah chuckled, seeming much livelier now. "Take some time; I'm sure you'll do the right thing."

I slunk past Zach towards the door.

"And Jasmine," Haamiah called. I turned to face him. "I have faith in you."

I rolled my eyes. That would be a lot more encouraging if I was a powerful angel, not a twenty-five-year-old hybrid jumping from disaster to disaster.

4

"Nobody can go back and start a new beginning, but anyone can start today and make a new ending."

Maria Robinson.

Jophiel

One hundred years ago

Jophiel skidded past Michael, her armor sliding in the wet mud. She kicked her leg out, catching the fallen angel in the chest and sending him back into another warrior, a sword slicing directly through his chest.

She jumped to her feet, rubbing the sweat from her brow with her forearm, and quickly ducked under a sword swing. She brought her own blade up in a wide arch, decapitating the angel attacking her, and she kicked the body aside.

A heavy weight knocked her back onto the ground, her head hitting the hard ground, hard. She pushed the body off her, pausing as she took in the terrified expression frozen onto the face of the dead nephilim girl. If she hadn't believed so much in Michael, she would have thought this was a terrible mistake.

Michael had led them to a vast land in the north where the fallen were gathered with the nephilim they had caught. The task was to destroy the fallen and return the children to their families, but it wasn't playing out so easy. The fallen had more numbers than anyone had guessed and some had begun killing the nephilim to throw the angels off guard, while others had already mind-warped them into working for evil and the angels had to fight both nephilim and fallen angel.

Jophiel was kicked in the ribs again and again, making it impossible to stand. She curled into a ball to better defend herself and waited. Eventually, one of the fallen angels was pulled away and she was able to twist around and shred the other into pieces. She spun, noting an angel struggling to hold off the second fallen angel who had kicked her, and she stabbed her blade through its chest.

"There's too many," a voice shouted. "We need to fall back."

"No!" Jophiel shrieked as the angels surrounding her began to step away from the fallen rushing toward them. "Michael has not given the order to fall back so curb your cowardice and continue."

She jumped into the fray, seeing a group of fallen angels pulverizing a warrior. She pulled one back, throwing him through the air, and got to work on the next one. Before long, she had managed to clear the space around the warrior, and beaten the fallen back enough for him to stagger to his feet.

She bit her lip in anguish as Zacharael spat a mouthful of blood on the ground. He swiped at the trail of blood running down his cheek.

"Are you okay?" she asked him, gasping for breath.

He snarled at her and grabbed at someone nearing him. He clutched a nephilim boy by the throat and shook him.

Jophiel grabbed hold of him and thrust him behind her. "Leave him alone."

Zacharael stepped closer, glowering at her. "They should die; they've led us to this."

Jophiel stood firm. "Those aren't Michael's orders."

"Fuck Michael!"

Anger erupted through Jophiel. She curled her lip up and threw her clenched fist at him, striking his jaw so hard he fell to his knees.

He stood and loomed up over her and punched back. Jophiel gasped, reaching up to her pounding cheek in shock.

"You hit me," she whispered.

"And? Get out of my way," he growled through clenched teeth.

He shoved past her, knocking her aside. Jophiel stared after him, an ache crushing her heart. They would never be friends . . . never.

5

"Don't worry; I won't bite. Well, at least not in the way you're afraid of."

Unknown.

I headed to the kitchen after Zach told me he was going to patrol the outside of the safe house. For now, it seemed we were safe and I had no desire to walk around in the dark outside at four in the morning. Also, I doubted that very much patrolling would be done.

Instead, I poured some strong coffee and pulled up a stool at the kitchen bench, trying to force my mind away from the thought of Haamiah getting down and dirty with a Goddess out on the lawn and back onto the impossible task of somehow avoiding the apocalypse.

I didn't even know where to start. I generally just went with my instincts, but those instincts had told me to try to save that person from being tortured, and everyone was telling me that would have been the worst thing to do. Should I try to find a way back into the vision? Should I request the Grigori find the man I spoke to? Why wasn't Haamiah sending his warriors to defeat the horsemen and prevent the apocalypse? Wasn't that his job?

The light began to rise, shining through the kitchen windows and the other residents poured in for their breakfast. The kitchen was soon full of chattering, and the smell of coffee and burnt toast. I moved to the sofa and sat quietly. When one of the younger boys put the news channel on, a few of the others groaned. Admittedly, the news channel was incredibly depressing now, full of self-righteous humans rioting, burning witches, and attacking anyone they thought to be acting suspiciously. We knew that at least ninety percent of those murdered were innocent. There was no way a Sorceress or a vampire would allow him or herself to be killed by a human mob.

I breathed a sigh of relief as a tall, bulky Nephilim going by the name of Phoenix flicked the channel over. Although the cartoons weren't exactly interesting, it was certainly less stressful.

I sat quietly, allowing the others to mill around. It wasn't that I didn't have friends here; I did. I guess I had never been the loudest or most sociable. Having been far too preoccupied with trying to stay alive and always being the odd one out, I had never found the time to connect with other Nephilim . . . except for my three best friends, of course, one of whom had just entered the kitchen.

I watched the light-brown-haired boy sneakily snatch the toast sitting on the bench and scampered over to sit beside me while his victim had his back turned. Sam stuffed some toast in his mouth, chewing loudly while staring intently at me. I knew he was reading my mind and though I should feel annoyed by the intrusion, I couldn't summon enough energy to care.

Sam, my best friend, was telepathic. He often bemoaned that his angelic gift had been something that would drive him insane instead of superior fighting skills or the ability to fly, like Gwen. Some of the other Nephilim were wary of him, and why wouldn't you be, having someone nearby who could hear every private thought you had? Only those who knew him well knew how much of a burden it was. To have voices playing in your head non-stop was awful—and I would know.

My valkyrie-self ensured I was able to harvest the abilities of those near me. I hadn't told anyone yet, but I knew Sam's telepathy was beginning to rub off on me. It hadn't developed fully yet—all I could make out were the occasional whispers—but I dreaded when it fully came into play.

Though few knew my abilities were now numerous and varied, it terrified me that I had limited control over them. I should really get onto that.

My original ability was the handy talent of opening portals and at my last check, I seemed to have a natural flair for spells; I could, and often accidentally, cause fires; I was stronger and faster than most of the Nephilim I had met; and now, apparently, I was beginning to have visions.

Yep, I was screwed. Why on earth did Haamiah think I could come up with a viable plan?

I glanced at Sam, noting that he was concentrating on his toast. These days he was much more quiet and solemn, and who could blame him after being betrayed in the worst kind of way possible? His girlfriend, a sorceress we had all adored, had lied to him, gaining our trust before her coven had captured Sam and tortured him to find the location of the Falchion of Tabbris—a weapon that somehow opened the gateway to the Heavens.

I grimaced. "Sorry Sam."

He shrugged and gave me a weary smile. "Don't worry."

I felt embarrassed. I had the worst habit of letting my thoughts carry me away. I needed to learn to rein my thoughts in and concentrate.

Sam grinned. "You'll never do that."

I looked up and started to laugh. "You're feeling better today?"

He nodded in reply and grunted around a mouthful. He had been injured during the torture and then had gone AWOL, but with a little healing from Elijah he was almost as good as new, except for his wounded heart.

I sighed. "I don't know what he wants from me." I didn't need to explain anything; Sam had heard it all as it played through my mind.

Sam pursed his lips. "You know Haamiah; there'll be a good reason for it. He knows something."

"Well, I wish he would share," I grumbled. He seemed to have plenty of time to frolic in the bushes with Mnemosyne so I would have thought he'd be able to spare a minute to tell us what was going on.

As Sam's eyes widened in shock, I clapped my hand over my mouth.

"Oops. Don't say anything," I whispered.

He chuckled and nodded his head. "You're *so* going to tell me the rest of that story, Jas, but later. This isn't just your problem to deal with; we're a team."

I looked up hopefully. He smiled and stood up. "Meet me later, say nine-ish in my room. I'll make sure Gwen and Trev are there."

I nodded and watched him push past our housemates and out of the kitchen.

I sighed and sunk back into the sofa cushions. That was another problem yet to be solved. Gwen and Trev had been closer than friends, so much so that I had begun to think they were sleeping together but after they had been captured by Asmodeus, Trev had been turned into a vampire and a rift of epic proportions had split them up. While Gwen wouldn't even look at him, Trev could do nothing but gaze after her, lost and heartbroken. It was devastating.

Now Sam was expecting them to jump on board with Haamiah's plotting? I didn't think that was going to happen any time soon.

6

"I do not believe in using women in combat, because females are too fierce."

Margaret Mead.

I knocked on Sam's door bang on nine o'clock and was more than relieved to see Gwen and Trev already inside, on separate sides of the room looking quite uncomfortable.

"You've already filled them in?" I asked Sam.

He shook his head. "I thought it best to wait for you."

I nodded. "Okay guys, I kind of need your help. I had a vision last night, maybe some kind of leftover magic from that spell." The one where I had found out my fiancé was a cold-blooded killer with family issues.

"What did you see?" Trev asked, falling silent when Gwen cringed away from him.

I bit my lip, feeling overwhelmed with sorrow again. Sam briefly touched my fingers with his, reminding me that he felt the same, and I continued.

"Someone was being tortured. I couldn't see them properly but the screams were . . ." I trailed off.

"Was it Asmodeus?" Trev glanced at Gwen and away again.

"I don't think so. There was this guy there and he said they were the four horsemen of the apocalypse."

"What?" Trev yelled.

Gwen stood up in shock. "You saw the horsemen of the apocalypse? They're real?" She gasped.

I shrugged. "That's the thing. I don't know for sure."

"Who was the guy? The one who told you who they were?" Trev questioned.

I shrugged again. "I don't know. He stopped me from rushing in to try and stop them. He told me they would kill me and sent me on my way."

"You actually listened to someone who told you not to rush headlong into trouble? Wow! He must be some guy," Trev quipped with a good-natured smirk.

I rolled my eyes at him. "The point is he shouldn't have even been able to see me. In those other visions I had, no one could see, feel or hear me, so how could he touch me?"

"He touched you?" Sam frowned.

"Well, he tackled me to the ground." I grimaced.

Sam and Trev exchanged a grin.

"And you *didn't* incinerate him?" Sam laughed.

"Haamiah wants me to sort this out. It was really bizarre but he wasn't even interested; he just told me to go away and come up with a plan." I tried a smile. "We all know I'm not exactly a great planner. I'm more of a fly-by-the-seat-of-my-pants kind of girl."

"Four heads are better than one. I'm on board." Sam grinned. "Besides, we could all do with some livening up. Lying low and hiding from the humans is so dull."

I turned to him with relief and love in my eyes. I knew I could always count on him. He was *so* going to Heaven!

"I'm in," Trev said quietly.

I smiled my thanks and looked to where Gwen stood, nervously shuffling her feet. My smile slowly disappeared.

"Are you in, Gwen?"

After a long pause she lifted her chin, her big, brown eyes staring up at me fearfully. Slowly she nodded her agreement. The tight knot in my chest eased somewhat, despite the constant worry that she was planning on leaving us that had gnawed at me for weeks.

"Where do we start?" Trev asked.

I blew out my breath. "There's a lot to work out—so much my brain hurts."

Sam tossed a pad and pen to Gwen who scowled in return, unappreciative of being made the minute secretary.

"Okay, I guess we should start with the four horsemen," I suggested.

Trev nodded. "We need to know more about them. Who and what they are . . ."

"What their agenda is," Sam added.

"Where they live, or at least where to find them," Trev continued.

I sighed. "And how to kill them," I added grimly. "We need to know their strengths and weaknesses."

Sam and Trev glanced at each other then back at me with solemn looks.

"Trev, can you ask your mother?" Sam asked. We all knew this was a touchy subject. Since becoming vampire, he hadn't heard from her. This was incredibly upsetting for him, seeing as his angelic ability was communicating with the Angels.

Trev nodded.

"Gwen, maybe you can do some fishing about in the library; see what you can find. I'll see if I can get any information out of the Angels. What else do we need to do?" Sam asked.

I paused. "The guy."

Sam nodded, lines creasing his forehead. "We need to know who he is and what he wants. It's too freaky that he could touch you in a vision. If something's changed we need to know."

I snapped my head around so quickly I felt dizzy. "What do you mean?"

Sam shrugged and began to pace the small room while Trev sat down on the windowsill, resting his feet against the frame. "A vision shouldn't be tangible. By its own decree is should only be visible. Both the viewer and anything or anyone in the vision itself is a figment. It's not real; nothing in the vision is real. You can't touch, taste or smell anything."

"But I could," I insisted. I wasn't sure what he was getting at.

"Maybe this guy has abilities to make visions more . . . substantial. We don't know what creature he is and we don't know if he is dangerous to you. What if he pulled you into the vision?"

"He didn't know who I was," I reassured him.

Sam cocked his eyebrow. "Are you sure?"

I bit my lip. "Yeah."

"We can't rule out anything until we are one hundred percent sure," Trev drawled. "It is you, after all."

My grin was slow in coming but I laughed. "Fair point," I agreed. "So how do we find out about him?"

"Can you try to contact him through another vision?" Gwen asked.

I shrugged and ran my fingers through my hair, twirling the ends through my fingers. "I can try," I conceded.

"Maybe you can ask the Grigori to find him?" Trev suggested.

I snickered. "Because they're totally going to do anything I ask them to do."

He pulled a face. "Could be worth a shot but yeah, unlikely."

"Maybe the valkyrie can find him? Between them and the amount of abilities they must have, surely one of them can search for him?"

I nodded thoughtfully, stepping closer to the desk to lean against it. "That's worth a shot."

"There is another question we need to answer: what if it wasn't a vision?" Trev added, shocking us all.

The thought hadn't even occurred to me and judging by the frozen looks on Sam and Gwen's faces, they hadn't either.

"What else could it be?" Gwen asked with wide eyes.

Trev rolled his eyes. "Haven't any of you considered Jasmine's first and strongest ability . . . opening portals?"

My mouth dropped open. A portal?

"A portal," I shrieked. I clapped my hand to my forehead. I was so stupid! Why hadn't I considered it? Sam, Gwen and Trev were staring at me wide-eyed. I nodded. "That would make sense. More sense than the vision, I guess." I frowned. "I don't know, though. There were vision-like qualities."

"Such as?"

I threw my hands up. "Mist, for one. The air was like this thick, almost white cloud. I've never had that when I've gone through a portal."

"Hmm." Gwen pursed her lips. "But if it was a vision, wouldn't you need to do a spell? Like you did with the Witch?"

"I think so. Maybe it's a lingering after-effect."

"Maybe we need to ask someone instead of guessing," Trev rumbled from where he was perched against the window ledge.

I snorted. "Yeah, I can just see Haamiah answering my questions about witchcraft and spells."

"Who better to ask than the witches?" Trev said with a wink.

I nodded, smiling. "True."

"So we're going to see some witches and some valkyrie," Sam said gleefully.

I grinned. "I guess we are."

"When do we go?"

"Tomorrow. I need to clear it with Haamiah first," I said. I hoped he wasn't going to drag his heels with this.

"And Zach?" Sam asked wryly.

I frowned. "Zach isn't the boss of me."

"Maybe, but you promised to tell him whenever you were going to open a portal."

I grimaced. "Ugh! Yeah, I forgot about that."

"Are you sure it's a good idea to be leaving the safe house right now?" Gwen asked, in a low voice, sullenly.

"Sure, why not? We're not going to find any of the answers here." I frowned.

She shrugged, dropping the pen and paper onto the bed. "Oh, I don't know, maybe the fact that there's a war going on. The human resistance is everywhere and we're on the wrong side of it."

"We're not on the wrong side," Sam argued. "We're the good guys!"

"You think the humans are going to stop and clarify that before shooting you dead?" she asked coldly. She stomped across the room, turning back to us before she opened the door. *"You* can go searching for the answers you need, but don't think for a second I'm entering a war zone just to make you feel better."

I froze. Why was she being like this? She had been off with us ever since being captured by Asmodeus. I knew what she was going through . . . I was the only one who really did, but it didn't totally explain her behavior. It was as though she'd had a personality transplant.

I didn't know whether to be upset or angry. Was I wrong? Was this whole investigation just to make myself feel better about not helping when I should have? It's true I felt beyond guilty. My heart told me I should have stayed and fought, not left that poor soul to be tortured.

"You don't need to come, Gwen. You can help us from here. But don't think for one second you're going to push us away," Sam said gruffly, startling me out of my miserable thoughts. He was scowling at her fiercely. "You, me, Trev and Jas are in this, in *everything* together. You're one of us and there's no going back. We're not going to give up on you."

I couldn't help but wonder for a split second if that wouldn't be for the best. After what she'd been through, maybe it was unkind to make her stay in our group. Sam and Trev were right that I attracted trouble everywhere I went. Gwen deserved peace. She didn't deserve to be pulled into more drama.

For a second, Gwen looked grief-stricken, her eyes wide and fearful, then she spun on her heel and marched out, slamming the door shut behind her.

Laura Prior

7

"Life doesn't give you the people you want, it gives you the people you need, to help you, to hurt you, to love you, to leave you, and to make you into the person you were meant to be."

Unknown.

Gabriel

Twenty-five years ago

Gabriel grabbed hold of Zacharael's arm. "I need to ask you something."

Zacharael huffed out his breath in irritation. They stood to the side, hugging the wall as the other angels filed out of the meeting room, pushing past them.

"Well?" he asked impatiently, when they were alone.

"There's a nephilim child in need of a guardian. I'm putting the call out but I need you for this task," she urged.

"I'm a warrior, not a guardian." He tried to leave, but was pulled back.

"I mean it. We're losing you, Zacharael. We need you back in the game," she insisted.

He grabbed her shoulders and shook her. "This isn't a game! People are dying."

"I don't mean it like that," Gabriel said, trying to wriggle free.

"Get off her!" Jophiel brought her hands down onto Zacharael's arms and ripped them free. She threw him back into the wall, watching as he slid to the floor. He kneeled and unsteadily pulled himself up.

"Stay away from me, and keep your manipulative bitch of a sister out of my way."

Watching him storm off, Jophiel turned to Gabriel. "Was he talking to you or me?"

Gabriel gave her a crooked smile in response.

"What are you doing, Gabe? I told you to stay away from him."

Gabriel held herself stiffly, lifting up her chin. "It's important."

"No, I told you not to involve him; that's important."

"You think it's easy trying to create a plan that has a happy outcome for everyone?"

"It's not your responsibility to create outcomes for anyone."

"It is. You're my sister and I love you," Gabriel cried desperately.

"This has something to do with me?"

"We're *all* involved up to our necks." Gabriel sniffed, her eyes turning misty. "Imagine you and your family are standing in front of a thousand doors. One will lead to Heaven, and the rest to Hell.

You know which one is the right one but they won't listen to you. That's what I'm facing right now."

Jophiel gasped as Gabriel began to cry. She pulled her close, wrapping her arms around her shoulders.

"I don't know what to do; no one will listen to me," she said between tears.

"You just have to let us go our own way, Gabe."

"But I know what will happen!"

"You've got to let us get on with it. You can't force us to do what you think is best. We'll face the consequences of our actions and deal with them as they come."

"You say that because you don't know . . ."

Gabriel wiped her cheeks, sniffing. She took a few steps back. "I'm not going to give up on you, you know. I'll never stop caring about what happens to you."

Jophiel sighed. "What is it you asked Zacharael to do? Maybe I can do it instead?"

Gabriel flashed a wan smile. "Not right now, but I'll take you up on that offer when you get back from your trip."

Jophiel nodded. "Very well. You have my promise."

8

"I myself am made entirely of flaws, stitched together with good intentions."

Augusten Burroughs

Sam sighed and threw himself onto his bed, uncaring that the pen and paper slipped to the floor. He stretched his arms above his head, his T-shirt riding up to expose his lightly-tanned skin. The springs creaked and groaned, seeming to sympathize with our awkward situation.

"Was I too harsh with her?" he asked eventually.

I bit my lip and glanced over at Trev. He remained silent for a second then shrugged. He swiveled on the windowsill, dropping his feet to the floor. "No, she needed to hear it. Maybe we have a chance at getting her back, or maybe she will be able to make a decision whether to stay or go now."

I nodded slowly, saddened at his words. "I agree. We had to do something; she's been pulling away ever since . . ." I flinched. "I understand what she's going through, but someone had to do something to get her back. She's going to make a decision either way—at least we've let her know where we stand on the issue."

Sam rubbed his hands over his face roughly and pulled himself up into a sitting position. Trev shuffled over and slapped him on the back a few times—very manly. I grinned. These two guys . . . they were amazing and I loved them. They were my family, as was Gwen, and even if she decided to walk away from us I would not let her without fighting tooth and nail to make her see it.

"So where do we start?" Trev asked.

"The horsemen," I replied when the boys looked to me.

They nodded their agreement and Sam picked up the list Gwen had left.

"I'll go to see the valkyrie and ask for some information on the horsemen and the boy," I suggested.

"We can't go today. We've got training with Daton," Trev reminded us.

Sam nodded. "With everything that's going, we can't miss it."

Daton, a warrior angel living with us in the safe house, taught the nephilim fighting tactics. As nephilim we would never be as strong as the Fallen, but we were all taught how to defend ourselves so we would have a fighting chance to stay alive until the Angels arrived to save the day.

Of course I now knew that I wasn't a nephilim and neither was Trev. Both of us were strong enough to take on the fallen and any other creatures that came our way. It was a good job too, now that we were in a war. Leaving the humans aside, Demon factions now fought each other constantly, often spilling over into our territory causing mayhem for all of us.

Most of the other nephilim were aware of both Trev and my change in circumstances, and while most tolerated our continued presence there were a few who thought we no longer belonged.

As much as I would like to be angry about it I could actually see their point. I had moments where I didn't feel as though I belonged here, and Trev had admitted to feeling the same, but where could we go? I loved the island but I couldn't live there forever, never seeing another soul, and Zach would never agree to live amongst the valkyrie. Trev had nowhere. He had no family and everyone he knew lived here. No, until I could come up with a viable alternative the other nephilim would just have to get over it.

I flinched as I realized Sam was repeating my name to get my attention.

"Sorry." I grimaced. I twirled my fingers in the air near my forehead. "Too much stuff going on since . . ."

Sam nodded with a sad smile. I could only feel relieved that my best friends knew how hard it was to stay focused. Since the Star Mist I had won and consequently been forced to ingest in the Tournament of Ascension, my abilities had grown in power tenfold, as well as my talent at acquiring new ones. Everything in my head was so loud, fighting for my attention, even with the magical ring that held the overflow of power in check.

Trev was already standing by the door. "Are we going? You know Daton will be furious if we're late."

I nodded and turned to follow him, smiling as Sam placed his hand on my shoulder, trailing after me.

We jogged down the stairs and wandered through the house until we arrived at the gym. We were a little early and there were only two other people there. I frowned as I saw Joe lifting weights in the corner, his friend Will standing nearby. They both looked over as we entered, scowling. Joe and Will were heavyweights in the safe house. They were popular, both loved and feared, and were very vocal with their dislike of Trev and I. I was used to it, but being disliked was something new for Trev.

I scowled in return and sauntered over to the stretching bars, Sam and Trev following silently. We warmed up in unison, saying nothing as more Nephilim arrived and stood at the other side of the room. The battle lines had been drawn.

Daton arrived in a flourish, seeming to appear out of nowhere, the air around him pulsating with power. He was tall, taller than Zach, and thickly built with tattoos coating his skin everywhere I could see. He wore black trousers and boots, and was shirtless. His muscles flexed with each movement, each thought rippling through him like a wave. He was a mountain of a man with the skills to terrify even Lucifer himself.

He ignored the tension between our two groups and began to instruct. He briefly repeated the lessons he had taught us the week before: dodge and evade, hide where possible, blend into our surroundings. Thankfully he soon moved on to defending ourselves. We were only to do what was necessary to keep us alive.

"Leave the heroics to the Angels," he said solemnly.

He stressed the importance of remaining focused—for my benefit, I was sure. I shifted on the balls of my feet, bored already.

"Today we spar with each other," he intoned.

I froze. Spar? With each other? We had copied fighting tactics, trained with weights in speed and endurance, and even sparred with the angels for practice, but the angels held a strict no-fighting rule amongst the nephilim in the safe house. That's not to say Sam, Trev, Gwen and I didn't practice—we just did it away from the other Nephilim. Judging by the smirks on Joe and Will's faces I presumed they had also found a place to practice.

Daton named two female nephilim. Giggling, they stepped forward onto the mat and followed the instructions Daton called out. They pranced around, laughing nervously, exchanging light taps and almost dancing around each other.

I glanced up at Sam, biting my lip to stop myself from smiling in amusement. A bitchy thing to do, yes, but seriously, who were they kidding? They would have been better off learning gardening for all the damage they could do to an enemy.

Daton seemed to feel the same way and shooed them back to the sidelines. He called out another pair and another until finally one pairing made my nerves shoot up. *Joe and Trev.*

What was he doing? Trev was stronger than any nephilim now and had very limited control over his vampirism. If he seriously hurt Joe he would never forgive himself, despite what a tool the guy was.

The Nephilim muttered, a spattering of shocked voices, as Trev slowly stepped onto the mat slowly. Joe had already jumped forward eagerly, and was flexing his muscles with a sardonic smirk playing on his lips.

"Trev," I called out.

Sam pulled me back, leaving his arm around me for comfort. Or maybe he needed the comfort. I stared, anxious, my eyes fixated on Trev's back as he balanced his weight on the balls of his feet. He ducked as Joe swung for him, jumping out the way of a following kick. With my heart in my throat I glared at Joe as he jabbed Trev in the kidneys, knocking him to his knees. He kicked him again in the ribs, laughing loudly as Trev rolled onto his side.

I couldn't take it any more. "Fight back!" I shouted angrily. "You're stronger than him."

Joe whipped his head round and bared his teeth at me. I clenched my fists, anger swirling through my stomach.

"Control it, Jasmine," Sam whispered.

I hadn't even noticed but black smoke had begun to leak from me, spreading through the air, until the room began to turn foggy. I took a deep breath and pushed the rage away, focusing on Sam's eyes, on the light-brown color, on the way he looked at me with such care and worry. I turned back to the center of the room, noting with relief that Trev had jumped up to his feet and was continuing the fake battle. He concentrated on blocking and evading Joe's hits rather than actually fighting the way I knew he could, but it was an improvement to lying on the ground accepting the blows.

The fight was uneventful, tedious to watch. I knew Trev wouldn't fight back properly, even if Joe deserved a good ass-whooping. Unfortunately, Trev seemed to realize the fight wasn't going to end any time soon and decided to give up the mild attempt to defend himself. Joe delivered a serious of fast punches, knocking him back, blood streaming from Trev's nose.

"Get him!" Will hollered. Laughter followed. Joe spun and kicked Trev in the stomach, sending him flying off the matt and into the wall. Trev groaned and slid to the floor.

That was it. I stepped forward again, shrugging off Sam's restraining arm.

"You want a go, do you?" Will shouted, jumping forward onto the mat. He beckoned me forward, readying himself to fight.

I grinned, my rage marginally mollified at the expectation of beating the crap out of him. I stepped onto the mat, letting my rage simmer quietly, allowing a small amount of my power to seep into my limbs, energizing them.

I began to circle Will, anger pulsating through my body with every heartbeat. I stretched out my arms and pulled them back lazily. I let the energy rippling through me color my vision, narrowing my world until there was only Will and Joe and me.

A prickling sensation on my neck had me ducking and diving to the side, flipping up to my feet again seconds later. As Joe lunged at me I reached through, punching him in the jaw, grinning as he spun away and fell to the floor. I spun on my toes and used the momentum to lift my leg and kick Will in the head.

Seeing Joe getting to his feet, I ran and jumped over him, grasping his arm to my chest as I sailed over his head. I pulled him over me, hearing something crack as his arm bent awkwardly. He screamed as I let go, dropping him to the mat. I paused for a second, frowning down as he whimpered beside me.

I had waited a second too long, my distraction getting the better of me. I was caught in a headlock, my windpipe squeezed closed as Will loomed over me from behind, crushing me to his chest.

I struggled, trying to find a niche I could tuck my throat into to release the pressure. I wasn't finding one. Just as gray spots began to sparkle in my eyes, I fully turned to face him, cringing at the press of my body to his. I lifted my knee up to connect with his balls, grinning as he deflated like a balloon, rumbling to the floor with a moan.

I had won. I was powerful, stronger than they could imagine.

I immediately noticed the fallen angel in me crowing over the victory and did my best to reel it in. It resisted, wanting to elate in the win over the two nephilim.

I saw a figure approach me and turned, ready to rip them apart. I winced when I realized it was Zach. He shook his head so slightly no one else would have noticed it and brushed past, pulling Trev up from where he lay, dazed. His disapproval weighed heavily on me. I felt scolded, like a child.

"Lesson's over," Daton's low voice rumbled.

I bit my lip and stepped off the mat, away from the nephilim to follow Zach out of the room. Sam trailed behind.

I grimaced at Sam as Zach pulled Trev into the corridor, shouldering most of his weight. We followed silently as they stepped outside onto the verandah. I tentatively smiled at Trev when he was deposited on a soft seat overlooking the garden. I waited for Zach to leave, unsure of myself now, the victorious traitor in me fully cowed. I wanted to check Trev was okay, even though at the same time I wanted to shout and rant at him for not defending himself.

"Jasmine," Zach called impatiently.

I blew out a breath and looked at my feet before turning and walking to where Zach now stood on the steps.

Reassured I was following, he turned away and marched off through the gardens, pushing into the denser part right at the back, through the bushes and trees and away from prying eyes. I grumbled silently to myself, sure he was angry but unsure what he would actually say.

I pushed a rose out of the way, and ducked around the body of the rose bush, carefully avoiding the sharp thorns that stuck out.

Abruptly Zach stopped and turned to face me, his face dark with anger.

"What did you think you were doing?"

I scowled. "Joe was laying into Trev! You think I was just going to stand by and watch?"

"It wasn't your place to fight for him. He could defend himself."

I clenched my teeth angrily. "No he couldn't!"

"With all the extra strength in him now, you think he couldn't take down a couple of nephilim kids?" Zach challenged.

I shook my head. "That's the point. He won't defend himself against them because he doesn't think it's fair."

"Then you shouldn't take the decision out of his hands."

"You're so wrong! That's exactly what I should do. You think I'm going to just stand by while my friend gets beaten to shit? I'm not that person. Sometimes I don't think you know me at all! Or Trev, or Sam. Trev's *hurting*. He doesn't know who he is anymore. He's lost his whole identity. You think letting someone pound on him, just standing by and letting it happen is going to make him feel more like himself? God, even Gwen is terrified of him now."

"And rightly so. Vampires are evil and very powerful."

I paused, catching my breath. "And fallen angels aren't?" I asked quietly. "And valkyrie? I thought the angels thought they were evil, too."

Zach ran a hand over his face, rubbing at the stubble on his jaw. "That's different."

"How?"

"You've had time to get used to your powers. Trev is newly turned. Though you're still *volatile*—"I rolled my eyes. "—you've got more control. Trev can snap at any moment, making him much more deadly."

I squeezed my eyes shut and tried to think of the words I wanted to say. I didn't want this to end up as another argument, even though I desperately wanted to defend him and rail against these accusations heaped upon us both.

"Zach, regardless of someone's power, ability, race or species, if I see that they are being taken advantage of I'm going to help them. I can't just stand back and watch. I know it's different for you and the angels. It's ingrained in you to behave a certain way." I bit my lip as he raised his eyebrows. "No, I don't mean it as an insult. You are strong and brave. You're an angel warrior; you have a job to do, a duty, and you've done it for a thousand years, which means that aside from being really old, it's in your nature. You are who you are. This is who I am. Nobody said you had to like it, but I *am* asking you to accept it if you want to be with me, because that's not something I think I should change about myself."

Zach stared at me in silence with a bemused expression. I turned away and stared out at the garden. From back here I could see the high wall surrounding the house and the vegetable allotment right at the very bottom of the garden. Rose bushes grew really, and were currently in full bloom, hiding us from anyone in the house.

Eventually Zach let out the breath he had been holding.

"I know. I know who you are, but I still wish you would show some restraint. By defending Trev you will have made things worse for all of you. You have even more people to watch out for now."

I nodded and shrugged. "Like that bothers me. I know people don't like me. Some for the things I've done and even more just for what I am. I'm used to it. You think I can't hear what they say about me anyway? Zach, I've spent my whole life being disapproved of by everyone around me, so I really don't give a damn what a couple of bullies think, or if I've pissed off anyone else. They can just jump in line.

"What does frustrate me is when they try to interfere with me and you . . . I know what Zanaria and Maion have been telling you to do."

Zach lifted a hand to cup my face, stroking his other one through the fall of my hair. He was closer, towering over me, his black eyes pulling me in. He dropped his eyes to my mouth, smoothing his thumb over my lip.

"I don't care what they say. I'm in love with you."

9

"It takes nothing to join the crowd. It takes everything to stand alone."

Hans F Hansen.

Those words. Those beautiful words seemed to resonate in my soul. How could this man be mine? I wasn't worthy of him. He was . . . magnificent.

I closed my eyes and rose up on my tiptoes, pushing past his thumb until my mouth lightly, gently touched his. That soft merging of our souls lasted only a second before his tongue thrust between my lips, his hand cupping my neck to him, showing me no release.

His lips teased at mine, his teeth biting my bottom lip before making their way down my jaw to my neck. He sucked and bit, rousing my desires until I clawed at him, desperate for more of what I knew only he could give me.

I dug my nails into his shoulders, the sheer width of them enough to dominate me. I gasped as he slid my T-shirt down across my shoulder so that he could bite along my collarbone. He grasped my waist and slid his hands down around me, inside my jeans to cup my bottom and thrust against me.

I could feel him, his hard length pressing against me. I knew what he needed. I knew what I needed.

I reached down and pulled up my T-shirt over my head, shaking my hair loose behind me. Zach growled and slid one hand up to loosen my bra and let my breasts fall free. My nipples perked, begging to be sucked. And he did. He drew one peak into his mouth and flicked my hard nipple with his tongue while nipping at my flesh. My head fell back, my chest rising erratically. I moaned as the hand kneading my fleshy bottom slid down and entered me from behind. I could feel the slickness of my body welcoming him in, showing him how much I needed him.

He slid his finger in and out, replacing with two and then three. I could do nothing other than clutch on to his shoulders and pray I didn't fall when my release came.

"Shit! Sorry!" I heard someone say.

I gasped, my vision rapidly clearing, my body cooling.

Before I could wrench myself away from Zach, he had already thrown me behind him, baring his teeth at our intruders. I panted, covering my chest with my arms while hiding behind his body.

"What do you want?" Zach growled.

"I . . . I was looking for you. I didn't realize you were with *her*," a soft voice replied.

Zanaria. I cringed at the thought of what she must have seen. If I had ever hoped to change her opinion of me, I'm pretty sure almost fucking her brother in broad daylight in the garden wasn't the way to do it.

"I'll find you later," Zach replied, his voice tight and measured.

There was a small silence. "Don't bother. I can see who you've chosen to ally yourself with, brother."

"Zanaria!" an anxious voice shouted.

I cringed even more, wishing the ground would swallow me up. This was all I needed.

Maion soon crashed through the bushes and stopped beside Zanaria. I peered around Zach to catch him gaping towards us.

"What . . .?" He gasped.

"Don't, Maion." Zanaria turned away and grasped his arm. "He's a fool to think she will do anything other than damage his reputation."

When Zach said nothing in reply, they left us.

I felt so foolish, so stupid. Zach turned around to face me and leaned forward as if to rest his forehead against mine. I ducked away and pulled my T-shirt on, stuffing my bra into my pocket.

"What are you doing?" he asked, his dark eyes searching mine for something.

I shrugged bitterly. "You don't even bother to defend me?"

Zach groaned and lifted both hands to run through his hair, his muscles jumping. "Come on, Jasmine. What about what I just said?"

I bit back my tears. "You know what? Actions speak louder than words. You tell me you don't care what anyone says or what they tell you to do, and then you don't even defend me."

"I *don't* care what they say but that doesn't mean I have to start an argument with her. She'll get over it; it'll just take some time."

He was right, of course. I knew he was. He didn't care what they said. He was standing by me despite the things they said. It wasn't as if he were running off after her right now. He said he didn't care what anyone said about me or us and he had proven it. Was it ridiculous of me to wish that he *did* care?

I stepped back away from him. "I know," I said quietly.

"Then what's the problem?"

The problem was why couldn't he tell them to go fuck themselves?

"There's no problem. I need to get back and check on Trev. I'll see you later, okay?" I said, forcing a smile.

I turned away, leaving him with a frown on his face as I picked my way through the rose bushes back towards the house.

By early evening, Sam, Trev and I had reassembled in Sam's room. I had found Haamiah in his office and told him of our plans to visit the valkyrie to find out more about the horsemen. Worryingly, he had seemed incredibly nonchalant about it all. He had nothing to say except, "Very well. I'll see you when you get back," which was very un-Haamiah of him.

I decided to update Zach on our plans, but discovered from Elijah that he had left the safe house on an errand for Haamiah and wouldn't be back for a few days. He hadn't even said goodbye.

No one mentioned the fight earlier, and Sam was flicking through the bullet points we had made in the notebook, pretending to be busy. For a second my mind flicked to when Zach had been sucking on my breast earlier.

Sam's face turned beetroot. *Oops.*

I coughed loudly. "Is Gwen not coming?" I asked, glancing at the clock. It was getting late and if we were going to be up early, I wanted to get a decent night's sleep. I was exhausted from the vision the night before, and who knew what would happen once we left the safe house.

Sam looked up, his face slowly fading to his normal colour. "I saw her earlier. She hasn't found out anything about the horsemen and said she'd text us tomorrow if she learned anything that could help."

I twisted my face. "She's not going to say goodbye or good luck?"

Sam looked down. I pushed myself away from the desk that I had been leaning on, accidentally knocking over a pot of pens. I slowly scooped them back up, taking the time to mentally chastise myself for being emotional. Zach rarely said goodbye before disappearing; it was part of his mysterious, brooding charm, and Gwen had always been temperamental and feisty. It was ridiculous to get upset over any of it.

"We need to decide how we're going to get to the valkyrie," I said.

"Airplane," Trev spoke up.

"Portal," Sam suggested.

I shrugged. Both options were viable.

"Portal might not be the best idea," Trev mumbled. He glanced at me with a sheepish grin. "With everything that's going on, do you want to risk anyone seeing us?"

I grimaced. That was a good point. With the world ready to shoot any supernatural creatures on sight, I would have to be very accurate when opening a portal. It wouldn't do at all to have us appear in the middle of a shopping center, for example. That would soon turn into a blood bath.

"It's probably a better option than an airplane though," Sam said, shooting an apologetic glance at Trev. "You're not exactly Mr. Self Control, dude. Couple hundred people trapped thousands of feet in the air with a new vampire with control issues . . . probably *not* the best idea we've ever come up with."

I winced as Trev turned away to look out the window. I glared at Sam, who silently held his hands up in response.

"Okay, so that's one decision made then," I said brightly, trying to move the conversation on. "We'll open a portal and hope for the best."

Sam snorted as Trev turned around with a grin on his face. It *did* sound quite ridiculous.

"What are we going to do after seeing the valkyrie?" Sam asked after a moment.

"We need to go to the witches to find out about the vision and to tell them about Emily. Then I need to find the harpies," I answered.

"How do we find the witches exactly?"

"The valkyrie are friends with some witches so I figured we'd just ask them," I said.

"And the harpies?"

I shook my head. "We'll figure that one out when we come to it. What time should we head off?"

Sam took a deep breath. "I imagine it would be best to get there after dark; less chance of us being spotted then," he mused. "With the time difference, what about setting off about four a.m., then we'll get there by eleven or twelve at night?"

I nodded my agreement while Trev smiled.

"Okay, where from? Here?" I gestured around at Sam's bedroom.

Sam mock-scowled, drawing himself up indignantly. "That would be like inviting a whirlwind into my bedroom. How about we do it somewhere where you're not likely to trash everything I own?"

I laughed. "The garden?"

Sam grinned. "Sure, right at the back though."

A thrill of excitement rushed through me. Freedom seemed to resonate through the air. Because of the war raging on outside, we had been on lockdown for months. I couldn't wait to get out from the safe house and just be somewhere else. This place was driving me crazy.

I sauntered towards the door, and then turned back with a smile. "Okay, I'll see you both at four o'clock in the garden. Let's hope that even though Haamiah isn't interested in helping us, there are some other angels out there willing to guide us in the right direction."

Laura Prior

10

"I am strong because I've been weak. I am fearless because I've been afraid. I am wise because I've been foolish."

Unknown.

Gabriel

Twenty-five years ago

Sitting by the pool of cleansing Gabriel groaned in frustration, coming close to glaring at her younger sibling.

"Jophiel, please will you do this for me?" she pleaded, splashing her feet in the water.

Jophiel sighed. "I've promised to fight alongside Michael. Don't make me go back on my word."

"It's important. Trust me when I say that you will regret it for the rest of your existence if you do not listen to me."

Jophiel frowned. "Are you threatening me?"

Gabriel leaned over and clasped Jophiel's hands tightly. She stared into her eyes. They were similar to her own soft-green ones, but sharper somehow, more emotional and passionate.

"You are my sister and I care about you. I want you to be happy. You know this?"

Jophiel dropped back against the cushions that outlined the pool, sending a wave of water over the rim. She stretched her toned arms above her head, relaxing her muscles.

"I know this," she finally answered.

"I promise you, this will solve many of our problems," Gabriel urged.

"*Your* problems you mean. You think bringing the realms together to form one army will solve all of your problems?" she asked skeptically, quirking her eyebrow.

Gabriel remained unruffled. "Many of them," she answered.

The archangels fell silent as two of the seraphim strolled past in animated discussion. Gabriel smiled gently when they waved as Jophiel rolled her eyes and looked away, annoyed.

"Why does it have to be me?" she asked when they were once more alone.

"Because it does," came the reply.

"Nuh-uh. I need a better reason than that." Jophiel shook her head.

"Okay, for one, you are the Angel of Miracles. If anyone can unite the creatures of the supernatural realms under one banner, creatures who have despised each other for a thousand years, it would be you. Your mantra is to confront problems head on and solve them, no matter the difficulties you may encounter. This task is for you."

Jophiel stood up and stepped deeper into the cool water. It was shallow, only reaching to her knees. She held her hand up when Gabriel began to speak.

"Say I did this for you and travelled to the human plane to bring together the races; how do you expect them to react when an archangel appears before them, telling them how to behave and what to do? They'll decapitate me or incinerate me; that's what they'll do."

"I admit it has its challenges."

"No, they're not challenges. Challenges are producing antidotes to the plagues that keep infecting the humans. A challenge is persuading that thick-headed Noah to scoop up a herd of animals and keep them safe in a ship while the human plane drowns, when all he wants to do is bed women and drink ale. A challenge will be getting Raph to agree to this insane idea of yours."

"Raphael doesn't know anything about this. This is a secret between you and I."

Jophiel threw her hands up in exclamation. "And our big brother isn't going to notice when I'm missing for a decade?"

"We'll think of something," Gabriel reassured her.

A warrior strode by, casting a frown over at them, disapproving of their raised voices. They smiled serenely almost mirroring each other's expressions, and then scowled once more when he was out of sight.

"You're an idiot if you think any archangel can walk into a vampire den and ask to be friends."

Gabriel worried at her lip. "You're right . . . but you could go if you were something or someone else."

Jophiel's beautiful eyes narrowed on her sister. "At a thousand years old, I think my chances of morphing into anything other than myself are pretty slim."

"Not necessarily," Gabriel said quickly, her mind ticking over.

"You mean for me to pick a champion, someone among the races, to do your dirty work? No. Whatever you're thinking, it's not happening. I'm an archangel. I'm a leader, a fighter, an angelic being of the heavens and I won't be lowered to this. Your plan won't work." Jophiel turned away and strode through the water.

"I asked Zacharael to go," Gabriel called.

Jophiel froze and looked back over her shoulder.

"What did he say?"

Gabriel shrugged. "He said no for now, but he'll change his mind."

"You know for sure?"

She nodded. "He'll go for another reason, but the outcome will be the same."

"He hates anyone other than the angels, and even then he hates most of us . . . you and I especially," Jophiel said, a slight tremor in her voice.

"He's no longer the captain of the Heavenly army, but a lone warrior. He will do as I say when I order it."

"He doesn't want to be a part of us. After Zanaria . . . he'll never be how he was again. He will never trust you or I."

"He will," Gabriel vowed, standing up in the water, looking like a Goddess in her flowing robes, with her loose blonde hair.

Jophiel shook her head, her short, brown hair swinging around. "You're always trying to maneuver people, Gabe. You should know by now you can't put everyone in the exact positions you want them to be."

"I can nudge them into the position they're supposed to be and hope they will take the right steps, though." She changed tactics. "Haamiah agrees with me on this."

"Don't drag him into this," Jophiel chided. She assessed Gabriel's expression. "Is Bëyander in on this too? I don't like her. Just because she's a principality, you shouldn't go along with whatever she suggests."

"I don't," Gabriel said indignantly.

"I don't want to argue with you. This plan to unite the realms comes from a good place, I'm sure, but it's not realistic. I don't know what end goal you have in mind, but there must be another way to get there." Jophiel stepped up out of the pool. Before leaving, she turned back once more. "I'm warning you: don't bring Zacharael into this."

"You promised me," Gabriel called.

Jophiel's heart sank. She should have known Gabriel wouldn't forget. Had she known the terms and conditions would change from the offer she had made Zacharael, she probably wouldn't have offered to take his place.

"I promised you when I thought I would be watching over a nephilim child, not when I was expected to go the human realm and unite creatures great and small. The promise is void and you know it."

Gabriel stepped out of the pool and glared at Jophiel. "Fine, I'll take the last option available to me; I'll go, but *you* will have to cover for me."

Jophiel scowled back. "Fine."

11

"We are all here for some special reason. Stop being a prisoner of your past. Become the architect of your future."

Robin Sharma.

I was in bed by eleven, a backpack by my side filled with a change of clothes, muesli bars, a couple of knives and throwing stars, and my iPhone charger. Lord knew I had been in my fair share of mishaps. I'd learned from my mistakes and at the top of that very long list was to always take spare underwear when going through a portal.

I was able to get a little bit of sleep before my phone began to vibrate. Sleepy-eyed, I scrambled around the bed before finding it tucked under a pillow.

"Yes?" I growled down the phone. If they expected manners, they should call at a reasonable time. I rubbed my eyes, trying to soothe the ache from the abrupt awakening.

Silence answered me. I glanced at the phone, rolling my eyes at the blocked number.

"Who is this?" I demanded, anger rushing through me.

I was just about to hang up, when a voice yelled, "Get down!" down the phone.

I sat bolt upright and threw myself out of bed onto the floor as the window exploded, glass flying through the air all around me.

I screamed as the house shook. I fell against the door to my en suite, wincing as my shoulder struck it. Another explosion rocked me, screams ringing out through the house. I scrambled to my feet as I faced the man who had just come through the window.

I whipped a knife off my table and held it tightly, my knuckles turning white with tension. Someone flying through your window in the middle of the night had to be bad news.

"It's me. Don't freak out."

That voice . . . *Aidan*. "What the hell, Aidan?" I screamed. "You just smashed through my window." I felt too on edge to avoid stating the obvious.

Aidan stepped out of the darkness, closing the distance between us and began to drag me across to my now glassless window.

I snatched my arm away from him and started to pull off my pajamas, sliding into the black combat pants I had set aside for the morning. I wasn't even remotely bothered about Aidan seeing me naked; he'd seen me in much more compromising positions before. Who cared about nudity after what we'd been through?

"We don't have time," he complained, even as his eyes drank me in.

"What's going on?" I asked, ignoring him.

He coughed, clearing his throat. "The house is under attack. We have to go now."

"Yeah, by you."

He rolled his eyes at me.

I snorted. "You think I'm leaving Sam, Trev and Gwen?" I rolled my eyes at his silence as I strapped on my sword holder, crossing it over my back. I pulled my backpack on over my shoulders and slid a sword out of the sheath.

"They're already in the house." Aidan hissed.

"Aidan, you can come with me or go back out the way you came in. I'm not forcing you to do anything, but at the same time I'm not leaving my friends here if we're under attack," I snapped.

I spun around as my bedroom door was kicked off its hinges. It slammed into the dressing table, falling to the floor at an angle.

A shape filled the doorway, huge and broad with at least six limbs that I could make out. Snarling filled the air, as well as growling, hissing.

I stepped forward, swallowing my fear, letting my power flow over me. I was ready to attack when the beast was yanked back out into the hallway. Savage roars filled the room, screams echoing from further on in the house . . . the unmistakable sound of a body falling to the floor with a wet thud.

"Are ye staying here then?" a low, lilting voice called out.

"Drew?" I whispered..

I clambered over the fallen door and rushed out of the room, skidding to a halt as I spotted the lycan standing casually over the beast's body, cleaning his blade off on his T-shirt while nephilim ran down the corridor in panic.

"What are you doing here?"

He glanced behind me at Aidan, shooting me a grim look. "Getting ye out of here," he said.

I glanced behind me at Aidan. He looked threatening, a scowl on his usually sweet and smiling face, his muscles bulging from under his clothes. I turned back to Drew who lifted an eyebrow at me in question.

I shook my head, irritated. *Men!*

"What was that?" I asked, pointing to the body on the floor.

"A demon plaything," Drew replied.

He began to stalk down the corridor which was by now empty. The other nephilim must have fled already, but what of Sam, Trev and Gwen? Would they be outside or still in the house?

"There are more of them?" I asked, glancing in the open doorways. I expected another one to jump out at any second.

"I saw about eight circling the house. There may be more."

"We need to get out of here, Jasmine. Sam and the others are probably outside by now," Aidan called from behind.

I ignored him and pushed on, creeping through the corridor after Drew. We edged towards the stairway, peeking over the bannister to see shadows moving below us.

I screamed as a force hit my back, flinging me through the wood and down to the stairs below. I held out my arms to cushion the fall, groaning at the pain that ran up my wrists. I rolled to the side as the bannister I had fallen through crumbled and fell down, smashing down where I had fallen

I jumped up to my feet and leaped over the bannister to face fallen angels swarmed around me.

I reached behind me and pulled out another blade, swiping at the first fallen angel who tried to tackle me. I cut through the tendons of his arm, noting the way he howled, clutching his lower arm as he dove away. I spun, ducking away from a sword swing, lifting my own up to counter another blow. This one was strong, his strength bearing down through the metal as he hurled me back against the wall. I gritted my teeth and pushed on the sword, forcing it up and away from my throat. I kneed him in the stomach then used my flat foot to boot him, breathing a sigh of relief as he sailed through the remaining bannister into the wall.

I was knocked to my back, a fallen angel straddling me while trying to dislodge my sword to reach my neck. I searched deep for my power and pulled up fiercely, grinning as it flooded through me like intravenous euphoria.

I knocked him sideways and slid my sword through his throat, decapitating him cleanly. I could hear shouts from upstairs. I couldn't expect any help from Aidan or Drew if they were dealing with their own fight.

Another fallen angel stepped forward and was roughly shoved aside.

"No, boys, this one's mine."

My eyes searched the faces of the fallen for the one who had spoken. It was the voice of my nightmares. It was horror and death and torture all rolled into one creature.

The fallen angel stepped forward. He towered over the others, at least seven-foot tall. He wore dirty, ripped jeans that molded to his legs, and was naked from his waistband up. Gold writing covered his upper body, ending just below his jaw. Thick, long, black hair fell in a mess around his face and he pushed it aside as he perused me.

"I'm not yours," I snarled, hearing my voice tremble.

A slow smile spread across his face. "You'll always be mine."

I shook my head and clenched my fingers around the hilt of my sword. "I can't wait to kill you."

A laugh rumbled through his throat until he roared out loud.

In a flash of a second he was on me. He punched me in the jaw so hard my eyes almost rolled back, my vision sparkling as I almost passed out. I forced myself to hit back, punch for punch. I spun around, trying to catch him off guard but he deflected the blow easily. I bent and scored a jab in his stomach, though his abdomen was so hard I bet he hardly felt it.

He lashed out again with a snarl as I fell backwards, smacking my head on the floor. As he rushed towards me I lifted up both legs and thrust him back, rocking forward onto my feet. With my power pouring out of me I sped forward and buried a shorter knife in his heart. I left it there and leaped back.

He lifted his hand to the knife and pulled it out, staring at it. His black eyes found mine and he grinned. "Oh, that feels so nice. Do it again."

My mouth dropped. Why hadn't that hurt him? I had stabbed it in to the hilt, and . . . nothing! My body began to tremble; I had lost my only weapon. Why on earth had I left it?

"What do you want?" I shouted.

He smiled. "Why would I tell you that? Actually, maybe I should. I might find some way of . . . getting it out of you."

I stared in stony silence.

"Where is the Falchion? And the dagger of Lex?" he asked.

"Lilith said you had the Falchion," I replied.

He laughed. "Lilith is an idiot."

Though I didn't know exactly what the dagger of Lex was, I knew that Zanaria was the key to getting it. *She* knew where it was. As for the Falchion, the last I'd heard it was hidden in the White House, but that was before it had been attacked.

"I can't help you, so I'd suggest that you leave," I said quietly, foolishly hoping he would.

"Oh, no. I found something that I want much more than the dagger or the Falchion . . ." His voice reached out to me and found some terrified part of me, bringing it forward until I couldn't do anything, couldn't move a muscle or say a word.

While I stood frozen, he caught me by the shoulders and threw me away. I hit the wall, the plasterboard shattering beneath my weight, and I fell to the floor in a daze.

I got to my feet shaking, and kicked out at him, catching him in the face. He snarled and his fists flew again. I dodged the first but the second had me bent over, winded. He grabbed my arm and wrenched it behind my back, throwing me against the wall again. He held me there, squashing his body up against mine even as he crushed my arm in his grasp.

I grimaced and gasped, trying to push him off me. I couldn't see a way out of this. I couldn't picture a single move I had been taught to loosen his grip. I was quickly losing control, and for that matter, all hope. Maybe that was the problem. I was fighting like one of them. Maybe I need to fight like myself.

I lifted my free hand and grabbed him by the throat, letting my fingers slide until I found his windpipe. There, I dug my nails in as hard and quick as I could. I groaned as my fingers slid into his flesh. I squeezed my fingers tight and pulled.

With an anguished squeal, Asmodeus let go of me and thrust my hand away, falling backwards. Now was my time to go for it. I grabbed his arm, forcing him to bend, and kicked him in the stomach, striking again, rewarded by seeing him fall to the floor. He rolled away and jumped up. Spinning, he threw a kick at me. I knocked it away easily and booted him in the balls, laughing out loud as he fell to his knees, his hands clutching his groin.

Moving closer, I grabbed him by both arms and threw him into the crowd of fallen angels who roared angrily.

"Let's go," a voice bellowed behind me.

I turned to see Aidan and Drew were standing at my back. Aidan grabbed my arm and dragged me down the corridor. Unwilling to stay and fight, I sprinted with him, running through the house until we were out in the garden and running to the very bottom. All around the garden, angels stood with their swords raised and their angry expressions on the house.

I screamed in relief to see Sam, Trev and Gwen standing in a huddle behind Haamiah and Elijah. I threw myself into Sam's arms, then hugged Trev and Gwen.

Gwen looked at the wounds down my arms and legs and my rapidly bruising face. "Oh my God, are you okay?"

I nodded and turned to Haamiah. "Asmodeus is in there."

He grimaced. "I know. He won't find what he's looking for."

I pulled back, staring at him. "How do you . . .?"

At his look of warning, I fell silent and answered the question for myself. He was a principality angel. It was his job to know what was going on and to organize counter measures.

"You need to go," he said to me.

I frowned, insulted. "What about everyone else?"

"He won't find what he's looking for, so he'll not be happy until he leaves with something he wants."

I trembled and stepped back. "I can't leave everyone in danger. I can help. I can fight."

Haamiah sighed. "You can't fight him. So go. That's an order."

Well, that was like a blow to the head. Hadn't he just said that he trusted me? That he knew I would do the right thing? I winced at his words and blinked away the hot rush of tears that stung my eyes. Asmodeus was scary, but to know that even after the years I'd spent here, I still wasn't trusted or appreciated? I helped destroy the witch on the werewolf plane, killed a heap of demons in the tournament and won the damn thing, fought off Lilith and her pack of wolves . . . and I still wasn't good enough to help?

"She sure as hell can kill them deader that ye, Grandpa," Drew drawled.

I turned and stalked through the bushes, away from them. Sam, Trev and Gwen ran after me.

"I'm sure he didn't mean it like that." Sam grabbed my arm and swung me around, dropping his hand when I winced at the bruise he had just squashed.

"Yeah, he didn't mean it. He knows you're one of the best fighters here," Gwen said.

"He did mean it. He thinks I'll just get in the way," I said stiffly. I held myself rigid. If it wasn't bad enough that Asmodeus was here, invading my home, Haamiah had just said I couldn't fight. I wasn't good enough. Was this because I wasn't a nephilim? I wasn't an angel; I wasn't anything. No one like me existed. I was in no-man's land.

"We need to leave this place," Aidan stared down at me.

"I guess I don't have any choice," I said bitterly.

"Come with me to the lycan. You'll be safe there," Drew said.

I shook my head. "No, I need to go to the valkyrie. I was headed there anyway." I turned to look at Sam and Trev. "I'd understand if you can't come; if you wanted to stay with Haamiah."

Sam bit his lip. "I want to come with you, but . . ."

I smiled as he glanced towards Haamiah. He saw Haamiah as a father figure; he wouldn't leave him when he was under attack. I glanced at Trev who looked equally uncertain.

"I'll come with you," he said finally.

"You don't have to," I said, though I was actually pleased he was coming. Trev was the only other person here who knew what it felt like to become something other, something reviled and hated amongst everyone else.

"Ye'll no' be going with just another nephilim. Whether ye're some sort of valkyrie warrior or no'," Drew said, glancing back towards the house as fire began to lick at the roof.

I glanced at Trev. "I'm not a nephilim," he said. "I'm a vampire."

Drew swung his sword round to face him. "A vampire?"

"Stop!" I hissed. "He's still a nephilim. He was bitten recently, but he's still a nephilim."

Aidan stepped forward and pushed on the sword, lowering it.

"I'm coming."

Drew laughed. "A fallen angel going to see the valkyrie? Do ye expect to leave with yer head still upon your shoulders?"

Aidan squared up to him. "I've been there before as Jasmine's guest."

"Stop it," I said, holding my hands up to them. "Aidan, you can come if you really feel you need to."

"I *will* be coming," Drew added.

I sighed. "Fine, but let's go before . . ."

Screams erupted as the fallen angels poured from the house into the garden. The angels roared and met them head on, swords clashing, body parts being ripped off. The nephilim were huddled between the angels. I spotted Joe and Will, Daton standing in front of them, protecting them.

Aidan steered me away. "How are we getting there?"

"Portal," I answered.

Surrounded by my friends, I concentrated, pulling on my power, forcing it out through my body. The ground shifted and I staggered before the world righted itself. I grinned with relief as Sam placed his hands on my hips, looking down at me with a soft smile.

"I'm with you." He mouthed.

I felt my friends close in, leaning as close to me as they could get, then the ground dropped away and together we fell.

12

"It is your reaction to adversity, not the adversity itself, that determines how your life's story will develop."

Dieter F. Uchtdorf

We landed in a rush, smacking into the ground and each other. I found myself turning at the last minute and grunted as I landed on something hard, then something even harder landed on top of me.

"Sorry," Drew groaned, sliding off me onto the pavement.

I looked down into Aidan's eyes. He had turned me, cushioning the blow as we had fallen. I bit my lip and slipped off him, staggering to my feet. I reached out, grasping his hand, and pulled him up after me. He said nothing, but turned away to quickly help Gwen to her feet.

"Um . . . Jas?" Sam mumbled.

I turned to look at him, taking in his wry and faintly worried expression. I glanced around.

We were in the right place, thankfully, though perhaps I could have picked a better spot to land. We were standing in the middle of the road, a few houses down from the one I was aiming for. Thankfully we'd managed to get off the road and onto the pavement before any cars turned onto the street. I led the way to the front of the valkyrie house.

"This is it," I said with a nervous laugh.

Sam whistled. "You never said your folks were rich."

I rolled my eyes. "Come on."

I stepped up to the gate and pressed the button on the small gold speaker dial. There was a long pause before someone answered.

"You're speaking to a representative of the House of Pain. Press one for immediate death via decapitation, two to release the hounds and three to be hit by the ugly stick," a sultry voice purred over the intercom.

I bit my lip and glanced at the others. I pressed down on the speaker key. "I'm here to see Caleb. It's Jasmine."

Another pause.

Silently, the tall, black gates swung inward, an invitation to enter. I led the way through them, marching up to the house.

The door swung open and a pink-haired woman peered out at us. A tall, blonde man pushed past her and jogged towards us with a grin. I sighed with something close to happiness as he neared. He was ruggedly handsome; no pretty-boy looks or fancy hair, but he was tall, muscular and stocky. His short, blonde hair would have been the same colour as mine, if I didn't regularly dye it, and his blue eyes were like the colour of arctic water—piercing and intense. He was dressed casually in jeans and a T–shirt.

I let my face relax, my mouth stretching wide to smile as he wrapped his arms around me and pulled me into a bear hug.

I blushed when he put me down, rolling my eyes as Drew and Aidan closed in from either side.

"Hi Caleb," I said, smiling.

He returned my grin and gestured for us to follow him into the house. "Come inside. I'm pleased you came, but it's better to stay out of sight for now."

"You're having problems too, mate?" Drew asked with a frown.

Caleb nodded. "It's everywhere. This human resistance is making life difficult for all of us."

"They don't know about you though, right?" I asked, my heart pounding painfully.

Caleb flashed a reassuring smile. "Humans are no match for the valkyrie, but I take it they've found the angels?" He raised a brow in question.

I nodded. "They've found us a few times but they've been diverted."

"Until now. I'm pretty sure a horde of demons and fallen angels attacking the safe house isn't going to be so easily covered up," Sam muttered.

Caleb stopped in his tracks and spun around. "You were attacked?"

A flash of lightning split the sky. The house looming over us lit up for a second. When my eyes adjusted I jumped. Caleb had been surrounded.

Beautiful warriors—my valkyrie kin—stood with their teeth bared and their weapons drawn. Aidan and Drew stood battle-ready while Sam, Gwen and Trev looked shocked to the core. I noted that Trev's fangs had protruded and he held his mouth open slightly as though he were ready to sink his teeth into anyone who dared to approach.

Caleb lifted his hand to ward off the valkyrie. "It's okay," he growled.

He turned and stormed off into the house while we followed at a safe distance, surrounded by the warriors.

We pushed through the crowd and followed Caleb down the winding hall into the kitchen. It was spacious and modern, with a large kitchen table that ran almost the length of the room. Most people would think the sheer size of it was absurd, but I knew that at least twenty valkyrie lived in this house, with other valkyrie coming and going, and many other visitors, such as the witches, with whom they were allied.

I refused to acknowledge Aidan's protective stance and Drew's disapproving glower. It was clear for all to see that they felt threatened by the valkyrie here, and truthfully, if I wasn't one of them, I'd probably feel a little overwhelmed myself. My family was large, loud, exotic and incredibly terrifying.

Sam bumped into me from behind, apologizing. I glanced up at him, breaking into a grin when I saw how huge his eyes were as he took in the dozens of faces that appeared in the hallway, on the staircase and peering out of adjoining rooms into the kitchen.

Trev and Gwen had similar expressions but it was Sam's that I treasured the most; lust and amazement. This was the first time I realized Lilura hadn't broken him with her betrayal. He was still Sam. I hadn't lost him after all.

"So what brought you here? Did you come for protection? I promise you'll be safe here. You and your friends are always welcome," Caleb said, grabbing a bottle of Jack Daniels from the shelf and beginning to pour into a cluster of glasses. He poured in some Coke and handed them out.

Gwen frowned at hers and placed it on the shelf behind her while the boys exchanged varying looks of glee and drank deeply.

I stared down, swirling the brown liquid around in the glass for a second, then back up at Caleb. He raised his eyebrows in question.

"It's first thing in the morning," I said.

Caleb laughed. "It's eleven at night."

I flushed red. *Of course the time had changed. Rookie mistake.* I shrugged to cover my embarrassment and took a sip. It was cold and tangy . . . the perfect post-attack beverage.

I paused for a second before answering him. "We didn't come for protection; it was just a coincidence that we were headed here at the same time as the attack." I took a deep breath. "I think I had a vision about the four horsemen. They were torturing someone. There was another guy there who could see me and touch me. I've never had a vision like that before."

Caleb's eyes closed as he thought. "Are you sure you didn't travel through a portal? It doesn't sound like any vision I've ever encountered."

I sighed. "I know. That's why I'm here. I'm pretty sure it wasn't a portal, but I don't know what else it could be if not a vision. If it was a vision then maybe I was meant to see it so I can go and stop what they're doing. If not . . . if it was a portal . . . then I just left that person there to die." I bit my lip.

Caleb's expression softened while Aidan put his arm around me, squeezing my shoulders. I quickly found myself removed from Aidan's grasp by Drew, the lycan towering over me disapprovingly. Sam quickly pulled me into an embrace as soon as Drew had let go of me. As traumatized as I felt about the whole situation, I could find some humor in the quiet growl Drew released. I refused to allow myself to be bothered by the fact I had just been manhandled by three huge guys in the space of a few seconds; there were more important things to worry about.

"Lass, there's nothing ye could've done against the horsemen anyway," Drew said.

I pulled back and nodded, turning to Caleb with what I hoped was a serious expression. "I don't know that because I don't know what it means to be a valkyrie. I want to know more about who and what I am. I need to know what I'm capable of."

Caleb's teeth flashed in a white grin. "There's my girl. Us valkyrie are inquisitive and demanding and in control. I'll tell you anything you want to know."

13

"There's nothing wrong with you. There's a lot wrong with the world you live in."

Chris Colfer

"If you want to know what you're truly capable of, I'd start by getting rid of that ring," he said, pointing to my hand.

I glanced at my engagement ring first, annoyed at his easy dismissal of Zach. Anger flared briefly; how dare he decide to now play the father role in my life? I blushed as a second later I realized what he meant.

I looked down at the beautiful silver and opal ring Zach had given me. At first I had thought he was crazy when he had told me it helped to contain my power, then I had been annoyed. I had been brash and arrogant, thinking I could control the magic flowing through me and had been pretty annoyed he thought I needed to be controlled. After drinking the Star Mist and almost destroying numerous people and buildings, I had decided it wasn't such a bad thing to wear. My valkyrie side kept harvesting talents, adding to my magic ability, while my fallen angel side ensured a pot of anger was kept boiling deep inside of me at all times. It was a terrible combination, one that resulted in me flinging my magic out whenever I was mad. The ring was definitely handy and since the Star Mist had worked like a turbo booster, it had been the only thing keeping me from destroying the people I loved.

"I'm too dangerous without it," I said, refusing to blush or cower away. One thing I knew about the valkyrie: they never admitted to any weakness whatsoever but this was something different. The ring, or lack of it, would result in death the moment I fired up.

"Take the 'too' out of that sentence and you're right," Caleb said gently. His eyes softened and he showed me the hint of a smile. "Valkyrie *are* dangerous. We're strong, fierce warriors and can level a city with our fury. Our war cries spark lightning; a sign of the gods joining in our wrath. In *our* world might is right . . . and the valkyrie are the strongest of them all."

Aidan and Drew huffed behind me. I grimaced at them sheepishly. Although I loved to hear about the valkyrie, and it was a pretty cool heritage to have, it was a little embarrassing to have your father claim to your friends that you and your kind were stronger, meaner and better than them all.

I twirled a piece of hair around my finger, something I did when I was nervous. I scowled; I shouldn't be nervous about anything. I did what I wanted and that's the way I had always been. If I didn't want to take the ring off, no one could force me. "If I took it off and I lost control— which I *would* do—I would hurt someone," I said wryly, reading his disappointed expression. I didn't know why I hated that look so much. Why did it matter if he was disappointed I wasn't willing to go psycho at the drop of a hat? I needed to stay in control of myself and I could only do that with the ring. Besides, it was super-cute, and my rock-hard fiancé had given it to me. It was mine.

Caleb shook his head. "Not here. The angels are undoubtedly afraid of your power, afraid of you becoming a true valkyrie. I imagine they would try to destroy you if they saw you at full strength."

I flinched, remembering Maion as he'd said I needed to be "put down." *Asshole.*

"Before I had the ring I had accidents with portals. *Numerous* accidents."

Caleb shrugged. "You're stronger now, more aware of your abilities. Think what you could do if you had more power behind you."

Maybe I could open portals directly to any location I chose. Maybe I could transport whole groups of people, not just a few. I might be faster, stronger, deadlier. But was that what I wanted? Did I want to be even scarier than I already was? Did I want more people to be afraid of me?

"I'll think about it," I finally said.

We stood in silence for a long minute. I wasn't sure what the others were thinking but my mind had spun into overdrive, listing pros and cons like they would never end. If I let my power take me, would I be myself anymore? Would I turn into a crazy, pink-haired soul harvester like my family? Would I turn from the angels, ridiculing them? Would I disgust them so much that my friends would turn from me? Would Zach be disappointed?

During the tournament I had lost myself in the fighting and the pain. I had become someone else completely. After the Star Mist, my power had increased a thousandfold and Zach had given me the ring to help contain it. I'd had a slight taste of the power before I had been thrown into the Never Ending Forest and it had tasted like . . . euphoria. It was like freedom and excitement, with any negative emotions eradicated completely. It was like an icy blast of pure control. I don't know what would have happened if my power hadn't been contained when I was imprisoned.

Drew brought me back to reality. "What of the horsemen? We've all heard the tales but until the wee lass spoke of seeing them, I'll admit I thought they were long gone."

I felt behind me for the kitchen table and pulled out a chair. Eyes weighed on me as I pulled it out slowly and sat down. I needed to sit. Whatever Caleb was going to say was big; I could feel it in my bones. Was this another example of my valkyrie power? Was I copying Haamiah's future-predicting skill, or was I somehow telepathically hearing what he had to say like Sam?

"Everyone knows that the four horsemen are the heralders of the apocalypse. What most people don't know is that they've actually been to the human word twice before, to a plane called Avador once and a few others have been equally unlucky to host the hounds of hell," he said.

Gwen stepped forward, shaking her head. "What? How is that possible? The horsemen are the bringers of the apocalypse. There can only be *one* apocalypse."

Caleb snorted. "No, there can be a lot more than one. They aren't some futuristic, angelic myth like your up-themselves angels have been spouting for hundreds of years. They're fucking goblins! They're the henchmen of the goblin king."

My jaw dropped. My heart stopped beating for an entire second. Looking around the room from Caleb's exasperated expression across to Drew who was in the throes of hilarity then to Gwen who was scowling in utter disbelief, I could see that this wasn't news to just me.

"They're goblins? What a load of bullshit." Gwen rolled her eyes.

I frowned in her direction. "He's not lying, Gwen." I bit my lip when I realized that I'd spoken quite harshly. Gwen had been a bitch recently but there was no need for me to act like that too. I guess I just didn't like anyone accusing the only biological family member I had of being a liar.

Caleb scowled at Gwen. "If you've finished, then listen up. Goblins aren't the creepy little half-humans you see in the movies. They're soulless demons. They're your worst nightmare come true. Don't make the mistake in thinking they're cute little playthings." He turned back to me.

"The first horseman is called Conquest, the second is War, the third Famine and the fourth Death. They don't necessarily come in that order; they like to mix it up and fuck with us so you've got to keep your wits about you. Conquest likes to go after the top guns, anyone he sees as a hero or a leader. He likes to bring them down with a bow and arrow. He's a sadistic son-of-a-bitch, so watch out for him. War is a trickster. He's like your principalities; he plots and schemes to get what he wants. He can turn people against each other, and create hostility and confrontation out of nothing. Wherever he goes, mass slaughter follows.

"Famine is the quiet one. His agenda is pretty self-explanatory, and if you come across him you're pretty screwed. You kill fast or you get the hell out of there.

"Death . . ." Caleb shrugged. "Death is death. He kills, takes the souls and sends them to Hades to feed the fires. He takes one fourth of each army he destroys."

One fourth? I flicked my eyes towards my friends. If we crossed paths with them, would one or two of us be killed?

"So now we know who we're facing," Sam said.

I looked up at him, trying to gauge his feelings. His face was almost blank. Too much information to process?

I sighed and dropped my head in my hands. "So they're unbeatable?"

Caleb laughed. "Not against valkyrie. *We* are unbeatable."

I stood up, downing the rest of my drink. "So how do we kill them?"

Caleb lifted the bottle of Jack Daniels up, winking at me. "Same as any other demon; beheading will do the trick."

Yes. That would do it.

14

"If you can dream it, you can do it. Always remember that this whole thing was started with a dream and a mouse."

Walt. E. Disney.

"Now it's my turn to ask the questions," Caleb said sternly. "What happened at the safe house? You said you were attacked."

I held out my hand to Sam, accepting the bottle of JD he had swiped from the counter.

"Asmodeus raided the safe house looking for the dagger of Lex and the Falchion of Tabbris," Aidan answered.

Caleb whistled. "That's some pretty hefty loot. I take it he's keen on breaking his way through to the heavenly plane before the apocalypse hits then?"

I froze. "Is that what you think he's doing? I thought *he* was the one to start it."

Caleb shook his head. "No, goblins won't work for angels. No offense, but not many will work for angels, fallen *or* still standing."

I bit my lip at the rage that crossed Gwen's face. Why had she turned so self-righteous? It wasn't as if that was new information. Why had she bothered to come if all she was going to do was whine and argue? The angels didn't like anyone besides other angels; they barely tolerated the nephilim, so why wouldn't the feeling be reciprocated?

"What does the dagger do?" Sam asked.

"It's some kind of angelic relic." Caleb shrugged. "We don't really put a lot of stock in the angelic doings; we've rarely had anything do to with them until now. As far as I'm aware Tabbris was a principality and could put magic into objects. It's said that the Falchion can open doorways to other realms. The dagger, *I believe* is just another weapon, albeit a powerful one. We can only presume that Asmodeus means to break into the heavenly realm and use the weapon to bring down its leader."

"God?" Trev asked incredulously. "He's going to use a dagger to kill God?"

Caleb roared with laughter. "Don't be ridiculous! Your god isn't even in a physical form. He's going to bring down the archangels. Michael would be my best bet."

"We won't let it happen," Aidan vowed.

"Easy there, soldier." Caleb snorted. "This is all hearsay. The angels are full of bullshit; spouting prophesies and myths . . . you don't even know if the dagger and the falchion exist!"

"They do," I said, after a small silence. I grimaced as everyone stared at me in question. "Zach told me the Falchion exists and Lilith told me about the dagger. She said Zanaria knew where it was."

"Why didn't you tell us back at the safe house? We could have saved ourselves this waste of time," Gwen said.

I stood up angrily. "This hasn't been a waste of time! We didn't come here to find out about the dagger. We needed to know about the horsemen and about my vision. If you think for one second that Zanaria would have told us anything she knew about the dagger then you're oblivious. Zanaria hates nephilim. She hates fallen angels," I glanced at Trev. "She hates vampires, lycan and valkyrie, anyone who isn't an . She wouldn't have told us anything. She'd rather see us burn in hell."

Gwen rolled her eyes. "She doesn't hate anyone who isn't an angel, angels aren't like that. Stop being so dramatic; Zach could have asked her, she *is* his sister." She scowled, her dark eyes pinning me.

I clenched my fists at my hips. "Zach's with me. She wouldn't have told him anything," I said. "And I don't know why you think you know her so well. It's not as if you two have ever actually spoken; she isn't exactly *big sister* material."

"That's because you don't know her," Gwen snapped. "I might not have spoken to her directly, but she's an ; she's good and kind, and you're just—"

"I'm just what?" I snarled.

"Ooh, can you feel the tension in here?" A valkyrie stalked into the center of the room. Her candy-colored hair fell down her back in ringlets. Piercings in her nose, lip and ears glinted in the light. She winked at me and pursed her brightly-colored lips to blow me a kiss.

I took a deep breath and exhaled slowly. "Hi Shmaz," I said, when I felt I had regained my cool.

"How's it goin', sister?" she asked with a wink.

Laura Prior

I shrugged. "You know, apocalypse, human rebellion . . . the usual."

"Sounds it," she agreed. She reached up to snatch a bottle of Smirnoff out of the cupboard and sailed past. "We're having a cocktail night if you're in."

"Cocktails? At a time like this?" Gwen muttered. Her face was set in a scowl.

I felt anger flood through me. I had been ready to flip just a moment ago; there was no way I could take that damn ring off when the slightest thing she said could set me off. Her attitude towards the valkyrie was seriously pissing me off.

I crossed one arm across my chest, stretching my tense muscles as I racked my brain. We clearly couldn't agree on anything at the moment and there was a lot of information to absorb, so there was only one thing to do until someone came up with a plan of action.

"I'm in," I called. I grinned at Aidan, and Drew and followed the valkyrie into the lounge.

After a chorus of hellos, we all sat down to join in on the valkyrie cocktail night. The room was packed with dozens of women and one or two valkyrie men, who to be honest, looked just as beautiful as the women. It was like being thrown into some kind of wonderland where the tea was alcoholic and the creepy creatures were sex goddesses. Though I usually rocked my look, feeling confident with my blonde hair and bountiful breasts, being around the ultra-confident and deadly valkyrie made me feel quite inadequate.

Shrugging off my unease, I downed the first drink I was given and accepted another, gazing around the room, absorbing the sight. Everyone was pierced to the max, tattooed or had insane hair styles and colors. Despite the fact we were laughing and talking, each person wore a multitude of weapons; daggers strapped to thighs, swords sheathed at the waist, and some wore odd gadgets with stakes attached to their wrists and wires wrapped around their arms. I guess the valkyrie didn't like to be surprised.

Everyone sat at different heights; due to the sheer volume of residents, the lounge was packed with sofas, chairs, stools, bean bags—there was even a chaise lounge in the corner, with three of the scariest looking valkyrie perched on it. Shmaz, Kathleen and Izzy were the only three valkyrie who I knew besides my dad, and though the others had thrown their names at us, I couldn't have remembered any of them to save my life. Shmaz and another valkyrie were screaming obscene things at the TV while playing a fighting game on the Xbox, and the rest of us seemed to just be passing around cocktail concoctions.

I grinned to see Trev looking intensely uncomfortable as he sat on the floor with a girl stroking his fangs with her index finger. His muscles were locked and he held himself rigid, concentration creasing his forehead. Sam looked in the same direction and turned away, roaring with laughter.

"Can you imagine Haamiah letting us do this?" he asked.

I blew out my breath with a laugh. "Yeah right! He'd probably have a stroke if he saw any of us doing anything fun."

Sam shrugged. "He's not so bad, you know."

I smiled. "I know. Has he always been so intense though? I mean, you've been with him for years; have you ever seen him relaxed?"

He thought for a second then slowly shook his head. "No, he's always been the way he is. He's serious, focused and uncompromising."

"Then why is he acting so strangely now?"

Sam straightened a little so he could accept a jug half-filled with a thick green liquid. He drank deeply and passed it over to me, coughing.

I frowned down at it and took a sip from one of the dozens of straws. Who cared about germs; we were all supernatural here.

"Jesus," I muttered, swallowing back a grimace with the cocktail. It tasted like pure alcohol. It must have at least half a bottle of gin in it.

I passed it along and tried to remember what I had been talking about.

Sam laughed at me. "How is he acting strangely?"

"By letting us do this." I shrugged, letting my mind consider our leader for a second while my stomach rolled. "It's the weirdest thing! Why would he let us leave the safety of the angels when we were being attacked and travel through a portal to another continent when the world is in rebellion, and why would he trust us to solve whatever that vision was about? Haamiah is bossy, possessive, uncompromising, and always thinks he's right. Why would he trust me with this?"

Sam laughed loudly. "Chill out, Jas. He trusts you. He believes in you. We all do. Haamiah knows what he's doing. If he says that you can do this, then you can. He can predict the future, remember?"

I nodded and let my feeling of unease be washed away with the next cocktail.

We each took a turn on the Xbox, except Gwen, who sat in a stiff chair in the corner by the kitchen scowling and we continued to drink until the early hours of the morning, by which time we were all drunk enough to have lost our inhibitions and worries.

"Screw the human rebellion!" Shmaz hollered, spilling her drink all over the nearest valkyrie. A chorus of cheers followed, as well as the clinking of glasses and jugs.

I glanced at Caleb who sat soberly, looking unusually sad. With difficulty, I stood and made my way over to where he perched on the arm of a sofa.

"You're not joining in? You're not down with screwing the human rebellion?" I joked. I paused, an icy shiver running through me as I realized by the expression on his face that he was contemplating royally screwing them.

"We need to talk," he said. He stood and pulled me away from the drunken valkyrie towards the back of the lounge.

I followed willingly, more than a little curious. The humans were killing anyone out of the ordinary, even other humans. They were burning them alive, decapitating them. They'd gone crazy in this mad witch-hunt, but what did he expect us to do about it?

Caleb faced me, glancing over my shoulder. His eyes narrowed in a scowl. I spun around, seeing that Drew had followed us.

"Can you give us a minute?" I asked, after glancing back at my dad.

Drew slowly shook his head. "I've got a feeling I'm going to be interested in what he says."

Caleb nodded, stepping back to make room for Drew to join us fully instead of just hovering behind me. He ran his hands through his messy hair. "Do you really think the humans are to blame?" he asked, surprising me.

"For killing hundreds of innocent people?" I asked, skepticism lacing my tone.

He shrugged in reply. "How many have we killed?"

"Me, personally . . . none," I retorted.

"Jasmine, this started because destroyed almost every government building in the human plane. We don't know why, we weren't part of it, but it was still *us* that started this war."

"You're being very general there, mate," Drew said. "I can assure ye the lycan had bugger all to do with the blowing up of the White House and the rest."

"I'm not saying the lycan are to blame, or the valkyrie, for that matter. But the supernatural world started this, and we need to finish it," Caleb said.

"You think we should destroy the demons?" I asked.

He nodded, glaring at me "We should. We should also take down those who are taking us out."

I frowned, confused. "You think we should kill the humans?" I was astonished. I certainly didn't expect him to suggest that. I had guessed wrong, I was sure of it.

"The mystical world and the human world should remain separate. They should never have found out about us. Killing the rebellion is the only way to stop our persecution and killing the demons involved is the only way to ensure our continued survival."

"Ye can't be serious?" Drew looked aghast. "Ye canna just kill every human who knows about us. They *all* know about us now, thanks to the bloody Internet."

Caleb turned away from me in a flash and threw a glass bottle against the wall, shattering it. In the silence that followed, the sky outside was lit up with enough lightning strikes to tell me he was seriously pissed off, possibly verging on psycho-Jasmine-style.

Drew pushed me back so quickly I almost fell into Aidan, who had appeared behind me. I ignored the faces of the valkyrie who now surrounded us and stepped forward again towards Caleb.

"What are you saying, Caleb?" I asked, my eyes narrowed on him.

He spun around to glower at us. His mouth was set in a grim line. "The humans aren't the only ones to blame, but some does fall on their shoulders too. The evil on our side of existence has been allowed to prevail for too long. Goblins, the fallen, demons, sirens . . ." he spat. "We will go to war. We will destroy them, every last one. The valkyrie won't allow these beasts to share in this plane. The valkyrie won't shame the Gods by allowing blame and disgrace to fall on our name as the shadows extend from the demon realms to taint us. By Woden and Freya, we will be victorious! It is time the valkyrie drew their swords and made the world remember us. Once the demons are sent back to the Hell that spawned them, we will take apart this human rebellion and once again, this plane will be at peace."

War cries erupted around us. Valkyrie screamed their retribution, their anger, their thirst for vengeance against the otherworldly creatures that had wronged them.

Fright sent spikes of alarm up and down my spine. This was definitely a plan, and I certainly was on board with the first part, but taking apart the rebellion . . . that was *not* okay.

Caleb focused his eyes on me. "Are you with us?"

15

"Be yourself; everyone else is already taken."

Oscar Wilde.

I bit my lip, drawing blood. "I want to be. I want to kill the fallen and the demons as much as you. I want to say I'm with you but I have a mission of my own."

"The valkyrie is your family and your allies. You would do well to stand with us."

I scowled. "The valkyrie aren't my only ally. I have others to think of and if the valkyrie attack them then I have a problem."

Caleb scowled at me, questioning me with his angry eyes and downturned mouth.

"I'm allied with the Feral witches of Longly, the harpies of the human plane, the angels, the nephilim." I looked up at Drew. "I owe my allegiance to the lycan, and though Aidan is a fallen angel and Trev is half vampire, they too have my protection and friendship for life. And as much as I would love to kick some demon ass, remember I have my own . . . I don't want to say the word *quest* because that's really nerdy, but I have a mission. I need to finish it."

"We have no argument with witches or the harpies. We will leave them alone if that's what they wish, or, they can join with us, as many of the covens will," Shmaz turned to Drew. "The valkyrie would welcome an alliance with the lycan . . ."

Drew glanced at me then back at her. "The lycan are allied with Jasmine, and that won't change. If she is allied with ye then ye come with her." He held his finger up. "Only for as long as she is fighting with the valkyrie. We go where she goes."

Caleb and Shmaz exchanged a smile. "Agreed," Caleb said. He gestured to Aidan. "You have saved Jasmine's life, I extended our gratitude and friendship to you last time we met . . . it still applies. As for the vampire," he smirked at me, "we have no quarrel with a baby vampire, as long as he keeps his fangs to himself."

"I don't know, I quite like them," a black-haired beauty whispered loudly amid a scattering of laughter.

Trev blushed, clamping his mouth shut tightly to hide his sharp incisors.

"You should continue to find out more about the vision. I've told you about the horsemen and I've given you advice on how to discover what you're capable of. Valkyrie power and ability differs in each case; you will never know the true extent of what you can do unless you let yourself be free, let yourself be a valkyrie. We live without boundaries, without restraints. We embrace our natures and our strengths. You are holding on to your angelic side, keeping the valkyrie within leashed tightly with that ring." Caleb shrugged. "I can't tell you if what you saw was a vision, or portal travel or a premonition. It could be any of them, and only you can work that out. I do think that we can work together in this, though."

"How?"

"You mentioned you were headed to the witches next, then the harpies. Spread the word that the valkyrie is gearing up for war. When you've finished with the harpies, come back and we'll update you on our plans. We'll send word to our allies and when we know who's with us, we'll attack from all sides."

I slowly nodded. It seemed like a good enough plan but I still felt wary about not consulting Haamiah first. Although, he did say that he trusted me to solve it. *Ugh.*

"Okay," I agreed.

"I'm not okay with that," Gwen fumed. She narrowed her eyes at me. "You told Haamiah we'd be going home after we'd seen them. I'm not even supposed to be here."

Sam huffed. "Gwen, it's not as if we had much of a choice other than to bring you with us, and the house probably isn't even there anymore. Do you actually remember the fire and demons the size of bears?"

"They'll fix it. They always fix it."

"And if they haven't? We don't even know where they've gone now."

"We'll find them. They won't abandon me."

"But they'll abandon *us*?"

"Enough already!" Drew shouted. "You're acting like a spoiled brat. Get over yourself. If you don't want to come with us then find your own way home or stay here."

Gwen looked around. "I'm not staying here."

"Then shut your trap," Drew finished.

Sam, Trev and I exchanged a long look. What were we going to do with her? She was pushing us further and further away, and each time we argued it seemed less and less likely we were going to get her back.

"So we're going to see the witches?" Aidan broke the silence. I nodded.

"How are we getting there?"

"They're not on this plane, so we'll need magic." I couldn't risk opening a portal on another plane of existence. Who knew where we would end up? "Can your witches help?" I asked Caleb.

He shook his head. "No can do. They're in hiding. Most of the supernatural world have hidden themselves away because of the humans."

Shit. "I was hoping they would help us find the harpies of the human plane," I muttered.

"We can help you with that," Shmaz grinned, pulling her hair up into a ponytail. She stretched out her arms. "They are not that far from here."

"Great, where are they?"

"New Zealand. Where else?"

Sam coughed. "That's not exactly close."

She shrugged. "I guess it's all pretty relative, it just depends on how far you've travelled."

"How do we get there?" I cut in before another argument started.

"Um . . . airplane," she quipped.

I grimaced. "There's no other way?"

"I wouldn't risk trying a portal. Not with the war brewing," Caleb advised.

I groaned. "I know; if I haven't been there before the chances of arriving where I want to are pretty slim anyway, but what about Trev?"

He looked up at me. "I'll be fine."

"Are you sure? When we're up there you can't go all—*grr!*" I bared my teeth at him.

He chuckled. "It's only a couple of hours. I'll be fine."

Within the hour we had arrived at Melbourne International Airport. Gwen had a face like a slapped arse, Drew was merrily drinking his second whisky and Coke at the bar, Sam and Trev were sitting in stony silence, nursing coffee, and Aidan had barely taken his eyes off me.

"What?" I snapped. "Why do you keep staring at me?"

Aidan blushed. I felt mortified. "I'm sorry. There's just so much going on and I'm tired. I wish for one moment we could just relax and be normal instead of always jumping from one problem to the next."

He nodded. "It's difficult being who you are."

I narrowed my eyes. "Being who I am?"

"Being . . . supernatural I mean. In our world there's always d. . . drama," he stammered.

"Oh. Yeah, I guess so." I smiled gently. "Sorry. Again."

He chuckled and crossed his arms over his chest.

"Flight NZ306 is departing from gate twenty. Please make your way to your departure gate."

We all breathed a sigh of relief. Drew downed his drink while Sam and Trev took the last sips of their coffee, and we all began to walk to our gate.

Any other time Gwen probably would have wanted to look in all of the designer stores, but she remained silent, staring straight ahead as she marched onwards. We reached the gate in no time and stared up at the board. We had twenty minutes.

As the others took seats, I told them I needed the bathroom. I quickly stepped out of their line of sight and headed as far away from the gate as I could. I found a corridor leading to the bathroom and jogged down it, leaning against the wall. At this time of the morning there was no one coming and going, I could be alone for a minute to think.

Could I do it? Could I take the ring off and not lose control?

"Should I try it?" I whispered.

"You should."

I jumped away from the wall, startled.

Aidan stood there, a shy smile on his face. "Sorry."

"You think I can handle it?" I asked, holding up my hand to show him the ring.

"I think you can do anything you put your mind to. If you have trouble, I'm here," he said with a gentle smile.

I squashed my lips into a thin line and breathed in deeply through my nose. I clasped my hands together and slid the ring off, clutching it in my palm. I took deep, calming breaths, desperately trying to feel nothing.

It worked. I was free. I was nervous, yes, but not insane with rage, or currently mid-flight to a hellish dimension. I grinned at Aidan.

I glanced past him, feeling eyes on me. I smiled, wanting to show Sam and Trev what I had done, only it wasn't them.

A tall, middle-aged woman stood only a meter or two away from me. She was flanked by an older man and two younger guys; I could only presume they were her husband and sons.

"Well, look what we've got here," one of the young guys said.

I froze, my heart pounding. Aidan took my hand and pulled me away from the toilets, intending on existing the empty corridor. He stopped abruptly and I bumped into him.

"What is it?" I whispered.

He jerked backwards.

"You demonic scum. You don't belong here, and we're going to send you back where you came from." I heard a deep voice say.

I felt the blow to Aidan as he stumbled to the side. I was in shock. These people were attacking us! At least, they were attacking Aidan. Why did they think he was demonic? How did they know?

I took a second to take him in. He was huge. He was tall, incredibly muscular, with tight-fitting clothes that showed off the cords of muscles across his body. Who *wouldn't* think he was supernatural? He was gorgeous, heartbreakingly beautiful, and kind. He was so gentle and sweet.

It was too late. I had no warning. Rage, pure and white, rippled across me in such a way that I actually felt my body undulate repeatedly. The airport was no longer dull and grey with stark fluorescent lights—it was angry and blunt, painful to my eyes. The corridor we stood in seemed to flex, expanding then closing in on me. My power felt itchy, desperate to be released. It pulsed at my inside, demanding to be freed. I couldn't stop.

My mist poured out, beginning to envelope me as I strode past Aidan and grabbed his attacker by the throat. Though I wasn't exactly tall, I was able to lift him off the ground and choke him. I forced myself to stand still as I crushed my fingers together squeezing, suffocating, and breaking. It was . . . delicious. It tasted wonderful. Something akin to contentment raced down from the hand that held him, soothing my arm, my soul.

I felt a blow to my arm and I turned, dropping the boy to the floor. I ducked away from a punch and grabbed the second son with two hands, lobbing him further down the corridor. The woman screamed and pulled at her husband, dragging him away from us. They pushed open the door to a disabled toilet and locked it behind them. I narrowed my eyes at the door, feeling a vacant smile take place on my lips. I turned to pick up the young man she had left, ready to crush the life from him when I was pulled backwards and spun around.

I used the momentum to lift my fist and make a decent blow to the person who had just grabbed me. At the groan that followed I felt a stream of merriment sparkle inside me.

Lips touched mine. Soft. Hard.

I pulled back, angry, my rage melting my insides. I was ready to scream and sink my teeth into the beast that dared to touch me when a hand snaked around my back, down the curve of my spine, holding me carefully.

I gasped as the rage simmered, becoming more intense and different. Passion warred with it, thawed it. I began to panic. What was happening? I ached . . . *everywhere.*

I reached up desperately, needing to feel real, needing to feel the crush of lips again. There wasn't reality for me anymore. I was dreaming. I couldn't find myself. I needed something real, and what was more real than Aidan? He was smooth energy, all soft smiles and hard muscles.

I ran my hands up to his shoulders, digging my nails in, urging him closer. *Needing.*

Our lips met, soft at first, then harder. I bit sharply on the corner of his mouth, making him open to me. His tongue swept in as his hand cupped the back of my head gently. I felt soaked in his energy, beyond turned on. I needed more.

I felt my rage recede, rapidly turning into lust, every hint of rage and violence turning to a sparkle inside my abdomen, rushing through me like electrical pulses. Aidan. This was Aidan.

My eyes opened and I pulled back. I could breathe again. I stared into his light, pain-filled eyes and down at the hand he held. He'd put the ring back on my finger.

I pulled my hand out of his. "Aidan . . . I'm so sorry. I don't know what I'm doing." I stepped back, mortified, and covered my face with my hands, turning away. "I'm sorry."

"It's okay," he whispered.

"It's not okay. I practically threw myself on you."

"It wasn't so bad." He shrugged, smiling. "And I did kiss you first."

"That's not the point. I can't do this." I rubbed my forehead, a headache starting to pound away. "You saw what happened to me when I took the ring off. How can I be whoever I'm supposed to be if I can't control myself? You saw what I nearly did."

Aidan pursed his lips. "Maybe you can't control it because you're trying so hard to suppress it. Maybe you need to let go completely and just go crazy for a while."

"Oh yeah, that's a great idea," I said sarcastically. *Yeah, why didn't I just go crazy and kill everyone around me, then maybe afterward I'd feel better . . . not.* "How did you even know that would work?"

He cast his eyes downward. "I know you, Jasmine. I just know you."

"Are you coming?" I heard Sam shout.

I jumped away from Aidan and stared down at the men I had assaulted. They were both breathing but unconscious.

"What should I do?" I gasped.

"Nothing. They attacked you. You don't owe them anything."
Aidan dragged me away from where he lay. "You don't owe them
anything, least of all your pity or your regret. We need to get out
of here before security come our way. I don't think anyone saw or
heard us, but you never know."

He took my hand and pulled me down the corridor. We sped
across the terminal and slid in amongst the other passengers.
Ahead of us, Sam and Trev appeared.

"The gate is open," Sam said.

"I'm coming," I answered quickly; maybe too quickly.

I smiled broadly and marched off in the direction of the gate with
my ticket at the ready.

16

"A true lady doesn't start fights, but she sure knows how to finish them."

Unknown.

I didn't think I'd ever felt as nervous as I did when boarding the plane. Any second now, someone was going to start shouting and tell everyone what I'd done. I felt so guilty; I was sure everyone could see it on my face. What did I think I was doing? I couldn't control myself and I'd clearly just proven that. All I'd done was hurt an innocent human or two . . . well, not so innocent I guess, but what about Aidan? I'd hurt Aidan all over again. I was such an idiot. I was an awful person.

I rubbed my forehead with the palm of my hand and buckled my seat belt. I sat in the middle seat, Sam next to the window and Drew on the other side. Gwen, Trev and Aidan sat across the aisle.

"You okay?" Sam whispered.

I closed my eyes. He would know anyway. Why was I even bothering to try to hide it? Hello—hiding secrets from a telepathic friend was the most futile exercise ever.

"You have secrets from me?" he whispered.

My heart sank. And I'd just hurt another of my friends. I whipped my head around as I felt his shoulders shake. He was laughing.

"What?" I hissed.

"You're such a loser. I'm not offended. Although, I am now curious about who else you think you've hurt."

I gave him a mock scowl. "Everyone," I replied. "Everything I do somehow seems to result in someone being hurt."

"Aw, poor Jasmine. You want me to play a violin for you?" he teased.

"Quit it! I'm being serious." I glanced at Drew who was eyeing up one of the air hostesses . . . or the drinks cart, who knew which one.

The lights flickered and we sat in the glow of the emergency beams.

"What's happening?" I hissed.

Drew rolled his eyes. "We're taking off."

"Oh. Okay then."

I sat back in my seat and held on to my armrests as the plane began to taxi down the runway. I winced as the engines screamed when we belted down the strip and took off. As much as I was relieved to be out of the airport and away from the humans who had attacked us, I was becoming only too aware that if anyone chose to attack us up here, it was a long drop down.

I sighed and turned my head. Sam was still waiting for his answer.

"I took the ring off."

He glanced down at my hand then back up at me with confusion.

"What happened?"

"We were attacked and I couldn't control myself. I nearly killed someone."

"Wait, why were you attacked?" he hissed angrily.

"Drink?" Drew asked.

I shook my head.

"She'll have a whisky on the rocks," he told the air hostess for me.

The air hostess, a perfectly prepped and perked blonde with massive boobs, giggled and poured out a glass. Without making eye contact with me, she leaned over Drew and placed the glass in front of me. She turned inches away from him.

"If you need anything else, don't hesitate to . . . ring my bell."

Sam immediately started to choke, liquid spewing out of his mouth. I slapped him on the back and rolled my eyes at Drew.

"Do you get that everywhere?"

He chuckled and lifted his glass to his mouth. "Only on good days."

The plane had quieted a little so I couldn't continue my conversation with Sam without everyone overhearing. Or could I?

I rested my head back on the headrest and began to form the words in my mind.

Aidan was attacked by some guys in the airport. I couldn't hold in the rage. It took over and I nearly killed one of them. They ran away just as you called to say that the gate was open. I just left that guy there almost unconscious on the floor.

I peered over at him. Did he get it?

He smiled and nodded.

Well, that was that. He knew my guilty secret.

You've got nothing to feel guilty about.

I sat up straight, my eyes wide open.

"Easy! What's with you?" Drew asked, moving the drink in front of me to his own tray.

I bit my lip and smiled. "Nothing."

"Alright, but ye seem a bit jumpy. Ye need a drink in ye." He held up the glass.

"It's, like, six in the morning."

He shrugged. "And? You need permission from your mother?"

I rolled my eyes. Why did people keep accusing me of being boring? I took the drink from him and downed it.

I coughed. "Happy?" I wheezed.

"Ecstatic," he drawled.

You're not boring. I heard Sam's voice in my head.

I glared at him. *Stop it!*

When did you start being telepathic?

Agh! I'm not telepathic. I just hear things sometimes. This is the clearest it's ever been. Usually I just hear whispers and to be honest, I thought I was going crazy at the time.

Sam smiled.

I guess I really am a valkyrie.

Sam's eyes found mine. He squeezed my hand. *Yeah, stealing the abilities of your best friend . . . that's harsh.*

Feel free to take it back, loser.

***

I slept fitfully. Sam woke me when we were about to land and I wondered if I would have been better just staying awake. To say I felt groggy was an understatement. Still, it was better to get a couple of hours sleep now; who knew what would happen once we saw the witches.

We filed off the plane and headed through security. I had an anxious moment as three security guards passed us slowly, looking Aidan and Drew up and down. I held my breath but we passed them with no argument.

Outside we stopped in shock. Having never been in New Zealand before, I hadn't known what to expect, and to be honest I hadn't had a moment to think about where we were going, what with the fight and the rage.

Snow-topped mountains surrounded us on all sides while the sun beamed down on us from a completely blue sky. We piled into a taxi as Drew read the address Caleb had scribbled down. Within a half hour we had pulled up outside a dingy hotel at the outskirts of the city. The taxi driver peered at us, then out the window.

"You're here," he announced, accepting money from Drew.

I looked past Gwen to see out the window and grimaced. This was where Tanya's harpies lived?

Loaded trash cans lined the pavement outside, and soggy cardboard boxes littered the floor beside broken glass bottles.

I blew out my breath and slid out the taxi, stepping onto the sidewalk beside the others. Drew stepped forward, reaching for the front door. It was locked firmly.

"I could kick it in," he offered.

"No. It would draw too much attention," Sam said.

"From who? The homeless people?" Drew laughed.

I smacked him on the arm. "If this is the home of a harpy pack, do you really want to kick their door in? Idiot!"

He shrugged. "Fair point."

"There has to be another way in."

"Didn't Caleb give you a number?" Gwen asked.

I lifted my arms in exasperation. "You were there. He wrote down their address and that's it."

She sucked in a breath and turned away.

"There's no doorbell." Sam turned back from the door to us. "Want to try around the back?"

"Couldn't hurt," I said.

He took off to the right, following the hotel wall down an alleyway, which looked as disgusting as the front. How could they live like this? Tanya seemed to know a lot about magic . . .

"You'd think they could magic it clean, huh?" Sam called. When I didn't answer he turned back. I glared at him pointedly.

He winked and kept walking. I sneakily glanced up at Aidan, who stood beside me. He raised an eyebrow in question. *Shit. He knows*. I didn't need anyone else to suspect something weird was going on with me. When would the abilities stop? I couldn't handle many more. If I took the ring off with all of these abilities running around my body while I had zero control of any of them, I'd probably destroy the entire world.

A dumpster lay on its side, blocking the alleyway. Sam looked at me and grinned. We ran for it, jumping at the last second. I cleared it completely, landing in a crouch on the other side. Sam landed on top of the dumpster and jumped down from the edge, laughing. Aidan and Drew leaped over seconds later, neither looking very happy with me. Trev jumped over afterwards, while Gwen landed beside Drew, folding her wings in behind her.

"That was childish," she said.

"Jesus, who brought Grandma?" Drew drawled. He had a point.

"Come on," I said, sauntering off down the alley. "We're looking for a way in, or at least a door."

We picked our way across the rubbish, startling a homeless man lying under a sheet of cardboard.

Sam let out a shout and beckoned us forward. We gathered around him. There was a side door, maybe used as a service entrance, wide open.

"Looks like it's been kicked in."

17

"Pain is inevitable, suffering is optional."

Unknown.

I stared at the cracked door that was resting awkwardly off its hinges. Not a good sign.

"Is it really the best idea to go in there, seeing as something bigger and badder than a harpy pack looks like it's been here first? What if they're still around?" Gwen hissed.

"I'm no' scared of a harpy, or of anything else," Drew said fiercely. He turned to me. "If you say the word, we're going in."

Aidan shrugged. "We have no other lead. This is where Caleb said they'd be."

"What do you guys think?" I asked, looking across at Sam and Trev.

They both peered into the dark interior. "I say we go in," Trev said.

Sam nodded in agreement. "With a vamp, a valkyrie, a lycan and a fallen angel, I think we've got a shot at getting out alive."

"You're idiots. I'm not coming with you," Gwen growled. "You could be throwing away your lives. Who cares about harpies? Who wants to be friends with thieves anyway?"

"They're not thieves. They have to steal to survive," I exclaimed.

Gwen threw her hands up. "Yeah, that's a valid argument."

"It is! Stealing is in their nature. They have to steal. The drawback of their powers is that they can't take anything for themselves if it's offered. If they didn't steal food they wouldn't be able to eat it. They'd just starve to death. Now do you think they're evil?"

"They're not angels are they?" she said, narrowing her eyes.

"Whoa! Hold on here. You think anything other than an angel is evil?" Drew glared. "Then what the hell are you doing here?"

She smirked. "I didn't exactly get a choice in the matter."

He laughed. "I'm giving you a choice right now. Fly home, little bird!"

"Drew," I shushed.

"No, Jasmine. It's time she made up her mind," Trev said loudly. We all turned to look at him. "Gwen, you're one of us. We love you, and you're pulling away, doing everything you can to make us hate you. Well, I'm done. I'm through with being called *evil*, with you flinching every time I move. I'm sick and tired of your whining and your negativity. I . . . I think I'm done with you, so go. If you don't feel the same love for us that we feel for you, then go. Sam, give her your credit card."

"What?" Sam asked, his eyes wide, even as he pulled out his wallet.

"She can't exactly fly back. Flying through the air using her wings like a bird is a bit of a giveaway that someone's not human," he said. "She hadn't planned on coming here, so give her your credit card so she can get a flight back to the safe house, or her father, or wherever." Trev stared at her as though memorizing her face before turning and stepping through the doorway.

"Trev, wait!" I yelled.

"It's okay." Aidan jogged inside after him, followed by Drew.

"Gwen, come on," I pleaded.

Gwen paled. She stared at me then at Sam as he held out his card. It was as though everything went in slow motion. She bit her lip and nodded. Reaching forward, she took the card from him. She said nothing. She turned away from us and walked quickly back up the alley towards the front of the hotel.

Arms encircled me. I turned my face to see Sam. He kissed my shoulder, resting his chin there.

"We'll be okay," he said quietly.

I nodded and gulped down the lump in my throat. "But it's Gwen."

"Trev was right; this has been coming for a long time. She'll either come back to us or she won't. Now come on, we need to find these harpies."

I turned in his arms and hugged him tightly. Holding hands, we entered the hotel together.

We stepped through the doorway, pausing to allow our eyes to adjust to the shadows. I wrinkled my nose in disgust at the putrid, rotting stench that enveloped us. It was a thousand times worse than the damp smell in the alleyway.

"God, that's awful," Sam huffed. I refused to open my mouth to reply, more than a little revolted at the thought of tasting what I could smell.

I blinked, trying to make out the objects that seemed to loom at us as we walked further into the room. Sam stumbled, the sound of something scraping across the floor as he righted himself putting me on edge. He pulled his phone out to shine the light down at his feet.

"It's just a box," he muttered.

I nodded, aware that he couldn't make out the movement but unable and unwilling to say anything. I clenched his fingers tighter and purposefully strode forward, holding my free hand out in front of me so I didn't walk into anything.

A few kicked boxes later, we had telepathically agreed that we were in a storage room or perhaps a delivery entrance.

How have they gotten so far ahead of us? I heard Sam whisper in my mind.

I flinched. I hated having someone's voice in my head.

"Sorry," he whispered.

I flushed. *No. I'm sorry, I didn't really mean that. It's not having you in my head that I don't like, it's the fact that the more abilities I acquire, the harder they are to control. I've got no hope of surviving this if the ring comes off.*

There was a tentative silence. *I believe in you.*

For his benefit, I squeezed his fingers and tried to relax. That was easier said than done though, while walking through an abandoned hotel in the darkness, hunting down a pack of harpies who were more likely to behead first and ask questions second.

Reaching up, I pressed my hand against the wall in front of us. I ran my hand to the side, not finding an edge. We seemed to have reached the end of the room. Sam lifted the camera flash on his phone from our feet to shine ahead of us to find the way out, and a door stood open just ahead, leading deeper into the bowels of the hotel.

I straightened my back, pushed my shoulders down and wished for the life of me that I still had a weapon. Unfortunately for us, we had to leave our knives and swords with the valkyrie as the airlines seemed to frown on such arsenal being carried onto their planes. I wished now that we had stopped somewhere to gear up before making our way here.

Sam stepped through the doorway first, shining his light around to make out our surroundings. We followed the corridor onward and stepped out into what must have been the hotel foyer.

I flinched as eyes flashed back at me, reflected by the light.

"Took your time seeing Princess Up Herself off," Drew drawled.

I frowned. I wanted to say something in her defense but how could I? What was there to say? She'd royally pissed off everyone here with her angelic holiness and discriminatory accusations.

"I know we don't really have another lead to go on, but I can't see a bunch of harpies living here," he added.

I shrugged. "Shmaz and Caleb said this was their last known residence. We'll just have to keep looking for clues."

Drew snorted. "This isn't a detective thriller, you know."

"You don't want to look? You can go home," I replied, heading for the stairs.

I stepped up onto the carpeted steps. It was one of those grand staircases that split off in opposite directions at the top. I frowned, wondering which way I should go.

With a crack, the step disintegrated below me and I plummeted through the staircase, screaming.

I was yanked upwards aggressively, more wood snapping as I was dragged out of the hole. I clutched onto Aidan, burying my face in his chest as he held me aloft, his wings keeping our weight from touching the staircase.

Breathing heavily, I told myself to calm down, ordered my heart to stop fluttering and to settle into an ordinary rhythm.

"Jasmine, are you okay?" Sam and Trev shouted in unison.

"I'm okay," I said, my voice wavering.

Aidan flew me to the top of the staircase and let my feet touch the ground, keeping a tight hold of me. "I'm fine now," I reassured him. "Go get the others."

With a frown, he unwillingly left, swooping back down the stairs. As soon as he was out of sight, I leaned down and rolled up my trouser leg, wincing.

I was covered in a spattering of cuts, wooden splinters sticking out and thin trails of blood running down into my shoe. I pulled as many of the splinters out as I could. I pressed my palm to my calf and pulled on my power. It came easily this time, flowing through my fingers into my flesh, beginning to knit the fibers together.

I shrieked and jumped back, letting go of my trouser leg when Sam and Trev appeared next to me. "You scared the crap out of me," I hissed.

"Sorry, what are you doing?" Sam asked with a grin that told me he wasn't in the least bit remorseful.

"You're hurt," Trev guessed.

No. He hadn't guessed, he could smell the blood. My heart turned cold and I stepped back as his fangs protruded.

"I'm fine. Just a scratch," I lied.

Sam looked from me to Trev, realizing what the problem was. "Easy dude, it's Jasmine, not lunch."

Aidan and Drew landed beside us.

"Thanks buddy," Drew clapped Aidan on the back.

Aidan stared at me, then at Sam and Trev. "Is there a problem?"

"No," I said.

"Jasmine's looking a little tasty to Trev right now," Sam said slowly, still eying him up.

"Tasty?" Drew echoed.

I stared up at Aidan in amazement as he let out a low, warning growl. He appeared directly in front of me, nudging me back away from the guys.

"It's okay." I ducked past him. "I cut myself on the stairs. It's only a scratch," I added as his brows creased in distress.

Aidan dropped to his knees before me and ran his hand down my thighs to my ankles. I shivered then winced as he clasped his hand around my calf. He rolled up my trouser leg.

"It's pretty bad," he said softly.

"I'll be fine. It looks a lot worse than it is."

He placed his palm directly on my skin and began to send his power through me.

"Don't, Aidan, I'm fine." I pulled my leg out of his grasp.

"Just let him fix your leg before Fangs here decides to take a taste and I have to put him down," Drew quipped.

I grunted and held my leg out to Aidan, nodding for him to continue. He ran his hand back up my calf to just below my knee and again, I felt his healing power pulse through me. I avoided everyone's gaze until he had finished, then thanked him with a small smile.

"You okay, Trev?" I asked tensely. He nodded, his body held stiff and tight.

"Okay, let's get going."

"If they were here, wouldn't they have heard us by now?" Sam peered into the dark.

I shrugged. "We have to try."

"Why again?" Drew asked.

I bit my lip. "I made a promise of allegiance to Tanya and I got her killed. I need to tell her family what happened to her and I need answers about my vision. Also, remember, Caleb wants me to propose an alliance between the valkyrie and the harpies."

"Why would the valkyrie think we would take them up on that offer?" a husky voice called out.

Aidan knocked me to the floor as an arrow embedded itself in the staircase bannister behind me. In the darkness, I could see moving shapes headed straight for us.

18

"An eye for an eye will only make the whole world blind."

Mahatma Gandhi.

Aidan rolled, taking me with him. He stood, grabbed my hand and pulled, helping me to stand.

With a roar the beasts descended upon us, the likes of which I had only seen once before: in the tournament.

The first beast to reach me had wings that spanned my length twofold. Bulbous yellow eyes and spikey, jaundiced-looking skin made me think of insects . . . evil giant insects, but insects nonetheless.

I ignored Aidan yelling at me to run and instead filled my palms with my power, grinning as I felt my body recharge while my mind narrowed and focused on the demon. I shot forward, skidding between its legs. I had the impulse to slash at it from beneath . . . but I had no weapons.

I rolled to the side as another slammed down next to me. I could make out the fighting figures of my friends and hear the screams and shouts of the others, but for the life of me, I couldn't see anything I could use as a weapon.

I got to my feet and spun, throwing my weight behind a high kick, sending it crashing through the bannister to the foyer below. Before I had a chance to be pleased it reappeared before me, its wings holding it aloft and level with me.

Feeling a presence at my back, I turned and lashed out, my fists landing blow after blow on the creature that snarled and snapped at me. Jumping up and using a box on the floor as leverage, I sailed over its head and ripped at it's head with all my might as I flew over the top. I screamed with the effort as the flesh finally gave way with a disgusting sucking noise. I fell back, dropping it to the floor beside me.

One landed, crouched on top of me, caging me in as its pincer-like teeth clicked and snapped close to my face. I hit and wriggled, trying to create some space to bring my leg up so I could kick it off me. Just as I was about to resort to something else, Trev's face appeared behind the beast's.

If anything could have scared me more, this was it. Trev's eyes, now black with red rims, were menacing and his face held a snarl, not out of place on one Hell's minions. His fangs had protruded further than I had seen them ever before, sharp and already coated in slick blood. I could only watch in horror as he sank his teeth into the creature's throat, clamped down and ripped the entire neck wide.

Blood pulsed across me in waves, coating my face, filling my open mouth. Cartilage and flesh dropped onto me as Trev loosened his hold and spat the flesh out.

A large bang, followed by six more gunshots in quick succession, had me lying flat on the floor, covering my head with my arms. I was thankful to see that Trev hadn't been completely swept away in the blood lust and had the sense to also drop to the floor . . . and not to sink his fangs into any of *my* body parts.

Roars and wounded snarls echoed through the darkness as I scrambled away from the gunshots. I pressed my cheek to the floor, cringing away from the sound.

A hand grabbed my ankle and I was dragged across the floor. I kicked, catching what I presumed was a demon's head, and dived away. I slithered onto my back and sat up, trying to make out the creature that couldn't be too far away.

I gasped in fright when Drew appeared beside me, close enough that I could make him out in the darkness. He glared past me and let out a low, warning growl.

"What is it? I can't see it," I said anxiously, letting him push me behind him. If I could only see what was there, I'd know what to do . . . but how could I fight something in the dark?

Drew didn't answer; instead he sprang forward with a howl, launching himself at my attacker head on. Snarls and roars deafened me as I desperately searched the shadows for the lycan. He was defending me, I knew it and I didn't like it.

I cowered again as more gunshots fired close by.

Something tight, hard and painful cut into my neck. I shrieked as it pulled taut, cutting into the skin around my throat. I slid my finger under the wire, trying urgently to loosen it but found myself dragged backwards across the threadbare carpet, searing pain tearing at my throat.

I dug my fingers past the wire and held on, easing the hold it had on me, and swung myself around, forcing my legs out in front of me so I could stand. I ran my hand along the wire, finding the person holding it.

Relief spread through me; it wasn't one of the demons. My relief quickly changed to annoyance and my anger flared hot and fierce. We had come here to broker an alliance with the harpies. I had been allies with one of their own, and they wouldn't even hear us out? Perhaps the demons worked for them; one species enslaving another certainly wouldn't be anything new. I had seen an entire pack of werewolves manipulated by one witch . . . was that what was happening here?

I forced my body to go limp, then head-butted the harpy when the wire dropped, scoring a well-aimed hit. They fell back with a grunt, dropping the wire to the floor. I spun and kicked, getting in another blow to the head. Surely only one more and I could knock him or her out. I blocked a couple of poor punches and gave a right hook, cackling when they dropped to the floor.

Lights beamed on my face and I turned, dodging out of the way. The room brightened, torches and flashlights appearing all over. I could finally see what was going on.

I froze in place, my eyes widened to the point of pain. It was chaos. In the darkness I could hear the noises but I hadn't envisioned this.

The hotel was crawling with activity. People fought everywhere I looked; some on the stairs, some down below in the foyer and more still all around me on the balcony at the top of the staircase. Bodies lay strewn across the floor, mostly demons, thankfully, though one or two other creatures were mixed in.

The people fighting looked human, and I would have presumed them all to be harpies if they hadn't been fighting each other. One group of people seemed to be organized, uniformed, with black fighting suits and matching guns and silver knives. The others looked just as fierce, but wore a mismatch of civilian clothes and favored personal weapons.

Which group were the harpies? Who should I be trying to help? Where on earth were the others?

While I had been standing with a dumbstruck expression on my face, someone had crept up beside me. She kicked out, sending me stumbling to my knees. I righted myself and glared at her.

She was small, wearing what I could only describe as a fitted, black ninja suit. Her hair was black, pulled back and plaited. She carried a black handgun which unfortunately was now pointed at me.

I instantly swept my foot up and in an arch, knocking it out of her hand. I sprung forward, kicking and punching, fury riding me hard. I sucked in my strength, determined not to kill a harpy, even though this was clearly not going the way I had intended it to.

"We haven't come here to fight you. We came to make an alliance," I said through gritted teeth.

She sneered at me. "You came to make an alliance with the demon scum, not us."

I ducked a blow, returning my own. *Okay, not a harpy.*

"What are you then?" I snapped, wondering if this meant I could unleash my rage. The effort of keeping it inside was killing me. It felt like I was trying to hold in a bucket of acid, though it was eating away at my insides.

"You're looking at the human resistance, bitch," she replied tartly. She gave me a smug smile. "We're going to wipe you freaks out of existence."

19

"Whoever fights monsters should see to it that in the process he does not become a monster. And if you gaze long enough into an abyss, the abyss will gaze back into you."

Friedrich Nietzche

Rage, hot, blinding . . . it poured through me, filling up every hollow in my body. I felt as though I was on fire. My vision hazed over, glitter jumping from my skin like sparks. Mist seeped from my pores, invading the air between the human and I.

I spun, catching her off guard. I slammed my elbow into her face, knocking her to her knees. Grabbing her long plait, I pulled her head backwards, exposing her neck.

She screamed. It seemed to penetrate me, piercing through my rage . . . and I loved it. I wanted more. I wanted her to beg for mercy and forgiveness, and there would be none. She thought to cross me? She thought she could wipe *me* out of existence? She was dead wrong, just like everyone else who underestimated me; Maion, Asmodeus, Lilith, Lachlan, even Gwen. I wasn't going anywhere.

My skin tingled, liquid pooling beneath the surface. Smoke began to simmer around me, rising up angrily. The screaming got louder and more ferocious but I could barely hear it. I felt comforted by the heat, excitement and raw pleasure tickling my skin softly.

I hit the floor.

"Snap out of it," I heard a voice shout. Then everything went black.

***

I blinked slowly. I could feel myself moving but still I felt apathetic, not quite sure what was going on. I focused on the face beneath me. I was sitting on someone. *Sam.* I jerked back, rolling off of him. I gasped, shocked. What was I doing?

Sam let his head fall to the floor with a rushed and loud exhale. "What happened?" I asked in a strangled croak as I looked around to see that the fighting was over.

He tilted his head and gave me a weary smile. "Don't worry. We just lost you for a second."

I frowned. "What?"

"You were minus your ring. It's okay, I found it."

I looked down at my hand, twisting it around my finger.

"What's happening?"

I turned in the direction he pointed. It took me a second to search the crowd for something that stood out. Aidan knelt before the small human I had been fighting, *healing* her.

I clapped my hand to my mouth. "Oh my God! Did I . . .?"

"No," Sam said firmly. You singed her a bit, but Aidan already said it isn't that bad. He can heal her."

I stared at him, aghast. I'd almost burned a human alive! But she was attacking me . . . did that make it okay? It wasn't as if she was weaponless—she tried to kill me first, trying to decapitate me with a wire then aiming her gun at me. Still, I hadn't set out to kill anyone. That wasn't me . . . although I couldn't deny it seemed to be who I was becoming.

"Jas." Sam sat up and took my hand. I pulled away instantly, not wanting anyone to touch me. He sighed. "You lost control, yes, but you're not the only one." He flicked his eyes to the left.

I knelt, turning. Trev stood with Drew, breathing heavily. He was coated in blood, and by coated, I mean he looked as though he'd taken a bath in it. Streaks of red had begun to dry in trails down his face, his dreadlocks had soaked it up like a sponge and his clothes . . . well, he looked like he was wearing a red onesie.

"He tried to rip your throat out," Sam said, shocking me even more. "He completely lost it, way worse than you did. Drew seems to have calmed him down though."

"Trev tried to rip my throat out? What's happening now?" I whispered, my eyes still fixed on Trev and the way each breath shook his body, the way his hands clenched and unclenched as he fought for control. That was one thing to be pleased about, I figured. I might lose control and go all Black Widow, but at least I snapped out of it pretty quickly with only remorse and guilt as a lingering effect.

Sam shrugged. "A stand off?"

I finally pulled my eyes away and surveyed the post-fight remains. Now that the fighting had stopped, bodies lay all over, bloody pools soaking into the carpet and dripping down the bannisters. The human resistance had gathered behind Aidan and the injured human, while the harpies glared and shouted insults from their various locations around the hotel.

"Between you and Trev, I think you took over the show. The fighting stopped soon after you went all . . . *valkyrie,* with your mist and lightening."

I flushed in embarrassment. Way to look good in front of potential allies. Caleb would be so proud.

Actually . . . he *would* be. Valkyrie valued strength and ferocity above all other abilities, as did harpies. Could this be salvaged?

I forced myself to stand, even though my energy was beyond depleted. I bit my lip and offered my hand to Sam, who took it. Together we stalked closer to the human resistance, where I could protect Aidan as well as address both groups. They quieted down and waited for me to speak.

"We're not your enemies," I began.

"Bullshit!" someone hollered.

"We're not! We came to make an alliance. I come from the valkyrie. They told me to tell you that the apocalypse is upon us. I think you heard me earlier say that I met a friend of yours and I'd like to extend my offer of friendship to you," I spoke loudly, forcing my voice to remain calm.

One harpy jumped down from where she was perched high up on the wall, clinging on to the cracks.

"We heard you. We also heard you say our sister died," she said solemnly, with royal bearing. She held her head high, brown hair swinging behind her.

I nodded. "She did. We were . . . friends. I can tell you what happened if you like."

The harpy stared at me before relenting and shaking her head. "As long as she died fighting."

I nodded, pleased I didn't have to explain anything. How could I tell them that I didn't even know how she was cut down? She could have been asleep for all I knew . . . it certainly looked that way.

The harpy nodded. "You're strong and fearless, and if you are truly from the valkyrie, and they do want us as allies then we'll think about it. The humans, however, we'd rather rip apart before allowing them to leave."

The humans immediately drew their guns, aiming them around the hotel at the harpies stationed in various locations.

"Stop!" I shouted. "You're not enemies."

"They came here to kill us," a harpy shouted out.

"Yes, but instead of killing you they helped us fight off the demons. They know now that we're not the bad ones here." I turned to eye up the small band of humans. "Right?"

The girl Aidan had been healing pushed him aside and stomped forward. She eyed me in disgust before turning in a circle, appraising the room.

She turned back to me and paused, before nodding reluctantly. "I guess so."

"See?" I turned to the harpies. "They're not our enemies."

"So they're not going to move on and find a new pack to hunt down and murder?"

I worried at my lip, eying up the humans. I shot a warning glance at the girl who seemed to be in charge, the one I had burned.

"No. We need to reevaluate things. Those . . . *monsters* were unlike anything we've come across before. They were here to kill you and you know the saying: an enemy of my enemy is a friend," the human said. She tossed her gun from hand to hand and stared at me.

This seemed to be going better than I had expected. "Good," I said. "Then we're allies?"

She nodded.

The harpy snorted. "You may be allies, but the harpies need a bit more convincing."

"You need more convincing? I saved your life. My friends and the humans have helped defeat a demon pack that came to annihilate you, and before today, Tanya and I were allies. The humans have already admitted they made a mistake and that they won't attack the harpies again. Are you going to turn down the manpower they can offer right before the apocalypse?" I growled.

There was some whispering and muttering among the harpies before the leader turned back to us.

"Fine," she snarled. "But our alliance is limited and balances on a knife edge. Never before has a harpy pack been indebted to humans or to valkyrie. Don't think I'm not aware that there is a fallen angel, a lycan and a vampire among your group. We would be fools to turn down such a potentially advantageous alliance, just as we would be if we trusted you completely. One wrong move and we'll be hunting *you* down."

I released the breath I had been holding and nodded.

One by one, the harpies backed away, melting into the darkness.

20

"Fearless is getting back up and fighting for what you want over and over again . . . even though every time you've tried before you've lost."

Taylor Swift.

The humans seemed to relax collectively, and began tending to their wounds once the harpies had left. The woman Aidan had healed gestured to herself.

"I'm Nikita."

I took a deep breath. This was *so* happening. We could have worse allies, even if they were next to useless.

"I'm Jasmine. That's Aidan," I said, pointing. "Sam, Drew and Trev."

Nikita made a face as I pointed to Trev. It was an, *oh my God, you're friends with the psychotic vampire* kind of look. I could see where she was coming from and to be honest, I was surprised that she wasn't giving me the evil eye for setting her on fire.

"You said you were going to reevaluate things. Where are you headed? Or will you be staying here?" I asked.

"Not *here*," she said with a laugh. "We'll find somewhere to lay low. We have contacts, and when we're ready we'll find you."

I raised my eyebrows. How did she plan on finding us, exactly? As for having contacts . . . well, wasn't she playing coy?

"Are you sure you want to? With everything that's going on, the apocalypse . . . maybe you would be safer staying in hiding until it's all over," Sam suggested seriously.

I rolled my eyes. These morons, who had willingly joined the human resistance to kill anything other than humans and in some cases actually killing humans too, weren't going to hide in their houses.

Nikita held up her hand to stop him. "Wait, the apocalypse?" she snorted as the other humans laughed. "Are you for real?"

I flashed a scowl at Sam. I didn't like this girl.

He grimaced. "They deserve to know. If we're allies . . ."

I rubbed my forehead. I knew that. I knew they had a right to know and it wasn't as if *they* had set the apocalypse in motion. I nodded at Sam and stepped back, letting him talk.

"A reliable source told us it's coming . . . that we need to pick a side and choose our allies," he said to Nikita.

"And you believe it?" She rolled her eyes. "You actually believe the apocalypse is coming? That's just a myth, a fairytale told to frighten people."

"You believe in demons, vampires, even harpies . . . you believe in the supernatural so much that you would join an army to hunt them down, yet you won't believe in the apocalypse?"

"That's different. We've seen demons. We know they exist, and we know what they can do."

Sam shrugged. "Believe what you want, but we're telling you the truth. Things are happening, alliances are forming, and you don't want to be caught in the middle."

"We can handle ourselves."

"You have no powers. How can you defend yourself against vampires, the fallen or werewolves? You were lucky today; the harpies took out most of the demons, yet you still lost a lot of people."

"We've got weapons."

"Guns? They'll be no good against the fallen or vamps. I can't see any of you being strong enough to behead either of those, and guns won't work on them. You might wind them but that's about it."

Nikita scowled and bristled at his words. The humans muttered and whispered between themselves. She silenced them. "Like I said, we need to go and reevaluate. We'll be in touch."

"I'll go with you," Aidan said, out of the blue. He stared down at Nikita, towering over her.

"Aidan!" I exclaimed. What was he doing?

"You'll be fine, Jasmine," he said.

"That's not the point," I snapped. What was he thinking, leaving us? It wasn't as if I could tell him now, in front of everyone, that I needed him. What if I needed to take the ring off again for some reason? Who would calm me down when my rage took over? No Zach, no Aidan . . .

I gulped. I was being selfish. I was holding on to him, using him. God, this felt awful. It wasn't just that I was using him. I *loved* him. I loved him, just as much as I loved Sam and Trev, and I certainly wouldn't be jumping on board with either of them escorting the humans anywhere. And that wasn't fair to him. If he wanted to go, to leave, I had no right to demand that he stay. Really, did I actually think I could make him stay just by asking? Aidan wasn't a little lost puppy following me around, doing anything I asked. Though I was sure that was how he seemed to other people, I knew better. I knew him.

Aidan . . . he was *mine*. Could I not keep anyone for myself? Was I not allowed to be selfish in the face of the apocalypse? Was I going to lose Gwen and Aidan in one day? I didn't doubt for a second that Gwen would be gone from the safe house, wherever it had been relocated, when we returned.

I wished I could persuade myself that none of my thoughts were self-centered. After everything I had been through, everything I had survived, the amount of times I had almost been killed . . . I wish I had the right to demand that he stay with me. I didn't have that right.

Aidan could see the turmoil on my face. "I need to do this," he said softly. He turned away from me and gazed at Nikita. "I need to see you safely to wherever you're going . . . if you'll have me."

To my disgust, Nikita blushed. "I'll have you." She cleared her throat. "I mean, we would be happy for you to accompany us."

Without a backwards glance, Aidan guided Nikita to the staircase and followed her down to the foyer. While I watched from the balcony, unable to pull my eyes away, he left.

21

"When something goes wrong in your life, just yell, 'Plot twist!' and move on."

Unknown.

My heart ached. My whole body seemed to tense in sadness and something akin to betrayal as I stared after Aidan down where he had disappeared.

"You okay?" Sam wrapped his arm around my shoulder, squeezing gently.

"I'm fine," I forced myself to say.

"He'll come back," a hoarse voice said beside me. I turned my head, seeing Trev. He had managed to control himself enough to stand close to me, to comfort me. I wasn't afraid of him, not in the slightest. He was Trev. He might go psycho and try to rip my throat out on occasion, but then wasn't that the flavor of the month?

"Maybe," I replied absently, turning things over in my mind. What did we do now?

Drew coughed, clearing his throat. "Umm . . . I hate to be the bearer of bad news, but you didn't ask how to find the witches."

I swung around, my mouth open in some kind of shock-frustration-fury mixture. I couldn't believe it! What was wrong with me?

"Are they still here?" I asked.

Drew grimaced. "They left."

If I knew anything, it was that I could trust in a lycan's sense of smell. There was no point searching the hotel; they were gone.

I could feel my friends' eyes on me. I had no answers to their silent questions. I didn't know whether we should run after them and try to find the answers we had come for. I didn't know if we could find the witches another way. I didn't know what Haamiah was going to say when we returned and said we had failed.

I shook my head, lifting my shoulders to shrug. "What do we do now?"

"We should go to Haamiah; tell him what's happened, and what we've learned," Sam said quietly.

I bit my lip. Go home with my tail between my legs?

"We're together in this. Gwen was originally going to stay behind and find out information on the horsemen from the angels, so why don't we head back home and see what we can find out?" Sam said.

"We can't go home," Trev muttered.

I couldn't help but agree. We had found out *some* information, yes, but nothing that was going to help us solve the vision I'd had. I shared a look with Trev, pulling my gaze away as it dawned on me.

"The house is gone. We don't have a home," I hissed.

"I can text Haamiah, see where they are. They rebuilt after the last fire pretty quickly; maybe they're back there already."

I shook my head. "I don't think so. This wasn't just a fire; the humans found us a few days ago, and now Asmodeus and his demons . . . it's not safe to go back there."

Sam pulled out his phone and began to type. He pressed send and we stood in silence, staring at each other.

"We need to get out of this shit-hole before it collapses," Drew said, breaking the silence.

We headed towards the staircase. Standing on the top stair, I grimaced. There would be no rescue now if any of the steps broke. Still, the humans had gotten down safely so there was no reason why I should plummet to my death . . . except for the fact that I'd almost plummeted to my death not that long ago.

I stepped lightly, following Sam and Trev, with Drew bringing up the rear. The stairs creaked and groaned, but held until we reached the bottom.

We headed in the direction of the corridor we had come through originally. I paused, hearing a groan behind us. I stopped and looked back, Drew hissing as he bumped into me from behind.

"What're you doing, lass?" he grumbled.

"Listen," I shushed him.

The groan got louder, so loud I could actually feel the vibrations through the floor.

"What the . . .?" Drew gasped. "Run!"

He grabbed hold of my arm and dragged me down the corridor after the guys. We soon caught up with them and barreled through the storage room as the ground bucked and rolled. I spotted the open door ahead, the light beckoning to us. I leaped, strengthening my stride at the last minute.

A roar found us. The ground heaved and we flew through the doorway, landing in a heap in the alleyway, just as the hotel tilted. Oddly, once we were out, the ground stopped moving.

I panted, anxiously staring at the hotel with vengeance in my eyes. Was it a safeguard of some sort? Magic, to ensure we left?

Sam started to laugh. "I've never been in an earthquake before."

I glared at him. "An earthquake? Is that what that was?"

Trev shrugged as Sam continued to chuckle.

"Trust *us* to be in a decrepit old building that could fall down at any minute when we're in an earthquake for the first time," I said, still glaring up at the building with distrust.

Sam whipped his phone out and grinned. "They're in Ulaanbaatar."

"Where?"

"Mongolia."

We decided to head to the airport. Since none of us could fly, it was either that or swim to Mongolia. We were able to get a flight to where another plane would be able to take us to our destination. Haamiah would arrange transport from there.

I reluctantly boarded the plane, taking the window seat, and buckled my seatbelt. Sam jostled me on occasion, and him and Trev chatted about a movie they were watching; a gangster film based on characters from the 50s. Sam ordered something to eat, Trev copying soon after.

I rested my head on the corner of the headrest, pulling down the window blind when it got too bright, much to Sam's complaint. I felt exhausted, drained. I needed to sleep for a hundred years. No . . . I needed Zach. I hadn't seen him for days, or at least it felt like it. I felt like I hadn't seen him for days, and it ached.

I missed him so much. I missed everything about him; his bad temper, his dominating presence and brooding demeanor. Most of all, I missed the way I felt when I was with him. Yes, I felt the usual girlfriend things: lust, happiness, whole, and the expected feelings related to having my very own guardian angel: safe, cherished, indestructible. But more than any of that, when I was with Zach I felt as though I was power embodied. Not that I was a power-junkie, but I seemed as though I had a full tank of energy fueling me. I felt in charge and potent, as though I could finally be myself. Until Zach, I had never felt that I was enough; somehow, I wasn't fully me. Now I knew I never would be without him.

I closed my eyes and relaxed into the seat cushions, forcing my body onto standby despite my uncomfortably upright position and the constant stream of chattering going on around me. I let my mind go, drifting on a sea of dreams and white noise.

Slowly, an insidious tone of discord slithered into my body, alerting me to danger. It took a few seconds for me to fully comprehend and that was all it took for the scream of torment to penetrate my mind; the scream from my vision, that tortured soul being torn apart for its secrets in the forest . . . by the horsemen.

I opened my eyes and gasped for breath, seeing Sam's brown eyes inches from mine, his arms around me and his mind in mine, searching. I stared at him, horrified, anxiety rippling through me, then up at Trev and Drew who loomed over me menacingly.

The cabin was silent, except for the shriek that continued to rip through the air.

It was me.

I clamped my mouth closed and sealed it with my palms. Lightning crackled outside, the vibes of electricity filling the air with static. I heard a low moan and someone crying further up ahead in the row of seats.

I would have been mortified if I hadn't been so scared. Terror prickled at my neck as I leaned forward in my seat, protected from prying eyes by Sam. That voice . . . so scared. Was that me? Was I seeing the future, past or present? There was no way out of this mess, yet I needed to do something. The soul who the scream belonged to was beckoning me, calling to *me*.

"What's going on?" an obnoxious voice shouted, nearing me.

I cringed away as Sam searched my mind for an explanation. He turned to the air hostess.

"Just a bad dream, nothing to worry about," he said with a convincing air of innocence, his smile apologetic.

I vaguely heard the spattering of conversation going on around us, and knew the danger I had unwittingly put us in. Despite Sam's assurances that I'd had a nightmare, my scream combined with the eerie lightning had even the most skeptical of passengers eyeing us with uncertainty. I made out a few snatches of conversation, whether telepathically or the usual way. I definitely heard more than one echo of the word "demon".

Aside from the demon comparisons from the other passengers, my horror had set both Trev and Drew on edge. Trev was having difficulty hiding the fangs that had sharpened, his body trembling with the effort to restrain the psycho he hid inside, while Drew's body had suped up in the way the lycan's did when faced with battle; his body had grown larger, his eyes almost glowing blue, and his expression beamed pure menace. We were definitely in trouble.

Sam knew it too. I struggled to concentrate on his thoughts but I could hear wisps of sound as he directed his words to me, simultaneously texting Haamiah.

Too dangerous. Urgently need help. Nearly there.

I shook my head. I couldn't make out what he wanted me to do. I needed directions, instructions. My body was till aching from the torment-laced voice that had torn through me. My throat throbbed, and my eyes stung.

"Get up," Sam hissed. He slid out of his seat, pulling me with him.

The boys cocooned me between them, all pretense of civility gone with the first passenger that approached us.

A tall, lean man with graying, shaggy hair and a several-day-old stubble stomped aggressively toward Trev, who stood at the front of our little huddle. His fists were clenched, one holding a wooden stake. How had he even gotten that on the plane?

Sam tried to push past Trev, his hands held up in a placating manner.

"It's okay, we're not here to make trouble; we're normal people who just want to land safely at the next airport, just like you."

Trev, denying Sam the right to defend him, pushed him back into me, his eyes wide and his mouth open, snarling with his clearly unhuman fangs very much displayed.

The man snorted loudly. "Yeah," he cried. "You look *just like us*."

Trev's fangs were the catalyst that set off the rest of the passengers. No matter how passive some of the humans were, or how cool with the supernatural they claimed to be, no one wanted to be trapped on an airplane thirty-thousand feet up in the air with a rabid vampire.

The human was flanked on all sides by more of the passengers; I could even see the airhostesses handing out knives and other instruments that could be used as weapons to people nearby.

With Drew looming behind me, snapping his teeth together and growling, and Trev in front of Sam snarling savagely, I didn't need to be telepathic to understand Sam's wild-eyed message.

We're fucked.

22

"Guess what? You have a brand new week ahead of you to slay dragons, achieve goals, sweat more, gripe less and ditch the fear! Go!"

Unknown.

This was so *not* the way I was going to be taken out. An epic battle where a hundred swords pierced me, sure; giving my life to save one of my friends, in a heartbeat; as a grandma surrounded by my family, preferably; or having my head sliced from my shoulders by a demon, most likely. However I absolutely refused to have my story end with being murdered by a bunch of old, pathetic people who were obsessed with the idea of a human revolution when they didn't have a clue what was really going on: humans who were completely discriminatory of other species.

No . . . this wasn't how my story would end. I had heard somewhere before that only I could decide how I would bow out. Well, I sure as hell wasn't making an exit here.

"Trev," I snapped. He didn't turn to face me, but I knew he was listening. "Call your mother. We need her."

I knew it was a long shot, but if he could reach her I'd feel much more confident we would have a chance at keeping our lives. Trev hadn't been about to contact his angelic mother since he had become a vampire, but surely she wouldn't forsake him now?

I crossed my fingers, and leaned past Sam; huddled as we were, it wasn't such a long stretch. I lightly pressed my palm to Trev's back, unsure if it would work but keen to give this everything I had. I forced my power through my body to my skin, and pushed it out through my pores until my sparkling mist began to tap into Trev.

I was either revealing myself further to the humans, or giving Trev a power boost. Either way, I guessed it didn't really matter if we were murdered here.

As far as I knew, nothing happened. There were no flashes of light, no miraculous escape by teleportation, no angels appeared and the humans didn't fall down dead.

Trev flew into action, the vampire in him pushing him over the edge. He took hold of the nearest human and lobbed him over the heads of the others. Drew shackled my arm with an iron fist and lunged backward in lycan mode, protecting me.

The passengers behind us screamed and scrambled over each other to get away from us. Drew pulled me to the emergency exist, just three rows down, and pulled it open. I hung onto the nearest seat and shrieked as the open doorway sucked at me, wind whipping my hair into a frenzy.

"What are you doing?" I screamed.

Drew stepped closer, clutching my face tightly. He leaned down and kissed my lips firmly.

What was he doing?

"You need to save yourself," he shouted over the noise of the engines.

I shook my head. Not until there was no other choice.

"Ye can do it!" he shouted. "Jump and open a portal. Ye can't die here. This isn't how ye die."

I frowned. This isn't how I die? I should think not; no one wanted to hurtle from a plane to their death, but still, his words . . . he sounded like he knew something. Did he know something he wasn't telling me?

I glared suspiciously. "I'm not leaving without you all."

"Go!" he snarled, trying to loosen my hold on the chair.

I blasted him with my power, shaking him off. He fell back against the open doorway, clinging onto the nearest seat. Frustration and anger were etched onto his rugged features. He was trying to convey something but I was much more concerned with where Sam and Trev were battling, trying to reach us.

I presumed they had seen the open doorway and thought either Drew or I had a plan; one that involved more than me jumping out and saving myself.

They fought their way to our side. Sam's eyes were panicked.

"Are we jumping?"

"She's going to open a portal," Drew supplied.

I glared at him. "Even if we all jump out together, we won't be able to hold on to each other. I won't be able to get us all through the portal window. There must be another way."

Sam looked from me to Drew, then back at the passengers who, somehow were clinging onto their self-righteousness and their courage and were advancing on us while the plane soared on.

He shook his head, his eyes soft as they touched me. "I don't think there is." He pulled me close, kissing my forehead, his eyes reddening. "I love you, Jas."

Tears spilled into my eyes and were immediately ripped out by the wind. I sent a prayer up, begging for someone to hear me and save us. We couldn't die like this; not when there were angels sitting around up in the heavenly plane doing nothing to help. It wasn't fair.

Sam pulled me into a tight embrace, and together we fell through the sky.

23

"The things you are passionate about are not random, they are your calling."

Fabienne Fredrickson.

Gabriel

Twenty-five years ago

In the Library of Choices, the archangels had gathered to discuss the fate of the humans, and their place among the creatures of the human plane of existence. Books and parchments filled shelves and lay open on tables. Some remained where they had been left, open beside armchairs and upon rugs by the small pools of water that were dotted around the floor. Beside the archangels, the vast space was empty.

Gabriel wiggled her toes in the cool water, smiling gently at the way the water lapped at her calves. She ran her fingers through her long hair, listening to the discussion, bordering on argument. It was an impossible situation, and one that she was certain wasn't going to go her way.

Though the humans believed they had founded the planet, actually, the angels had been there first. While the angels worked with the humans to ensure peace and love reigned throughout they soon veered off in their own direction of agnostic and alternative religion. While disappointing at first, the common values were upheld and the angels were sent to guard all humans, regardless of their beliefs.

This harmony soon attracted the attention of other creatures who, having lived in war-torn realms, quickly migrated to the land of promise to live in comfort and peace. With the migration of so many supernatural creatures and no way to monitor their movements, it wasn't long before the world was corrupted, cults forming, diseases spreading.

Not all of the non-human species were to blame; most were at peace, keen to be ignored by the humans and simply live among themselves. It was only one or two of the demon faction that were to blame.

Thousands of years later and the problem still hadn't been solved. The archangels had convened many times, and still no outcome had been decided on. Raphael and Chamuel were of the opinion that the species should be separated. The witches, wolves, valkyrie and other more civilized beings should be sent to another realm while the demon factions were eradicated, and the angels could control the human plane once more without outside influences. Uriel agreed in a roundabout way, but was mostly focused on destroying the nephilim disease the angels had infected the plane with. Raguel was against destroying the nephilim, but thought they should be placed under arrest on another plane; he had suggested using the waiting room for this.

Gabriel felt very alone. She was the only one who thought the angels should protect the nephilim and work with the species to bring harmony to the human plane. She truly believed that if the angels would only ally themselves with the factions, then good would triumph.

Unfortunately, all of the others were strongly opposed to this. The only argument that seemed to be up for discussion was what to do with the nephilim.

While the meeting had progressed with the archangels expressing their views and making their arguments, Michael and Jophiel were yet to speak.

Jophiel wouldn't lean either way unless Michael forced her to, of that Gabriel was certain. She was a fighter, a warrior, only following instructions, sitting on the fence in all discussions. She clung to Michael, seeing him as the be all and end all. Though Gabriel and Jophiel were close and the only two female archangels, Gabriel knew that Jophiel would agree with anything Michael said.

When Michael finally stirred, Gabriel's heart leaped, pounding erratically, bringing her focus back to the creatures sitting around the pool with her.

"My brothers and sisters," he began. "Again, we reach in impasse. We each advise things that cannot exist together. Some of you wish to save the nephilim and ally ourselves with the supernatural beings." He glanced at Gabriel. "The rest of you consider varying degrees of extermination to deal with our problem; destroying some or all of the creatures for criminal activities, moving them or arresting them. I think it is fair to say that after years of pondering the matter, something must be done now; an action must be decided today.

"After the seers revealed that the heavenly realm faces invasion and destruction in only a few short decades, we need to formulate a plan of attack. Not knowing who it is that will come to our doors hinders matters, we can presume the fallen will have some part in this, but as for their allies . . . I am uncertain. Can we blame all of the creatures in the human realm for the coming apocalypse or do we attempt to guess at who will bring about the end of the world? The decision to destroy not just one species but a huge number of them, possibly making them instinct, is a difficult one when based on speculation, emotion and prophecy." Michael stood in the water, towering over the others who remained seated, staring up in anticipation. "I need to think about this. I will meet with you at sunrise with my answer."

He stepped up out of the pool and strode off while the archangels continued to glare at each other.

Feeling more than one set of eyes watching her, Gabriel stood, shaking off the droplets of water onto the hard floor and nodded to the others. She took hold of Jophiel's arm and pulled her away from the pool towards the back of the library, winding between the bookcases. Hearing a swift intake of breath, she silenced her sister with a quelling look.

Jophiel rolled her eyes and allowed Gabriel to lead her between the stacks. To what end, she didn't know. There was nothing that could be done to change Michael's decision now.

At the back of the room, they pushed open a door and headed out down a corridor towards the residences. Stepping lightly, they evaded notice from the patrolling warrior angels and headed into Gabriel's chamber.

Gabriel's chamber was a reflection of her aura; multicolored, numerous fabrics both contradictory and complimentary, with soft lounges and cushions on the floor, a huge bed draped in material, and crystals from floor to ceiling.

Gabriel closed the door firmly and lay with her back against it, her foot kicked up flat on the door slat. Biting her lip, and wringing her hands together, she looked nervous.

Jophiel tilted her head and scowled. "What are you plotting now, Gabe?"

Gabriel bit her lip. "Zacharael has accepted a task I set him."

Jophiel stomped her foot. "I told you not to involve him in any of your plans."

"He's the only one I can rely on for this."

"Stop!" Jophiel held up her hand. "Whatever you, Haamiah and Bëyander have thought up, cancel it. I'm not playing games with you."

Gabriel turned, hearing a noise in the corridor. She stepped back from the door, silencing Jophiel with a look.

The door swung open, hitting the wall with a bang. Raphael strode in with a mean look on his face.

"Trying to convince her to join your team?" he asked.

Gabriel rolled her eyes. "We're all supposed to be on the same team."

He shrugged. "Well, we're not." He gestured to Jophiel. "What is she using to persuade you with?"

Jophiel glanced at Gabriel, then away, guiltily. She worried with her lip. "A friend."

Raphael shook his head slowly. "Archangels have no friends. They are a complication, the same as soul mates; dangerous, harmful difficulties that should be avoided."

Gabriel flinched, while Jophiel glared at him. "I can have friends without my beliefs being compromised, Raph."

"Then what are you talking about?"

Gabriel stared at Jophiel, nerves sending tingling sensations to her palms. She hoped Jophiel wouldn't say anything. It was true; her strengths lay in planning for the future. If she hadn't been born an archangel, she would have been in the principality class for sure. She was adept at predicting and in guiding humans into their destiny. Unfortunately, the plan had many obstacles to overcome. If Raphael knew what she was planning, he would do everything he could to shut it down.

"We weren't talking about anything," Jophiel denied, much to Gabriel's relief.

Raphael scowled and slowly backed out of the room.

Once he was gone, Jophiel turned to Gabriel. "Don't involve me or Zacharael in your plans. I mean it."

24

"If opportunity doesn't knock, build a door."

Unknown.

As soon as we left the plane the wind whipped at me, sucking at my hair and slapping at my clothes. I clutched Sam tightly, fisting my hands into his shirt while we swung, our legs tangled. Gravity sucked us down, my sense of up and down lost as we spun around and around. Within seconds, Sam lost his grip on me and we fell separately towards the ground. I threw my arm out, desperate to catch hold of him again, but he was too far away to reach.

I screamed, unable to hold it in. I half choked on the bile that filled my mouth. My heart thudded painfully, instinct making me thrash my arms and legs. Now would have been an excellent time to develop an ability to fly . . . it wasn't forthcoming.

As I rolled, I could see shapes around me: Trev, Drew and Sam, I presumed. I could hear Sam give in to the nightmare of plummeting to his death; his screams were as loud as my own. My body tensed, terror, living and breathing inside me.

I needed to open a portal, but how did I do that when I didn't even know which way was up? I'd end up sending one of my friends to another planet while I fell to my death. Still, I had to try. I reached for my power, feeling it curling in my abdomen in the same area as my nerves and the sickness that made me want to vomit. I pulled, succeeding in only feeling more and more ill, my eyes beginning to roll as the light winked in and out.

A band of iron wrapped around my stomach, the pressure hideous enough to make me think I would be cut in half. Was it the plane? Was it something else? Was something attacking us? I threw my head back, trying to dislodge whatever had hold of me.

"Going somewhere, babe?" a low voice rumbled in my ear.

Relief poured through me, filling every crevice. Oh. My. God. *Zach.*

My lips stretched, pulling wide until I was grinning. He wouldn't have even known we were here unless Haamiah had told him. And he wouldn't have come alone.

I tilted my head and looked across my shoulder. I could see Sam fist-pumping the air. I heard him whoop loudly, his voice reaching me, an angel keeping him afloat. I laughed, unable to help the hysterical bubble of mirth that poured through me. Love, lust and something beyond freedom sizzled in my veins as I tilted my head back to connect with Zach's shoulder, the warmth of his flesh heating my skin, soothing me, despite the fear I had felt just seconds earlier. Zach wouldn't let me fall; he would never let me go. He was safety, shelter and protection all in one handsome hunk of a fiancé. My man.

I breathed deeply and flicked my gaze up to meet his. His face was nestled into the crook of my shoulder, his wings spread out behind him, beating strongly. He grinned into me.

"I need you," I said. I was sure the wind had whipped the words away but we dropped suddenly, my heart escalating its pounding rhythm as we swooped, turning away from the others and speeding diagonally down to the land below.

The ground below us was dark green, lush with vegetation, with a lake in the distance and mountains at the periphery of my sight. If the safe house was somewhere near here then I couldn't see it, or any other building for that matter. No city, town or farm was visible and Zach had dropped us pretty low to the ground. The trees grew thick and tight together, but if there were a building large enough to house our nephilim as well as the locals, I should be able to see it by now. I hoped they weren't living underground; that would be just creepy.

Zach must have seen a break in the canopy; he dropped vertically between the trees and landed, holding me off the floor for a moment.

I didn't see our surroundings. I didn't see the trees or the leaves or branches. I couldn't feel the coolness of the shadows or smell the woodsy scents. I didn't hear the rustle of the undergrowth or whispering of the treetops, nor the songs of the insects and birds living down here.

I saw none of it. Only one sense was on high alert.

I turned my body in Zach's arms, wrapping my legs around his hips, locking my ankles together to pull us closer. My lips instinctively found his and pressed taut to the silk of his lips, a complete contradiction to the stubble of his upper lip and jaw. I ran my hands up his neck to hold the back of his head, pulling him into me, not caring if either of us could breathe. Who needed air when we had this?

His rough hands ran up my back, tracing my shoulder blades, massaging my flesh, running down my spine. He dipped his hands under my waistband, pushing down until he could squeeze hold of my bottom, a cheek in each palm.

I sucked in a breath and tilted my pelvis, feeling him there, hard, between my thighs. I sucked at his bottom lip, nibbling when it slid into my open mouth. I licked his upper lip, reveling in the feeling of his hands massaging and squeezing, delving between my cheeks.

Time seemed to stop. The only thing in the world was his mouth, his lips, his hips and his hands. With my eyes closed I could smell him, could feel every hair on his body, every square centimeter of skin beneath my fingers.

He said nothing; he instinctively knew what I needed from him. I needed to feel. I needed this moment to just be myself. In this moment there were no demons, no human rebellion, no angels, and no apocalypse; just him and I. I didn't need to feel safe anymore, or feel protected like I had seconds earlier; I needed to feel powerful, capable. I *was* powerful. I was valkyrie.

I pulled my mouth from his, my eyes locking onto his face.

"Put me down."

Panting, he slowly withdrew his hands, placed them on my waist. He dropped me to the floor, the leaves crunching beneath my feet.

I reached down across my body and dragged my T-shirt up over my head. I reached back and unclipped my bra, not the sexiest thing I had ever worn; a training bra I usually used in class when sparring with the others. It held me in and up when now I needed to be loose and free. I dragged the straps over my arms and let the material slide from my open fingers to the floor.

Zach stared, openmouthed, his eyes wide and curious and his body tense. He watched, drinking in the sight of me. I could almost taste his emotion, his lust, the spike in desire when my breasts bounced. I reached down to my zipper, pulling my trousers over my hips and down to my thighs. I bent, sliding the flats of my palms down my legs, gliding the bunched material down to my calves and ankles.

I slipped one foot out, leaving my shoe on the ground beneath the fabric, doing the same with the other. I stepped forward softly. The crispness of the leaves meant nothing, nor the prick of sharp stones that I stepped over as I neared him.

I breathed shallow, my heart racing, my mind completely focused on Zach. I reached down to my panties and touched the material at my hip. I let heat rush through my fingers, singeing the material. I repeated my actions to the other side and slid the remaining material through my legs. It went the same way as my bra.

I paused, appreciating the way his eyes drank me in. He was able to make me feel the way no one else ever could. I could stand in front of him forever.

Who was I kidding? No, I couldn't.

I reached for him, sliding his T-shirt up. He moved, his hands lifting to touch me. I slapped his wrists away quickly. *I'm in charge of this, not you, Angel boy.*

He got the hint and flashed a smirk. I returned my attention to disposing of his shirt. I leaned forward and flicked my tongue over his collarbone, nipping down to his chest. I bit deeper on his nipple, sucking the flesh into my mouth.

Working on him, I ran my fingertips down the muscles of his abdomen, down to the *V* of his hips and across to his zipper. I undid him, and let them fall to the floor.

I pinched the fabric of his undergarments between my fingers, drawing on my power.

"Be careful," he murmured.

I ducked my head, hiding my grin. "I'm always careful," I whispered.

I released my power slowly, letting the material heat up, disintegrating it one piece at a time. The ashes flicked away, disappearing. I dropped to my knees before him, taking in the sight before my eyes. *Mine.*

I dug my nails into his thighs and drew them down to his knees, breathing heavily. I leaned forward, breathing my hot air on him, watching him twitch and enlarge even more before me.

I licked my lips and took him into my mouth, sliding him in as far as he would go. He was soft and silky, running over my tongue like water. I sucked, creating enough pressure to draw back and forward again. I left his thighs, tugging on his balls, cupping and squeezing, enjoying the feeling of the tightening between my fingers.

As soon as I heard him groan I grabbed his ass cheeks and dug my nails into his flesh, dragging him closer, giving him no option. I steadied my breathing, focusing on the feeling of the velvet slipping in and out of my mouth.

Laura Prior

Zach's hands slid into my hair, clutching at me, pulling me closer, moaning each time I drew back.

I wrenched out of his grasp and looked up at him. I reached up and grabbed hold of his arm, yanking him down until he dropped to his knees. He didn't complain about the rocks I had pulled him on to, or the twigs and debris on the ground. I smirked and pushed him backwards, climbing up over him until I had him pinned.

I sat over his waist, catching and holding his black gaze. I could see the smolder in them, the hunger, the desperate need to be within me.

He could wait, just a few minutes more.

I leaned forward, resting one breast over his mouth. He latched on, sucking, his tongue working the tip. I pressed my palms harder onto his wrists that I had trapped above his head. I arched my back, giving him full access to my breasts, letting him slide his tongue over to my other nipple and work his magic there. It was luxurious, scintillating and so erotic I could die. No more waiting.

I pulled back and let him have my lips, letting him suck on my tongue. I ensnared his eyes, held them tightly and slid down his hips until he was wedged between my lower lips. I slid my knees wider, sitting on him fully, slithering down his length until he was seated fully inside me, his balls cushioning me.

He pulled out and slid into me as I held him pinned, holding him still with my eyes. I moved over him, reveling in the fullness. I pushed up, relinquishing hold of his wrists to straddle him, pushing up and down with my hips. I didn't care that my knees ached and stung or that Zach had to be hurting, lying naked on the forest debris. I wasn't riding him because I thought it was sultry or sexy—though it definitely was—I was riding him to remind us where we belonged. I threw my head back, letting my hair slide over my shoulders. I adored this; being myself. With Zach, I *was* myself.

I languidly rode him, shivering when he placed his hands at my hips, gripping my flesh, forcing my body down to meet his.

He turned in one fluid motion, laying me on my back, driving into me with determination. He held himself up with one arm and delved the fingers of one hand between us, spreading my lips while thumbing my clit. He pressed firmly, squeezing and rubbing in a circular motion.

I trembled with heady desire; the fullness combined with his touch made for an erotically-charged sensation. My body clicked of its own accord, a well-known drumbeat rippling through me as I felt myself squeeze him tightly, milking it.

He leaned closer, his hands dropping beside my head, and tensed as he pounded into me, my thighs struck with each movement.

He came, filling me, our cream mixing, turning with me before he pulled out so that I lay on top of him, crushed with my ass bared to the forest.

I kissed his chest and tilted my head more comfortably. "I missed you."

"Hell, after that, I think you should disappear more often. It almost makes the stress worth it," he said, his breath coming in pants.

I heard the note of trouble in his voice. "I didn't disappear; Haamiah knew where I was going. If anyone disappeared, it was you."

"I was here," he answered my unspoken question.

"Why?"

He grunted. "There have been sightings of the fallen nearby and a demon attack in the nearest city."

"And I'm sure he knew you would be a handy parachute when I fell out of an airplane," I teased with a grin.

He laughed. "You've got to admit; it's handy having someone who can predict the future."

We lay quietly for a few minutes, our legs tangled, my soft curves mashed against his harder ropes of muscle.

"Is the safe house far from here? Should we be expecting someone?" I asked, my mind ticking over.

He shook his head, peering down at me. "It's near, but not so close you should be worried one of the nephilim will be out wandering and will see your prefect ass, or trust me, we wouldn't be still lying here."

Instinct made me scramble to my feet, shoving my legs into my trousers.

Zach leaned up with a curious frown, his brow wrinkled. "What are you doing?"

"I don't really want to fight naked. Get up."

"Fight?" He slowly rose, pulling on his own clothes. "Who are you planning on fighting?"

I paused. "I think I heard someone."

Zach froze, glaring into the trees. He shackled my wrist and pulled me close.

"Zach," I gasped. "We can fight whoever it is."

"No, we're going," he replied stonily.

"Are you serious? You'd rather run and hide, and leave whatever's out here to hunt someone else?"

He turned to me suddenly, gripping me. "How do you know there's someone out here? I can't see or hear anything."

I bit my lip. "My telepathy seems to have gotten a little . . . clearer."

He shook his head while staring at me, almost as if he were trying to read *my* mind. "We're going," he growled.

He wrapped his arms around me, bent his knees and launched us into the sky, torpedoing through the canopy until we were high and soaring.

Five minutes later we dropped through the trees. My stomach somersaulted at the abrupt descent.

Zach let go of our flying embrace but retained my hand, entwining his fingers with mine. I stepped back, looking up at the stone wall we now stood beside. It was high, so high I couldn't see where it ended. Weeds cropped up between the cracks, cobwebs splayed across the stones.

Glancing furtively over his shoulder, he pulled me along with him, following the line of the stone wall. In places, the forest grew thick against the wall and we had to push our way through the branches.

Zach picked up speed, the pressure on my hand increasing until I was jogging beside him. When he turned as if to pick me up I sent him a quelling look. I pulled my hand from his and grinned as I slipped past him, running in front. I followed the wall, rounding the corner when it turned.

The entrance was ahead. A wooden door with chain belts looped across it rose up at the top of eight or nine rough, uneven steps. Weeds grew stronger and thicker here, winding up the edges of the steps. The place looked ancient and abandoned. Was this really the safe house?

I stopped at the bottom of the steps and looked up at Zach as he brushed past, jogging up.

"People actually live here?" I muttered as I followed.

He smirked and wrapped his fingers around the circular iron handle. He tugged, and it pulled open easily.

I rolled my eyes. "No locks here either?"

"Come on," he said, striding through the open door.

I sighed and stepped through the doorway after him, entering the warm, yet dark interior.

It smelt musty, and old. Haamiah must have been clutching at straws when he decided to come here. I couldn't really see the other nephilim living here, and *Gwen* . . . Gwen would be lost without her en suite.

The corridor was only short, and I was surprised when Zach stopped against what appeared to be a dead end. The stone wall ran from the floor to the ceiling with no sign of a door or an exit of any kind. I was about to say something, maybe make a sarcastic comment or two when Zach ran his hand across the top of one of the stones, tracing the edge. He stepped back quickly.

My mouth dropped open. The stone slid apart seamlessly, silently, revealing a large room bustling with people. A few glanced our way; others scurried on with their business. Clearly, appearing out of a wall was normal here.

I was pleasantly surprised to see that this *real* part of the safe house looked clean and modern. The floors were still stone, as were the walls, but the room was lit with bright lights and a sweet, aromatic incense filled the room.

Zach turned back to me. "Let's find Haamiah."

"You can find Haamiah; I want to find Sam and Trev."

He nodded. "Head to the dormitory. I imagine they'll be there."

I took a step, biting my lip with nerves, only to be pulled back abruptly. Zach's lips found mine, his tongue sliding into my mouth, tasting me. I gasped when he pulled away, turning away from me to stride in the opposite direction to the one he had pointed me in. I breathlessly laughed and walked backwards, unable to tear my eyes from his body.

"Watch where you're going."

I spun around, an apology on my lips. It quickly disappeared. "Joe."

He sneered at me. "Great. You're here too."

I rolled my eyes. "Fuck you."

I pushed past, purposely slamming my shoulder into his, and kept my path, weaving through the throng of people. I pushed my hair back behind my ear, uncaring that I had mud stains all over, that I hadn't showered in what seemed like forever, and my hair was a beehive. I needed to find Sam, Trev and Drew and see that they were safe. I didn't even know if Drew would be allowed here.

I continued walking faster and faster until I was running. I turned away from the hall onto a small corridor which opened up into a gigantic gallery, pillars lined up on each side. It was dingy and not as bright as the other areas I had run through, but the light poured in through stained-glass windows on one side, casting colors in the shadows on the floor.

I spun in a circle, awed by the beauty of the room. I looked up, following the tall pillars with my eyes, stunned by the pictures of cherubs on the ceiling.

A figure appeared from behind a pillar. Cloaked in black from head to toe, they moved toward me. I didn't get the impression of danger, but I knew power when I felt it.

"Who are you?" I asked the approaching figure, squinting my eyes to try to see a face.

A soft, high-pitched voice answered, "Who are you?"

I frowned, unsure whether to answer. I let my power flare, tasting the aura of the figure. I still didn't sense any threat. "My name is Jasmine."

The figure closed in, still shrouded in shadows. "I didn't ask for your name."

What? I pursed my lips and scowled. "What?"

My head began to feel light. The ground dipped and tilted. "What are you doing to me?"

"Who are you?" the faceless person repeated.

"I don't know what you're asking. I came here with Zach. I'm with the house of Haamiah, the nephilim."

I staggered. The figure seemed to have lunged at me; they were so close, then they were across the room, and I . . . I was kneeling on the floor.

My head spun round and round. The floor wouldn't stay where it was supposed to be, and I was falling forward.

Who are you?

I braced my forehead on my knees, keening softly as my stomach heaved and my head whirled.

In slow motion I looked up, the cherubs smiling down at me, the colors flashing in sequence over my face. It slowed further, then stilled, then stopped.

I sat back, my legs folded beneath me and breathed deeply, cursing the nausea that rolled through me, burning my throat.

Who am I? That's a secret.

Laura Prior

25

"Be patient and tough; someday this pain will be useful to you."

Ovid.

I stood, taking one step at a time until I had left the gallery behind, leaving through the adjoining hall. What on earth had just happened? Was that a vision or a dream?

I shook my head and stumbled on through the hall, searching the corners for any other cloaked figures.

This safe house was unlike anywhere I had ever been. It was like an old church, a monastery . . . like the monastery that had been attacked years ago, just before Zach had found the island; the *reason* he had found the island.

I closed my eyes. This must bring back so many bad memories for him; the murder of all of those young children. I could sense the tragedy here, the pain resonating through the wide open spaces. It wasn't homely; it was anything but. There was no softness or warmth here. This wasn't a place for children to grow up, and yet it had been home to so many nephilim, and it was now home to us.

I had no idea where I was. Zach had pointed me in this direction but I didn't realize how huge this place was. I had no clue how to find the dormitory.

Laura Prior

Scrap that last thought. I narrowed my eyes on a group of three teenagers, maybe thirteen or fourteen, as they ducked into an opening in the wall, disappearing out of sight.

I jogged over, following them. I grinned when I saw the beds lining either side of the wall in the newest alcove I had found. The dormitory; it had to be.

My relief at finding the dorm was quickly replaced with dread as I noted the length of the room. The entire room was narrow and *long*. Bunk beds ran the length of the room, only a narrow gap between each one. There must have been a hundred or more. I couldn't even see to the back of the room. Were we all sleeping in the same room?

I began to walk, squeezing between the ends of the beds as I searched each one. Most were empty, the sheets neatly pulled back and tucked in, belongings stacked up in orderly piles; mostly books, although there were a few pictures too. Beside most beds there were statues of angels, bibles and crosses. Forget the iPhone chargers, magazines and empty bottles of booze strewn about in our old safe house—this was like being in school, only a much more religious and strict one.

"Where has he brought us?" I muttered out loud.

I needed to find Sam. Who were these people? Were they like us; just normal beings, or were they like, super-nephilim? I didn't see a single modern item here. Even the kids that were in the room were either praying or reading silently. There was no chatter, no laughter and no noise. No one met my gaze; no one answered the questions running through my head or made any comment about the shocked and probably quite disgusted expression on my face.

If someone came into my home and glared at everything like I was doing, I would sure as hell have something to say about it.

I'd been searching for a few minutes before I spotted them. I actually saw Drew first, and I would have started laughing if I didn't feel so uneasy about this place.

Drew was sitting on the edge of a bed, glaring around him, his teeth snapping together randomly. One kid who was also weaving through the beds, squealed and dashed away, almost falling over in his hurry to get away from the savage lycan.

Drew's eyes found mine, and relief poured over his features. He stood and strode towards me.

"Where were ye?" he demanded immediately.

I shrugged. "Zach and I had to do something."

He looked away. "I bet."

I grimaced. Awkward. "Where are Sam and Trev? What are you doing in here?"

"Ugh," he grunted. "The powers that be thought we needed a nap. They're in bed."

"Together?" I raised my eyebrows and peered behind him. They were in separate beds, the sheets pulled over their heads. "And what? You didn't feel tired?"

"They wouldn't tell me where ye were; only that ye were *safe*." He narrowed his eyes at me.

I shrugged. "I was. Safe as houses."

"Pfft. Not this one. Have ye seen the state of this place?"

I winced. "I know. I feel like we're in a boarding school for nuns."

He chuckled. "Right. I'm with ye on that one. Where's your angel?"

"He wanted to see Haamiah."

"And ye didn't?"

"No." I shook my head. "I wanted to see that you guys were okay."

He paused and smiled, genuine warmth emanating from him. "That's the thing about ye. Not everyone would be so concerned about a lycan, a vampire nephilim hybrid and a telepathic nephilim. Especially not ones who made ye jump out of a plane."

I grinned. "I'm not everyone."

He laughed. "You're like no one I've ever met."

I smiled and stepped around him towards the boys. Was he coming on to me? Or was I just being big-headed?

Sam poked his head out of the sheet and ran a hand over his face, yawning. "Dude, you need to get some sleep."

I leaned closer and kissed his forehead, thrilled to see him alive and well.

When I leaned in, he whispered, "Haamiah said there's big business later."

"Big business?" I echoed.

"Yeah, he was really weird about it. Actually . . ." He glanced around. *He didn't say it; he thought it. There's something happening later and we need our strength. He said to get some sleep while we could, because we had a long day ahead. Of course your lanky wolf insisted on staying awake until you got here.*

I pulled back instinctively. I heard it. All of it. It was clear, as though he was talking out loud. Previously my telepathy had been hit and miss, sometimes sounding as though I were listening through water. How could my telepathy improve so much in less than half an hour?

Maybe it's because we're here. Can't you feel the energy coming from this place?

I grunted. *Yes, and I don't like it.*

Get some sleep. We'll figure out what Haamiah meant later. We need to make plans too. We need to know what's happening with your vision and what the next step is.

Okay, I thought. *How long have we got?*

I got the impression we had a few hours.

"Fine, have your telepathics-only meeting. Now you're here, I can get some sleep," Drew said, throwing himself on a bed.

I glanced at him then back at Sam. He'd already pulled the sheet over his head.

I climbed into the next bed, pulling the thin, rough sheets up to my chest, and stared up at the ceiling. What was Haamiah planning? Or was he predicting? Was he trying to angle us into the right place for something else?

I turned onto my side, nestling the pillow into the crook of my neck. I should have gone with Zach. I wouldn't have this uneasy feeling now if I had. I needed to know more about the vision, and I was beginning to think that Haamiah knew more than he was letting on. He *always* knew things. What wasn't he telling me? What were his secrets?

I also needed to tell him about the figure in the gallery. Why was she asking me who I was? Didn't she know? Why was she even interested in me? Was she worried I would infect everyone here with my fallen angel and valkyrie blood? That had to be it. She had to have sensed that I wasn't fully nephilim and wanted to know what I was. She had just phrased the question weirdly.

I smiled to myself. If she wanted to know *who* I was, she was in for a long wait. Even I didn't know the answer to that one.

Sam nudged me awake. "You getting up?"

"Mmm," I groaned stretching my arms up over my head. I rolled in the sheets, my body begging to sleep for just a little longer.

"You don't want to find Haamiah? I'm totally down for sleeping for the next week." Sam laughed.

I groaned louder and sat up, kneeling on the bed. I felt like death. Every muscle ached; even my skin was sore. My neck was stiff from the airplane, my muscles aching from the shock fall through the sky and my back and knees were abraded from the forest floor. Not to mention my head was pounding from the lack of sleep.

I turned my head and glared moodily at Sam, who lay on the bed next to me with his feet resting on the slats of the bed above him.

"I'm up, I'm up."

I turned and slid out of bed, leaning against Sam's bed. I rubbed my face on the mattress, almost purring.

Someone slapped me on the back. I instinctively turned and bared my teeth at him. He jumped back, startled.

I caught myself and frowned, swallowing hard. "Sorry, just jumpy, I guess."

"Don't sweat it." He shrugged.

Sam raised his eyebrows. I held my mind blank, or as blank as I could make it. I didn't want him to know what I was thinking; not now.

He squeezed past me and led the way through the dormitory, Trev and Drew following closely.

How long had we been sleeping?

"Longer than we should have." Sam glanced at his watch. "It's six already."

"Do you have to?" I grumbled.

Sam grunted in reply. I bit my lip, wincing at the pain as drops of blood filled my mouth. I shouldn't have snapped at Trev, and I shouldn't have grumbled at Sam. It wasn't his fault he could hear what I was thinking; it wasn't as if he did on purpose. Growling softly at myself, I blew my hair out of my face and stomped on.

We reached the end of the dormitory and turned left. Absently I followed the boys, letting Drew steer me when my concentration drifted. They had to have been shown the way around while I was getting naughty with Zach, because within no time we seemed to have arrived in a library where Haamiah, Zach and someone else were deep in discussion.

My eyes fixed on Zach. My heart leaped when he stiffened, turning his head. His black eyes caught mine and he rose, parting his lips slightly. I was drawn to him, pulled in like a fish on a hook.

I reached him, breathing hard. He bent his head, his lips touching mine as my body went into overdrive. As I began to moan he pulled back, his attention focused and sharp.

"Why do you taste of—?"

"Shh," I hissed.

I pulled out of his embrace and stepped back, turning to Haamiah.

"Hi," I said, taking in a deep breath.

"How did it go?" he asked, his deep voice penetrating my mind.

I shrugged. "Well, we learned a lot about the horsemen; enough to know if it's really them in my vision we're in for a world of trouble."

"You've decided it was a vision then? The future, not a dream or a memory?"

I glanced at the man who spoke. I didn't know him. He had the bluest eyes; a light, sky blue. Lyrics and music notes were tattooed across his chest, while a sun was drawn around his navel. Facial hair swept artistically around his upper lip and down in a narrow line to his chin, then around his jaw. He gave off an arrogant air and I instantly disliked him.

"Who are you?" I asked belligerently, glaring and lifting my chin to show him I wasn't someone to be messed with.

"Jasmine," Zach growled.

I scowled at him. I would *not* apologize.

"This is Machidiel."

26

"It's better to walk alone than with a crowd going in the wrong direction."

Diane Grant.

So this was the last of Zach's friends, and the only one I hadn't yet met. He was a fighter, like Zach, when they were young—if they had *ever* been young. Now he was a teacher . . . here.

"I didn't think a tattooed warrior would feel at home in a monastery," I said.

He curled up his lip. "A warrior never feels at home anywhere. What about you? Where is your home?"

I glared, spinning around to pin Zach with my eyes. He had told him! Was my life a joke to him? Some bizarre story to be shared around like a nephilim bedtime story? The freak who was part valkyrie, part fallen angel, belonging nowhere and to no one?

"We couldn't find the witches, so we don't know what it was. We're going with vision for now," Sam answered for me. "But the valkyrie are allying themselves with us, and the harpies have kind of agreed to an alliance, as have a faction of the human rebellion."

"You've allied with the harpies?" Machidiel asked quietly.

As I drew breath to blast him, Trev and Drew boxed me in from either side.

"And the valkyrie," Sam added.

Zach fixed me with a look. "So we're gearing up for the apocalypse."

"Everyone seems to think it's heading our way," I said, my lips barely moving despite the growled words.

Machidiel took a step to the side, his eyes running over my body as he stepped around me slowly. "Very good. You seem to have accomplished something."

"What's that supposed to mean?" I said.

He shook his head. "You'll see."

He walked backwards, his eyes not leaving me until he was gone.

I glared at Zach. "What the hell was that? What was he talking about?"

He shrugged. "Machidiel's been missing for a while; he was talking about prophecies and missions. None of what he said made sense." He turned to Haamiah. "Did you know what he was talking about?"

"He said people are looking for the Falchion and the Dagger of Lex." Haamiah shrugged, "you sure you don't know where they are?"

Zach looked at me weirdly. His eyes seemed desperate. It gave me an eerie feeling.

"I don't know where they are. I thought you would, though," he said to Haamiah.

"I have no idea where they are," he answered, turning away.

That was weird.

Asmodeus had raided the safe house looking for the Dagger of Lex and the Falchion of Tabbris. For him to think that, surely there had to be some merit. Haamiah knew where the Falchion was, of that, I was certain. As for the Dagger of Lex, Zanaria was the only one who knew where it was. Haamiah knew that too; why was he saying he had no idea where they were?

By Zach's expression, I could see he felt the same way. Something was wrong with Haamiah.

27

"You've always had the power my dear, you just had to learn it for yourself."

Glinda—*The Wizard of Oz.*

We looked at each other, confused, uncertain what to say.

"Jasmine—" Zach began.

"Can we do this later?" I asked with a forced smile.

He sighed. "Fine. I'll find you."

He swept out of the room, the only way he could: brooding and dangerous.

The moment he left, Trev and Sam high-fived and burst into laughter.

"What?" I demanded.

"What have you done now?" Sam asked.

My face fell. I knew. I just didn't want anyone else to know.

"Yeah, you're so in trouble!" Trev laughed.

"He's not my dad, you know. He's not my boss or my teacher, or whatever else. I'm not in trouble with anyone," I said.

"Yeah right, you're so grounded." Trev chuckled.

Sam punched him in the shoulder. "Quit it, dude."

"What?" Trev's eyes were wide, his mouth open in shock. He shook his head in disappointment.

"Just leave it for now," he whispered.

"Geeks." Drew rolled his eyes. "I'm going to investigate this building. It's not often a lycan gets an invitation into a place like this."

"I'll come with you," I said, quickly turning to follow him.

"Jasmine," Sam called out with exasperation.

I paused. "Are you coming?"

Drew led the way through the halls, weaving between the people milling about, ignoring the weird looks he was given as they dived out of his way.

We found ourselves in the dining room; a brightly-lit hall with rows and rows of wooden benches where nephilim sat, quietly eating. I noticed some of our own nephilim sat there, blending in with their borrowed clothes. The sea of dull browns and grays completely ignored us. Not one person looked up. It was like we were invisible; like we were so different we weren't even recognized.

I grabbed Sam's arm and spun him around. "Oh my God."

"What?" he asked.

"Gwen. I'm the worst friend ever. Where is she?"

Sam cast his eyes down. "I was hoping . . . ahh, she's not here."

"Where is she?" I demanded.

"She went to live with her father. She's left the safe house for good. I was hoping you'd . . ."

"Forget?" I shook my head. "I did. How could I forget her?"

Trev put his arm around me. "Her part in this is over. She's safe, out of danger."

Tears filled my eyes and I felt my face flush. She was safe. I had to remember that, focus on it. God, why did I feel like my life was falling apart?

Sam tugged on my hand, leading me to an empty seat halfway down one of the rows of benches.

"I'm starving," Drew said, breaking the silence.

He and Trev headed off to the kitchen counter at the top right-hand corner of the hall and began to scoop up a tray full of food, probably more than necessary, while Sam and I sat in gloomy silence.

"Fuck, what are we going to do?" I muttered.

"Do you mind?" the nephilim next to me sneered. He wore loose, gray clothing, like most of the others here, and had his compulsory book next to his bowl of mush. "Profanity is not tolerated here. Take your crassness elsewhere."

"Jesus, man, chill out," Sam said with a friendly smile. "We're all here for the same reason."

"Shut your mouth," the boy opposite hissed. "You're nothing like us."

"Is there a problem here?" Drew banged his fist down on the table, his lycan-self rising enough so that everyone who was now staring at us could see the bulging beast beneath his skin, and his glowing eyes.

The nephilim around us stood, picked up their bowls and began to leave, muttering to each other and casting sly looks in our direction. Only the two who had spoken to us remained.

The first one, who had been sitting beside me, now stood and stared from Drew to me with disgust. "You're not welcome here. This is a place of peace and worship, not a home for delinquents and demons."

"Take your fellow freaks and get lost," the other added.

Rage erupted. Pounding, savage fury poured out of me like a volcano spewing ash. Mist steamed from me, filling the room, choking everyone on it.

Delinquent? Freak? Demon? Those words, they halted my breath, crushed my heart. They were so painful; I wanted to rip out my heart . . . or theirs.

I stood, clasping the edge of the bench. I flicked my eyes up from the old, damaged wood to the brown eyes of the nephilim closest who looked down at me, judging me. My knuckles whitened as I clenched the bench tightly.

I jerked in one fluid motion, tipping the entire bench over and hurtling it across the room as I roared with rage. The crackles of electricity made my skin tingle. Screams rang out as the light bulbs overhead popped, shattered glass raining down.

I wanted to rip open his chest. I took a step forward, oblivious to the screams, my mist forming a barrier between my friends and I, although I absently noted they were shouting something at me. I snarled, my focus pure, my fists clenching.

A hand landed on mine; cold . . . icy cold.

I spun, my left fist aiming for the face near mine. It was caught and lowered. My eyes were held captive by blue ones. Machidiel. Machidiel was here, touching me.

I wrenched my hands back.

"Come with me," he took my wrist and tugged, still staring into my eyes.

He pulled until we were out of the room and down the corridor. I was vaguely aware of Sam, Trev and Drew nearby but I couldn't turn my head or look away.

"What are you doing to me?" I asked, between gritted teeth. "What have you done to my eyes?"

"Don't you know the eyes are the gateway to the soul? And you have an old soul."

"You don't know anything about me."

"Don't I?"

Machidiel released me, and I fell back. Drew caught me and quickly tossed me to Sam. Drew held up a sword against Machidiel's throat. He must have pilfered it from somewhere, because he hadn't had it a few minutes ago.

"Let him speak," I ordered. "What do you know about me?"

He cleared his throat. "More than you think. I need to go."

"We're calling the shots, pal," Drew said, digging the sword edge in just enough to draw a prick of blood.

"I can't be around you," he insisted.

Well that was a slap in the face. "You know, I don't enjoy talking to you either. You give me the creeps."

"You're running out of time. You need to work it out."

I frowned. "What are you talking about?"

He turned his head slightly, grimacing at the soft cry of a girl as she approached us, then ran away.

Who are you?

I heard the words as clearly as I saw them, a glowing neon sign had just dropped into my brain. That was the second time someone had said that. What was going on?

"Tell me more."

Machidiel glanced at Drew then slowly lifted his hand, nudging the sword away from his neck. He kept his arm raised and reached for me, slowly touching my cheek.

I didn't know why I let him. There was something in his eyes, something deep in his expression that called to me. He trailed his fingers down my skin.

"You know me," he whispered. He pulled back suddenly, as if wounded. "And yet you don't. I didn't think this would happen."

"What are you saying? Jasmine, does this make any sense to you?" Sam asked frantically, dragging me out of Machidiel's reach.

"You're running out of time. It's taking you too long," he whispered.

I pulled away from Sam and stepped closer to the angel. "What's taking too long?"

He opened his mouth to speak then closed it again, backing away from me.

"What's going on?" a low voice growled.

When a hand grabbed the back of my neck softly I tilted my head up, locking eyes with Zach.

"That seems to be question of the day," I mumbled.

"Jasmine . . ."

I turned back to Machidiel, hissing with exasperation when I realized he'd gone. "Come on, I'll fill you in on how little I know. Take us somewhere quiet."

I took hold of his hand and let him lead me down the corridor.

"Jasmine," Sam shouted. I spun back. "We're going to keep exploring. We'll catch up with you after."

I nodded and looked up at Zach, grimly following him.

I lost count of the number of turns and twists we made, and was relieved when we finally stopped in a quiet corner. I looked past Zach's shoulder to see where he'd taken me.

My heart twisted, anxiety rippling through me as I took in the darkened room, the stained-glass windows now darkened, the waning sun unable to pierce through the trees outside.

"What's going on?"

"That's what I want to know." I fixed him with a stare. "Something is going on, and I want to know how it involves me."

"Well, there's an apocalypse brewing . . ." he said with a smirk.

"I'm not being paranoid! This is more than just the apocalypse. This is more than just my vision, or maybe it's all somehow linked."

"Easy," he soothed. He ran his thumb over my forehead, pressing on the spot between my eyes. "We just need to look at all the facts."

"The facts?" I murmured. "Okay, we know Asmodeus is after the dagger of Lex and the Falchion of Tabbris. Together, they somehow open the gates into the heavenly realm. So we can presume that the apocalypse is coming from that direction."

"We can presume."

I looked up. "He's going to bring Hell on earth, and then move it up to the Heavens."

"The vision?"

I bit my lip, thinking. "The vision was a prediction; I must have got it from Haamiah. Asmodeus has employed the horsemen to get one of the items he needs. He couldn't find them at the safe house; Haamiah said he didn't know where they were."

Zach frowned. "You're guessing."

"I'm analyzing the pieces and trying to make them fit together." I shrugged trying to ease the tension. I tilted my head to the side, relaxing as I felt my neck click. That was better. "The person screaming; they know where the Dagger and the Falchion are. They're being tortured for information."

"If it's a vision from the future, you can stop it."

I nodded. "Yes, I can."

"So we need to find the horsemen."

"There were four horsemen there. If I can find just one of them, I can follow him to the others. If I can kill them all, then I can stop the apocalypse."

"In theory."

I shrugged. "It's worth a try."

"How do you plan on finding them?"

"I have no idea."

Zach turned away and began to pace. I watched as he ran his hand down his face, rubbing over the stubble on his jaw.

"What about the boy?"

"The boy?" I frowned, my brow relaxing slowly as I remembered the young man who had appeared in my vision. "I don't know who he is. I've no way of finding him."

"Okay, so at least we have a plan. We start by finding the horsemen."

I nodded slowly, my mind spinning. I peered into the shadows behind the pillars. There was nothing here, nothing to be frightened of. "Why do people keep asking me who I am?"

Zach tilted his head curiously. "Who?"

"Machidiel, and this weird woman was here . . ."

He crooked his eyebrow. "Here?"

I nodded and gestured around us. "Here, when we first arrived. I was looking for the dormitory and I got lost. She came up to me out of the shadows and kept asking me who I was. And Machidiel told me I was running out of time, and that it was taking me too long."

"Too long to do what?" He scowled at me.

"Don't give me that look! I didn't know what he was talking about; he's *your* friend."

Zach sighed. "I'll ask him. But the woman . . ."

He tailed off into silence.

"Yes?"

He shook his head. "It's probably nothing. I'll ask Machidiel. If there's someone here making trouble, he'll know."

"I bet," I said, sarcastically, rolling my eyes.

Zach stepped closer, looking down into my eyes. He looked so troubled, and who could blame him; an apocalypse brewing, a psycho fiancée having visions of people being tortured . . .

"Sam said Haamiah indicated something 'big' is going to happen tonight. Now it's time for *you* to spill the beans on what's going on."

"There've been attacks on the safe house every night. I imagine there'll be more."

"Okay."

"Go find the others, head to the library and look for clues on how to find the horsemen; where they live, how to kill them."

"What are you going to do?"

"I'll find Machidiel and Haamiah. You're right; something's going on here that doesn't make sense."

I stood on my tiptoes and reached up. He leaned down and met me, kissing me deeply. I pulled back, sucking my breath in. I licked my lips, tasting him.

I took a step back, turning to go then turned back quickly. "Point me in the right direction?" I asked with a sheepish grin.

With Zach's help, I located the dining room and headed in the opposite direction—the only way my friends could have gone. I headed down the brightly-lit hallways, avoiding the angry looks the other nephilim gave me. Even the nephilim from our old safe house avoided me. It was typical really: it was looking like the apocalypse was balancing on my shoulders and did they have any clue? Did any of them care? I was just an invisible freak to them, someone who had little or nothing to do with them. Someone who they pretended didn't exist just so that they could feel like they were still good.

I knew I had the support of my friends and Zach, and I should have felt wonderful knowing that the harpies, human rebellion and valkyrie were on my side, but I couldn't help but feel that there shouldn't *be* sides. Why didn't the nephilim have my back? And why on earth was Haamiah acting so weirdly?

I needed to focus, like Zach said, and take one thing at a time. I needed to kill the horsemen; to do that, I needed to find them, and to find them I needed my friends.

Sam? I telepathically called. Would he hear me?

I ducked my head and continued to walk, trying to block out the chatter around me. There was no answer. I guess I hadn't really expected one.

I cleared my mind and reached for my power discreetly. I felt it flow in, tingling and sizzling through my veins. I opened myself up to the auras around me, feeling for Sam with my senses.

Where were they?

I moved forward, jogging down the corridor, peering into each room I passed. I halted at the end where the way forked into two. One was still brightly lit; the other was narrow and dark, and seemed to turn a corner as soon as you would enter it.

I ran my hand over the wall, unsure which way to go. A flash of movement down the right-hand one caught my eye. Keeping near the wall, I stealthily crept down the dark, narrow passageway, following as it curved around, the stones getting more jagged, less worn.

I glanced up at the ceiling: it was high up above me, despite the challenging width of the passage. I could feel the presence of someone stronger now, someone just ahead. I crept closer, faster, very much aware that I had no weapons except myself.

At that thought, I crumbled. I fell to my knees, the same feeling of nausea sweeping over me, just like it had back in the stained-glass hall. I groaned and bent my head to my knees. The swirling of the passageway made me want to hurl.

What was doing this? Was the woman back? Was she the person I could sense ahead? What brought on this sickness?

I gagged, keeping my eyes closed. No, I could do this. I could fight through it. Like I had just said to myself, *I am a weapon.*

My eyes flicked open, wide, staring, unseeing. I was a weapon. That's what I was. That's *who* I was. Was that the answer to the question? Who am I: a weapon?

The new question was whose weapon was I?

An odd feeling swept over me and I felt hands grab my shoulders. Instinctively I knocked them away, the heel of my palm slamming against the chest beside me. I felt the thud as my assailant hit the wall hard, and fell to the floor.

My vision restored, I snarled at the shape only inches away from me. I crawled over and slammed my elbow into the throat, holding him pinned to the floor.

"Who are you?" I growled.

My eyes widened, taking him in. I gasped and pulled back, my hands slamming to the floor behind me. I scrambled away, shaking my head.

"No, no, no. You're not here. You're not here!" I cried hysterically. I could feel my face heat up, my body sweating, my clothes sticking to my body.

"I had to find you. Jasmine please, it's important."

"I don't know what you're doing here, but you need to stay away from me. I don't want anything to do with you."

"Jasmine!" the haggard voice sobbed.

I held onto the wall and pulled myself up until I was standing. He was crumpled on the floor, pale and shaking, tears streaming down his face. He looked so scared. Did I care? Did weapons have feelings?

"You need to listen to me. You need to believe me. They're coming here. They're coming!" He gasped.

I looked down at my hands, holding them up. They were shaking, trembling, clammy. I guess weapons did care.

"What do you want, James?"

28

"A mind that is stretched by a new experience can never go back to its old dimensions."

Oliver Wendell Holmes, Jr.

I could barely believe my eyes. James, my brother, the same guy I had risked my life for, faced down death and mutilation to save, and who had been betraying me all along, was here. And he looked terrible.

He was pale and sweaty, his hair in disarray, his clothes dirty and ragged. His lips were blistered and flaking and his eyes looked so afraid, as though he had narrowly escaped the jaws of hell.

He reached for me, uncaring that I flinched away. He grabbed my arms, his fingers digging in, certain to leave bruises.

"You need to trust me. You don't know what you're up against," he hissed.

"I don't trust you and I never will. You're working for the fallen. You think I don't know that?"

He shook his head, shaking me by my arms. "Not any more. You have no idea the things I've seen, the things they do."

I tilted my head. "Did you just figure out your buddies don't count playing with kittens and charity work among their favorite things to do?"

He brushed my words aside. "You need to get them to trust me."

"Who?" I snapped, batting his hands away.

"The archangels. I need to speak to them."

I snorted. "You think I can get in contact with them? You're even stupider than I thought."

"Your leader, then, the commander of the army. They need to prepare for war. I have information that will help but I need them to promise they'll take me with them when they go."

"When they go where?"

"Back to their realm."

I paused, uncertain what to say. James seemed delirious, insane even. "We're already preparing for war. We don't need your help."

He shook his head, laughing manically. "You think you know; you have no idea who you're up against."

"Who?"

He turned his head, his body propped up lethargically against the wall. "There's a secret division hidden deep inside the fallen. Most of them aren't even aware they exist. They're a law unto themselves."

"The fallen don't obey any laws."

"They do; you just don't know them."

"We already know about Asmodeus's plan to invade the heavenly realm."

"Asmodeus has nothing to do with it. He's not with them. If he's trying to get into Heaven, it's so he can escape what's about to happen here."

I bit my lip. "What's going to happen?"

James's face crumpled, his mouth opening in silent horror as he began to sob.

"Hell on earth," he whispered hoarsely.

"What does that mean, James? You're giving me hints but not actually telling me anything."

He suddenly pushed away and began to stumble backwards down the passageway. "Get them to trust me. Make them listen; it's the only way."

"Where are you going?" I called.

"I'll find you again when it's safe."

He bolted, his feet slapping the stone floor noisily as he turned out of my sight.

Did I go after him? Did I catch him and persuade him to stay here until I found Zach and Haamiah? I couldn't be certain he was telling the truth, yet he seemed so scared . . . traumatized. What had he seen? What did he mean by "hell on earth?" That could mean anything; was he speaking literally? Figuratively?

Ten minutes ago, if anyone had suggested that I believe anything my treacherous brother said to me, I would have told them to go screw themselves, but now . . . I just didn't know what to think. The thought that Asmodeus actually wanted to hide in the heavenly realms was probably the scariest thing of all. It seemed ridiculous, yet when James had spoken his words had a ring of fact to them. It could be true.

I felt sick with fear at the thought that there was something else out there more frightening and evil than Asmodeus. He was the monster in my nightmares.

Where did the horsemen fit in now, then? I thought they were working for Asmodeus; were they still? Did anything Zach and I had discussed still apply?

I stared into the darkness for longer than I probably should have, but moving my feet seemed so difficult, almost an impossible task in light of what I had just heard.

Yet eventually I did. I backed out of the passageway, following the turns until I was out onto the main corridor again. I looked blankly at the opposite hallway the one lit so much brighter.

Where would I find Sam, Trev and Drew?

I berated myself. It was obvious where they would be. Where would any twenty-something-year-old guys be when they found themselves in an ancient safe house guarded by warriors? In the armory, of course.

I asked the first person I saw, and quickly found myself running down a wide staircase into the bowels of the monastery into a large gallery filled with every weapon imaginable, and some that looked so bizarre that I couldn't even begin to guess what they were used for. They were fixed up on the walls, in chests, in display cabinets and some piled up on tables. Guns, swords, knives, mace's, instruments of torture, gold and silver bows and arrows; they were all here. As were Sam, Trev and Drew.

They noticed me as soon as I entered, and hurried over to my side. I didn't need to ask why they looked so anxious; I had been sprinting so I was out of breath, flushed, and fear haunted my soul.

Sam read my mind before I had a chance to say anything.

"He's here? That son of a—"

"Who's here?" Trev demanded, his fangs glinting under the fluorescent lights.

"James," I panted.

Trev froze, his eyes wide. I could hear clearly that he wished he could read my mind like Sam.

"Fill me in, *now*," Drew snarled.

"My half-brother tricked me into entering the tournament of Ascension. I went in to help him, to save him, but he was working with the fallen to try to kill me. I found out, I won and I left." I took a deep breath. "He's here; I saw him a few minutes ago and he told me there's something much bigger going on. He said there's a faction within the fallen that are planning something."

"Invading the heavenly realm, we know," Trev said.

I shook my head. "No, he said Asmodeus is only doing that to hide from whatever else is going down."

"What *exactly* is going to happen?" Drew asked.

I shrugged. "He wouldn't tell me. He just kept saying I needed to get the archangels to trust him. He wanted to speak to them."

"It's a trap," Sam said, his eyes flashing fire.

Laura Prior

"I agree; we need to report him as an intruder," Trev said.

"Guys," I bit my lip. "He looked *so* scared. I think he's telling the truth. I think we need to hear what he has to say."

"Are you kidding?" Sam said. His expression beyond bewildered. He threw his hands in the air. "You know it's a trap. Nothing that guy has to say is true: *nothing*."

"What harm is there in telling Haamiah and Zach?"

"They might actually believe him and we'll be sucked into another mess, like the tournament."

I jerked back, hurt. "We had no reason not to trust him then."

"But we do now," Trev said quietly.

I shrugged. "I believe him, or at least I believe that he believes it."

"Oh, well, let's roll with it then. The guy's been hanging out with fallen angels for the past who-knows-how-many years and he's now afraid of them . . . that's a reason to go and get us all killed," Sam said.

"I know it sounds weird, but he wouldn't tell me anything else until he can speak to the angels."

"So he wants to get near them then kill them," Drew said, raising his eyebrow skeptically.

"I should have known you would all side with each other." I glared.

""That's not fair," Sam protested. "Your brother's a dickhead who tried to get you killed. He wants to get close to the angels to give them some mystery information, he says that the most evil guy we know isn't actually evil, he's actually trying to hide from something else . . . What are we supposed to think?"

"You didn't see him. I can't explain how I know he's telling the truth, I just know."

"Maybe if you can get Sam near enough to him to read his mind, then we'll know for certain," Drew suggested.

"You think I'm going anywhere near that bastard?" he protested.

"Sam, please. Don't you want to know if there's something else going on that we haven't found out about yet?"

He kicked his foot along the floor. "Fucking hellfire," he muttered. "Fine, how do we find him?"

"He said he'd find me."

He snorted. "Well I guess we'd better hope it happens before whatever Haamiah warned us about happens."

I grimaced. "I forgot about that."

"We didn't." Trev handed me a dagger.

I twirled it between my hands, looking up in surprise. "We can just take these?"

"Do you see anyone around to stop us?"

"Good point. What else can I have?"

Ten minutes later and we were loaded up enough for Armageddon. I eschewed the guns in favor of an assortment of blades and knives, and a sword that I strapped to my back. Sam went for a couple of handguns and stocked up on ammunition, while Trev and Drew gleefully strapped on a mixture of everything available.

We headed out of the armory and followed the stone passageways until we returned to the library. Six or seven nephilim sat studying; pouring over books and writing in thick note pads. There were some angels present, most sat in small groups talking amongst themselves, others standing guard, observing.

I looked around the room, again astounded at the size of the room and the thousands of books that were lined floor to ceiling.

"He's here," Sam said, rushing off across the room.

We pushed past anyone who dared to get in our way, knocking books off tables and annoying pretty much everyone.

Haamiah looked up as we reached him and frowned. I immediately got the impression that he didn't want us there.

"Yes?" he asked, his mouth forming a grim line. He remained seated.

"James is here; Jasmine saw him and he wants to speak to one of the angels, someone in charge," Sam said. "He says he's got information on the apocalypse."

Haamiah scowled. "I'm sure you're capable of dealing with it." He turned away, dismissing us.

Sam stuttered. "But he wants to speak to someone in charge."

"Isn't Jasmine in charge of your little group? Doesn't this fall into the assignment I gave her?" he asked with a frustrated sigh.

"I'm not an angel," I said crossly, folding my arms.

"No, you're not, are you?" he sneered at me. "There's too much going on right now; if you can't deal with it yourself, it'll have to wait." He stood and turned away, excusing himself from the angels he had been sitting with.

We stared at each other in shock. This wasn't Haamiah. What was wrong with him?

Sam leaped forward. "Wait a minute; you haven't even heard us out!" He grabbed his arm and pulled. Haamiah flung him off and glared at us angrily before storming off.

I felt so stupid, so small and belittled, and I couldn't help the rage that spread through me like a fireball. How could he be so awful to us? He was our leader, our teacher and our friend.

"Jesus, Jas!"

I heard the words and felt someone slapping at my arm but could only focus on Haamiah's retreating form.

As the noise beside me grew, I blinked and flicked my eyes to Trev. He was trying to extinguish the flames that had begun to singe through my sleeve. I hissed and concentrated on calming myself. Soon there were no flames, only the aroma of charred material. *Lovely.*

Trev took hold of Sam and pulled him out of the library, Drew and I following behind. The irony wasn't lost that a newly-turned vampire was taking control of the situation and assisting both Sam and I when we were losing it. I guessed we were all going through our own hell; the only things that differed were our personal demons.

We stood in the hallway at a loss for words. Drew looked furious and rightly so. He had allied himself and his species with the angels, and when confronted with an important matter, the leader didn't want to hear it. He was probably thinking what a bunch of irresponsible children we were and what time the next flight out was.

Trev looked bewildered and more than a little on edge, like Drew, while Sam was unreadable.

"You don't need to read me," he whispered.

"What?" Trev and Drew asked simultaneously.

He pointed to me. "She was going to try to work out what I was thinking, but she doesn't need to." His troubled eyes met mine. "That's not Haamiah."

I nodded, agreeing. Here I was feeling sorry for myself for Haamiah speaking to me with ridicule in his voice, when it must be even harder for Sam to see him act this way. They were so close; had been together since Sam was young. He was a father figure to him.

"I know. Maybe he's ill, or maybe the stress is getting to him. I know it's not fair for us to keep dumping all of our problems on him, but I guess we've just gotten used to him always knowing what to do—one of the benefits of being able to predict the future." I tried to smile.

"No," Sam said in a low voice. He shook his head slightly as though warning me about something. *"That's not Haamiah."*

29

"The most beautiful discovery true friends make is that they can grow separately without growing apart."

Elizabeth Foley.

We stared at him, unspeaking, unseeing. I could feel ice creeping up my veins, freezing me in place. None of us knew what to say in response to that. What *did* you say? I couldn't think of a single reasonable response to what he'd just said.

Before any of us could form the words to ask what on earth he was talking about an explosion ripped through the safe house, knocking us off our feet.

I was thrown against the wall then my knees hit the floor. I could feel the blood begin to trickle down from the cuts from the uneven, stone floor. Drew didn't give me a second to catch my breath; instead, he yanked me to my feet and bellowed for Trev to get Sam.

I felt the heat before I saw the flames. As we pulled to a halt, standing in a row, Drew, me, Trev and Sam, the hair on my arms rose upright, my power surging through my veins, my mist pouring out around me of its own accord. From where I stood staring down the hallway, I saw the white of the fire's tip peer around the corner before being joined by fiery oranges, red sparks, and a charcoal shadow. The colors blasted up the store hallway, scorching everything in sight as their greedy fingers reached for us, flaming jaws wide open to swallow us.

I shrieked, loud enough to send cracks splintering through the stones. I shrieked out my fury and rebellion. This wasn't how I was going out; I refused to be defeated.

I placed one palm out to the fire and thrust Drew behind me into Sam and Trev, and continued to roar my defiance.

I felt the flames touch me, ripping at my clothes, but I also felt the soothing caress of the embers inside, the glow of power as my body absorbed the heat as its own. They wanted to know who I was? I was fire, embodied.

The blast receded, leaving the hallway filled with smoke and the stones covered in scorch marks and soot.

I lowered my head, my entire arm shaking under the immense strength that it had had to maintain. Drew, Sam and Trev were cowering on the floor, looking up at me with wide-eyed amazement.

"I don't know why you're looking at me like that. I do weird stuff all the time," I murmured weakly.

Drew stood first and stumbled over to me, wrapping his arms around me so tightly it hurt. He pulled back and clasped my hands in his.

"It is an honor to serve you. I would pledge my loyalty to you a thousand times over. You have the love and servitude of every lycan in existence and none will forget it."

Trev rolled his eyes at Drew and slapped me on the back. "Yeah, I just like you. Thanks though." He winked.

Sam kissed me on the forehead. "I don't know how you do the things you do, but I love you, I seriously do."

I laughed giddily and ran my hands down my face, Haamiah's stinging words gone. "We need to get out of here before the whole place comes down."

It was then that my body adjusted back to my surroundings and I was able to distinguish the screams of the panicked nephilim who were running manically down the hallway, looking for safety. Everyone was covered in soot and some were bleeding from cuts, but thankfully there were no bodies around us. The nephilim wouldn't find safety; we were under attack.

"Do you know the way out?" I asked the guys.

"I think so," Sam said.

We ran back up the hallway past the dining room and found ourselves near the hall with the stained-glass windows. The room was pitch black, not a single fleck of light to show us the way, so we linked hands and ran together through the center, hoping that if anyone tried to attack us Drew would smell them, Sam would hear them and Trev would sense them. What would I do? Well, I'd light them up like a firework.

We made it to the other side, our flight only impacted by another bomb shaking the floor and one of the windows popping, spraying glass across us. I plucked the stinging shards out of my arm as I cowered against Sam. We ran through the doorway at the end and sprinted down the following corridor, some of the lights flickering, others off completely.

Laura Prior

When the last light puttered out Sam stopped, causing us all to pile into the back of him.

"Why have we stopped?" Drew shouted.

"Sam?" I hissed.

"Not this way," he said. "Not this way!"

He pushed hard and grabbed my hand, sprinting back the way we had come.

I heard an unearthly war cry behind us and gripped Sam's hand tighter, fleeing back into the pitch-black hall.

"We're trapped!" Sam cried.

I shook my head. "We can't be; we can go the way we came."

"They're already here."

I thought to the passageway James had fled down—it must lead to the outside, and that was why we were trapped.

"We're not going down without a fight, boys," I growled, filling my palms with invigorating, ferocious power.

I smiled, not allowing one pinch of doubt to enter my mind. I would protect my friends and I would rip anything that came near us to shreds.

I pushed the guys towards the windows, not wanting to be backed against a stone wall. I bent my knees slightly and slid the sword out of the sheath across my back. I held it just to the side of me, giving myself some room to put some force behind it. I quieted my mind, breathing softy and silently, waiting.

The first demon came quickly. Teeth snapped at my face and I blasted it with fire, letting the flames shed some light in the hall. When I could see more clearly I jumped to the side to give myself more room to fight.

Shadows burst towards us from all sides. My heart settled into a steady drumbeat and I channeled my power through my body. I felt a blow to my back and was flung forward. I dived and rolled, flipping back up to my feet.

I ducked away from a punch and threw my own, kicking hard to send the creature flying away into the nearest pillar. I grimaced as the force caused the pillar to crack, dust sprinkling down. I sprang closer and as the creature began to fall, I whipped my sword around and sliced cleanly through its neck.

I was grabbed from behind, my arms held trapped at my sides by iron bands of muscle. Heat and agony spread through my shoulder as teeth sunk deep into it, blood running down my chest from the wound.

I shrieked and threw my head back, cracking the beast behind me, but not hard enough to dislodge him. I struggled in his hold, kicking and stomping with my heel. I screamed again and lit myself up, fire streaming through my pores. The beast dropped me and ran back into the darkness, flames licking at his skin.

From the snarls and savage noises coming from behind me, I knew Drew and Trev were getting their fang on, I hoped they were keeping Sam safe because I was in no position to go back and help.

A hand wrapped around my right arm and hurled me into a pillar. I screamed as it crumbled against my weight. I landed heavily on the chunky blocks and rolled out of the way as more of the pillar and pieces of the ceiling fell down all around me. I was pulled to my feet, a demon on either side holding me still while a third began to pound on my face.

I coughed, spluttering blood, and lit myself up again, sure it would work. It didn't. Instead, the demons began to laugh and quickly lit themselves up, laughing, mocking my attempt. *Fire Demons.*

What on earth? Fire Demons and whatever that other creature was working together? There was someone else in charge here; someone big.

When one of the demons stepped closer I lifted my legs, counting on the other two to hold me up, and I wrapped my ankles around its neck, wrenching. It dropped to the ground and another demon took its place within seconds.

I gasped as it punched my abdomen, cramps shooting up through my chest. I bent over, heaving, as blood ran freely from my mouth and nose. Another pulled me back, teeth sinking in the already present wound in my shoulder.

I shrieked and lightning outside cast colored streaks through the stained-glass windows.

"I've got one more piece of the puzzle," a familiar voice rasped.

I opened my mouth, pure terror flooding out in a monstrous scream.

Asmodeus stepped out of the shadows, his face grim, his expression vague and absent . . . his eyes deadly. Here in the shadows he looked even taller, the blackness of his aura stretching his height over his usual seven foot. All he wore were black trousers, the gold images across his body free to glint in the firelight. His black hair fell over his shoulder, blown back by a mystery breeze that swept through the hall. His black eyes rested on me and focused.

"You will come with me. You are but one piece in a game, and I've almost got the other items I need." He nodded, almost to himself. "I've almost won, there's no beating me now."

"You'll never win," I swore venomously. "Never. Not as long as I have breath in my body."

"That can be arranged," he whispered, his voice echoing in the room the only thing I heard, despite the fighting going on around us.

"What do you want?"

"Many things. At this moment I want you," he said with a faint smile.

"What do you want from me?"

"There's a small task I need you to do."

"Getting you into the heavenly realm? Sorry, but despite the fact that that's not on my agenda of things to do today, it's also impossible. I can open portals but not into the Heavens."

He smirked. "That's what the other items are for. You'll get me there, and I'll have the key to open the door."

I tensed. I had been bluffing somewhat. Having never tried to get to the Heavens I didn't actually know if I could or not, but judging from Asmodeus's reaction, he'd already thought of everything.

I shook my head. "I'm not going to do it."

"You don't have a choice in the matter."

I let my power soar out, shadows and mist mixing together. "Come and get me then."

30

"You gain strength, courage and confidence by every experience in which you really stop to look fear in the face . . . you must do the thing you think you cannot do."

Eleanor Roosevelt.

Asmodeus remained still, staring, while fallen angels rushed out from behind him, attacking me. I bolted for the nearest pillar and ran up, flipping over and slicing with my sword as I flew back. I spun around, crouched on the floor when I landed and carved up on a diagonal, shredding the fallen angel next to me.

I rose up, ready for the next one when a punch to my jaw sent me reeling. My vision flickered black and white, the ground tilting as I fell to my knees. Fury ate through my body, turning me into a savage animal, a beast just like those attacking me. I snarled as I dropped the sword to the floor and used my hands to pry off heads, pulling apart bodies. I sunk my teeth into more than one of the fallen and ripped until the blood gushed down my body and theirs.

My world was gone. *I* was gone. I was mindless. All that existed was a swirling ball of rage, destroying everything in its path. I didn't laugh when I pulled the eyeballs from a fire demon, nor did I snigger as I sliced a knife through the face of a vampire.

I began to surface again only when I was kicked into the stone wall, and I slithered to the floor. I landed beside Sam. He was unconscious, blood dripping down from a laceration on his forehead. His body seemed relatively unscathed, but the head wound was a serious one.

I crouched over him, my soul reaching to his through the haze it had disappeared into. Sam, my Sam, my best friend. I wouldn't let him die here.

I stood up above him and searched for Drew and Trev. They were nearby, their clothes drenched in blood and their kill-count stacking up around them on the floor.

I was rushed by another vampire. I leaped to my feet and grabbed him by the throat, hurling him back into the others that crowded around.

"Drew!" I shouted. "I need help!"

Drew immediately found me and ran to my side.

"I can't lift him and fight," I bit out angrily.

Before he could answer the monastery shook again, the ceiling beginning to collapse. Huge slabs of stone crashed to the floor around us. I threw myself over Sam, covering him as best as I could.

I was pulled up by my hair. I clutched onto the hand, digging my nails in, trying to draw blood.

Asmodeus pulled me back so he could look down into my face. He glared at me, his eyes soulless, his mouth twisted into a snarl. He looked around, dodging out of the way of chunks of stone and dragged me across the floor. I twisted, kicking out in desperation.

He loosened his grip on my hair and moved his hands to my throat, squeezing. As I ran out of air, black and gray spots danced across my vision, warning me I was about to lose consciousness. If that happened, it was all over. Asmodeus would have me, and I would lose everything.

I tried to gasp for air, tried to pry his fingers open or push mine underneath his to loosen them, but his grip was iron and unyielding. There was no way I was getting out of this. Panic fully set in, my veins alive with horror at the thought of what he would do to me; I'd rather be dead. My heart ached with the stress it was under to deliver the oxygen it was missing. My knees buckled, giving in as my heart stuttered, my lungs screaming in agony.

I dropped heavily to the floor. My head hit the stone hard. I lay there, unable to move as air pushed into my lungs like slicing blades. My throat was hot and raw, pain pulsing through my chest as though my heart had been cut out.

I felt someone pick me up and I cried out, desperate to shake loose the hold. I freed my legs and dropped them to the floor, pushing away from the arms that held me.

"It's me. Don't fight me," a voice hissed.

Drew. Not Asmodeus.

I nodded and turned my head, searching for Sam. Trev had him slung over his shoulder, Sam's body limp, his eyes closed. I turned back to Asmodeus.

"I need to kill him. This can't go on," I rasped.

Drew bent close, his blue eyes troubled. "Not here."

"I have to. He's following me everywhere I go."

"No, you don't kill him here," he insisted.

I paused, my eyes slowly turning to catch his. *I don't kill him here*? Was that a prediction?

"*Drew* . . ." I hissed. He had said he was here to protect me. Why? Who was he working for? How did he know anything about me?

"Who sent you?"

Drew glanced back at Asmodeus, then at me. "Someone who told me that keeping you safe would stop the apocalypse."

I bit my lip and followed his glare back to Asmodeus, who was currently dodging stone blocks. The ceiling was giving in, the monastery was coming down. We needed to get out of here.

I turned to the windows just as Asmodeus roared at us. I ran, feeling Drew and Trev closing in behind me. I leaped up onto the stone windowsill and sailed through the glass, feeling the pressure then the release as it gave way, shattering into a million pieces.

Free-falling through the air with shards of glass stuck in my skin wasn't the nicest experience of my life. I had barely opened my eyes to see where I was falling before I had slammed into the ground. I scrambled through the pieces of glass as Drew, Trev and Sam fell around me; luckily, Sam had Trev as a cushion.

We ran through the trees, Sam still slung over Trev's shoulder, pushing through the leaves and branches as fast as we could. More than one branch whipped me in the face and I was sure I was causing loads to do the same to the guys who followed behind me.

We sprinted on, leaping over rocks, fallen branches and trees, thankfully not encountering any more of the bizarre mix of demons, fallen angels and vampires that had been attacking the safe house. I should have known that only Asmodeus would be able to unite them. He was so evil that Satan would probably do his dirty work.

Only, that wasn't true, was it? Because if what James had said was right, then there was something else out there, something that would eat Asmodeus for breakfast. I would have said that an enemy of my enemy was my friend, but if this monster was buried deep inside the fallen angels, so deep and so scary that Asmodeus would try to get into Heaven to escape it, then I didn't want to be anywhere near it. Maybe I would be better off looking for the Dagger of Lex and the Falchion of Tabbris myself and getting my friends and myself to safety.

Drew lunged at me, knocking me off my feet. He gasped, clutching at his shoulder and the long metal arrow that protruded from it.

"Oh my God," I cried. I crawled forward, placing my hands on him.

"Don't!" he roared.

"I can heal you."

"There's no time, we have to keep going."

He stood and sprang onward, pushing through the trees without a backwards glance. I looked ahead to where Trev had raced past us, still carrying Sam. This was quickly going to shit. Our only chance was to find the angels. Where was Zach? Where were Haamiah and the other warriors?

I caught the shadows of demons running parallel to us and shouted to the guys to turn slightly, angling away from them. We headed uphill, my adrenaline allowing me to continue. My lungs burned, and my legs ached with lactic acid build up, combined with the numerous injuries I could feel but hadn't accounted for.

We slid down a steep prominence, half-running and half-rolling until we reached the bottom. I checked everyone was still with us and we set off at the same speed—a flat-out sprint for our lives through the forest.

Eventually the sounds of battle dimmed and we slowed gradually without realizing it until we came to a stop at the edge of a clearing.

Trev dropped Sam onto the floor and threw himself down there with him, panting. Drew's left arm hung limply, as he leaned against a crooked tree, hissing out his breath while staring at me. Was he looking for directions? For instructions? He wouldn't find any.

"I don't know what to do," I said, panicked. "I don't know where we can go to be safe."

"We need to find Haamiah," Trev said.

"He doesn't care about us," I cried. "He doesn't give a *shit* about us."

Drew pushed off the tree and stalked closer. "You heard what Sam said. He said that wasn't Haamiah."

My mind ticked over. "You think he's been possessed?"

He tried to shrug, and swore at the pain. "Maybe. Only *he* knows." He pointed to Sam.

I ran a hand across my face, finding pieces of glass caught in the hair that fell around my ears. I pulled at it, sliding it out and dropping the shards to the ground.

"So we can't trust Haamiah. We can trust Zach. He'll know what to do."

"You know what to do," Drew said earnestly. He stood in front of me, eagerly staring down at me. "Think: you know what to do."

"What do you mean?"

"Out of all of us you're the strongest, the most talented. You can read minds, you can make fire, cast spells, you run with lycan and vampires and yet you've got a good soul. You see visions and open portals. You're stronger than anyone here, maybe anyone in existence. You're not like anyone else and there's a reason for it."

"What is the reason?"

He shook his head. "I can't tell you."

"Damn it, Drew! I'm not playing games. Look at us. Sam is unconscious, maybe dying, and we're all wounded and exhausted. Fire demons, vampires and fallen angels have been united under one son-of-a-bitch and are tracking us right now. I need to know what you know," I demanded.

"If I tell you then we'll all die here. You need to think and work it out for yourself. Tell us what to do," he growled.

I sniffed, my lower lip wobbling. My eyes filled with tears at the frustration and injustice of it all. I needed to think. What did we do? Everything I said was true.

"We need Sam," I said.

I dropped to my knees beside him and placed my hand on his head, stroking his forehead gently. I let my power seep out and begin to pulse into him. I could feel his body soak it in desperately, pumping it around his body to heal all of the hurts there. Soon the laceration on his forehead began to close from the inside, the fibers of his flesh knitting together. The millions of vessels there soaked up the blood that had leaked within as his body used my cooling strength to patch itself up.

Seconds later, Sam opened his eyes and frowned up at me. "Jas? What happened?"

I fought back a relieved smile and ran my fingers over his forehead, pushing his hair back. I took a deep breath and sat back on my heels. "Fighting, fallen angels, lots of blood and mayhem . . . you know, the usual," I said with faint humor.

He pursed his lips. "Oh, is that all?"

He groaned as he sat up. "So, where are we now?"

I looked around us, my heart sinking as I took in reality. Abruptly the happy, fuzzy feeling I'd gotten from healing Sam vanished, and I thumped back down to earth. "In the forest maybe fifteen or twenty minutes from the safe house."

"I meant where are we in terms of not being dead?"

Trev peered over my shoulder and grinned. "We'd be less likely to die if you'd get off your ass."

Predictably, Sam jumped off the ground, albeit staggering a little. "Who's that?" he asked, pointing into the clearing.

I turned and looked to where he pointed. A dark figure stood ahead with something on the ground beside him. I narrowed my eyes, trying to make out what was there.

"Oh my God," Drew breathed.

"Is that?" My eyes opened wide as my mouth dropped open in horror. My body exploded into action. Without thinking I shot forward, racing for the figure, sprinting as fast as I could possibly go.

Drew roared my name, furious. Sam and Trev shouted. I could hear footsteps behind me but I didn't care. Nothing mattered . . . nothing.

I skidded to a halt. "What do you want?" I asked Asmodeus, my eyes swimming in tears.

He smiled. "You know what I want."

"Fine. How do we do this?"

The boys reached me. Sam grabbed my arm and pushed me behind as Trev and Drew jumped in front of him, snarling and baring their fangs.

"Get off me." I pushed Sam away and tried to get past Drew. I settled for standing between him and Trev.

"Get her out of here."

That was Zach, trying to protect me to the very last; even when he was on his knees with a chain wrapped around his neck. He looked dazed, barely conscious as he swayed, blood coating his body with a dark-red sheen.

"I'm not going anywhere," I said calmly. "Make the trade."

"We're not giving you to him," Sam said.

"This is my decision," I snapped.

My eyes were drawn back to Zach and my heart almost broke. My strong, dangerous guardian was in the clutches of the most evil being in the universe. The man I loved and desired, the man who made me see stars would be destroyed if I didn't do this. It was an easy choice.

"It's not your decision. This is about more than just you," Drew growled. "The apocalypse rides on this very moment."

I frowned at him. "Drew?"

I tensed, glancing desperately at Zach. I needed to help him. I couldn't see him like this. I took a step forward and was jerked back again by Trev. He snapped his teeth at me with a savage snarl. I wasn't scared; he just wanted to keep me safe, and I would do anything to save Zach, *anything*—even giving up my own life. I'd do it with a smile on my face as long as I knew Zach was okay.

"I knew this day would come," Drew said to Asmodeus. "I waited and waited, and made preparations."

Asmodeus scowled. "Enough of your talk, dog." He caught my eye. "Come closer, give yourself to me and I will release him."

I took a step towards him only to be blocked by the lycan.

"You think the lycan would ever allow the death of such a beloved one? One we worship among all others?"

My eyes almost popped out of my head. Worship? Beloved? Zach wasn't exactly a fan of the lycan, or wolves or anything that wasn't related to an angel in someway.

"You worship him?" I asked skeptically.

Drew glared at me as Trev rolled his eyes.

Was he talking about me? No, he couldn't be. What the hell was he talking about?

"The lycan will die before we allow anything to happen to her, and the lycan cannot be defeated!" he roared, his bellow almost blowing me away.

His shout was echoed, repeated and multiplied a thousand times over.

Lycan began to appear, emerging from the trees, growling, their blue eyes focused on their prey: Asmodeus.

My heart leaped. I was terrified that Asmodeus would kill Zach out of spite or anger at Drew's defiance, or that Zach would be injured further, in the fight that was clearly about to happen, but a part of me glowed with excitement and glee. A thousand lycan against one fallen angel? What were the odds?

Drew's eyes were fixed on Asmodeus. The fallen angel hissed and squirmed before yanking at the chain around Zach's neck, making him cough and gasp for air.

Sam caught me as I tried to rush to aid him. I struggled for a second before complying with his demand to stand still.

Laura Prior

I was so scared, so terrified for Zach that when Asmodeus angrily looked down at him and bared his teeth, I almost fainted dead away.

Slowly, a smile pulled at the corner of his lips. Zach's chain fell loose and Asmodeus took one step toward me, dropping the end onto the ground. I watched, frozen in place as he took another step and another, almost in slow motion. Leaving Zach behind, he broke into a run and then a sprint, each thigh quivering with the strength he contained in his huge body.

He was running straight for me. Instinct told me to flee, to get out of there, but the other part of me couldn't possibly leave Zach on the ground, kneeling, watching everything unfold in a daze.

As I stood transfixed, my muscles locked down, preventing me from moving even if I had wanted to. Sam screamed my name. I felt him tug at me, felt the other guys forcibly turn me around, but above all else I felt the oddest sensation of being pulled sideways.

My clothes—what was left of them after being on fire—were whipped into a tornado around my body. I instinctively crouched, trying to get low to the ground. I could hear the loud beating of air pulsing, and feel the pockets of it being slammed down onto me, pushing me into the ground.

I fell to my knees and lay on my front, closing my eyes tight to prevent the dirt that flew around me in eddies from abrading my eyes. Anxiety rushed through me as I wondered where the boys were. I peered through my eyelashes at Sam, just a few feet away, doing the exact same thing.

I frowned and lifted my head a little when I realized he was mouthing, no, *shouting* something, though the wind was tearing away any volume. Was he telling me to run?

Darkness descended and the pulses grew so strong I found myself sliding across the ground with the dirt. I looked up and screamed. *Dragon*!

My mind exploded into fragments of terror and adrenaline. I had faced a dragon before, but that was tiny compared to this one. It was huge, beyond ginormous. I couldn't decide if it would be better to be eaten from behind, lying facedown on the ground, or whether I should roll over and face my death head-on. I decided to roll.

I regretted it instantly. It was directly above me with claws outstretched, ready to grab me. I scrambled on all fours, making for the cover of the trees. The wind its monstrous wings generated seemed to drag me backwards each time I gained some distance. Pure adrenaline drove me, made me dig my nails into the mud and pull myself away inch by inch.

The wind lifted and a spun me over onto my back seconds later, kicking me in the ribs. I groaned and rolled over only to be picked up by my clothes and thrown through the air.

I didn't land. Hard, iron-like bars closed around my torso and I was hoisted up into the air. I freaked. My power exploded, flames rippling over my flesh as I shrieked and shrieked, the pitch of my voice splitting my head. Lightning cracked the sky, the air sizzling with electricity around me.

It had me. It was going to kill me, rip me apart with its talons and teeth. I couldn't breathe.

Concentrate. Sam's voice reached me, cool and calm. *You've got this.*

Remember who you are. Drew's voice was the opposite of Sam's. It was laced with panic; I could actually feel the tremor running through it.

My body was sucked downwards; gravity pulling at me. I slid my hand under the talons on my hip and ran my finger down my thigh to reach the blade I had strapped on. I squeezed it tightly in my left hand, using my right to grasp hold of the talon ridge above me.

I bent my leg and placed my heel on the edge, hoisting myself up between the thick hooks and gripped hold of the dragon's leg. I lifted my legs and wrapped them around the scales. Gritting my teeth, I tried to slither up the leg. The scales were slick and I couldn't get purchase. I slid down again and again, growling my frustration. I was too high to jump down, too low to try for the only point weak point I knew of. Emily and Tanya had laughed when they had told me the only way to kill a dragon was to bury a sword in the small, soft area beneath the left forelimb. There was also a spot under the right, but only under the left could cause damage to the heart.

You need to get down here and heal Zach! Drew's voice came at me.

I clutched the scales tighter and hoisted myself up again. I clenched my thighs, gripping as tight as I could and pulled myself up inch by inch. It was slow-going, too slow.

Jasmine, you've got to speed it up.

Shit. What was going on down there? I put the blade between my teeth and fought to lift my body higher up the dragon's leg. I looked up at the dragon, a mass of dark-gray scales above me. I passed the joint and pushed my feet flat against it to slide up. I gripped the blade and for one whole second, prayed to anyone listening to give me the strength to stab it in far enough.

I took a huge breath, filling my lungs to the very bottom, fisted the knife and speared it in. With a deafening screech, we plummeted from the sky.

We had been up too high; I'd never make it. I twisted in the air, pushing against the flailing dragon. What was worse than falling to your death? Landing under a dragon, I'd imagine.

I took a deep breath, bent my legs, my feet against the dragon and pushed my power through my legs to fly off the side and through the air, my arms outstretched.

I stared down at the fast approaching ground and was able to register the mayhem that was going on down there. Hundreds of lycan clashed against Asmodeus's army of fallen angels. The dead already lay on the ground, a stain in the green and brown clearing. Where my friends were I had no idea.

My heart pounded, my head ached and my throat clenched in fear. Where were the ? Someone needed to catch me. They needed to catch me *now*.

I was frozen in fear, but I was closer now and could make out the faces of those I fell towards. One figure in particular caught my attention.

Machidiel. He stood with his arms folded, a scowl on his face. Sam lay at his feet, unmoving. He couldn't be dead. Not Sam.

Laura Prior

"Help me!" I screamed.

He lifted his chin and glared up at me, slowly beginning to smirk.

Bastard! I knew he could hear me, I knew it, yet he wasn't doing anything. He was going to let me fall. Oh my God, he was going to let me fall and die. He wasn't helping us, he wasn't a good angel . . . he was fallen.

31

"If you are always trying to be normal you will never know how amazing you can be."

Maya Angelou.

White-hot fury ripped through my throat and out my mouth. I shrieked my defiance, my anger and betrayal. My body was on fire, a side-effect of the fallen angel in me. My anger burned hot and furious, lighting up like a volcano. That asshole was waiting to watch me die, expecting to enjoy the sight of my body smashed on the ground. Had he been working with Asmodeus this whole time? Had he given Zach to Asmodeus too? Did Zach know one of his best friends was betraying them? I couldn't die, not when Zach needed me, and not before I'd ripped the smirk off Machidiel's face.

My power roared to life, invigorating and revitalizing every cell in my body until I felt as light as a ball of fire. I could feel the heat sizzling on my skin, the glittering shadow surrounding me, the flashes of green and black and tinges of red.

My back ached; my skin felt as though it was being ripped open by the flames. Agony fought with terror for my attention and focus.

A lightning bolt narrowly missed me, singeing the hairs on my arms as it passed by. I shrieked as it crackled by my face, almost deafening me. I seemed to slow somewhat; less falling to my death and more *floating* to it.

I still landed hard and fell to the ground with a thud, seconds before the ground split with the weight of the dragon. The dirt and rocks recoiled, rolling from the force. I scrambled away on all fours as the dragon thrashed and rolled nearby.

I staggered to my feet and lunged at Machidiel who stood smiling a few meters away. I relished the look of shock as I swung my fist at his face, landing a blow even Caleb would have been proud of. Machidiel reeled from me. He held his hands up, laughing. For someone who had just been caught out, he looked mighty pleased with himself.

I glanced down at Sam, then up at him.

"I'm going to make you pay for this. Zach might not have known who you really are, but I do."

"Easy. I'm on your side."

"You let me fall to my death and you're on my side? How is that exactly?" I sneered. He was a moron if he thought I would believe that.

He grinned, his teeth flashing. "You didn't fall to your death though, did you? Trust me, I'm on your side; your *real* side."

"I don't know what that means." I shook my head. I didn't have time for this; people were fighting all around me, ripping apart fallen angels, while the fallen tried to slash their throats. Fire demons were blowing up trees and setting loose flames everywhere, vampires held screaming lycan in their clutches, draining the blood from them. Whatever Machidiel was trying to say would have to wait.

I crouched by Sam and let my power flow into him. He opened his eyes and groaned.

"You're going to have to stop doing that," I teased.

"What?"

"Getting knocked unconscious. It's becoming a habit."

He moaned as I pulled him to his feet. "I'm going to put that at the top of my list, I swear."

He rubbed his forehead. "Where's everyone else?"

I spun away from him to search the fighters. Where was Zach? And Trev and Drew? I turned back to Sam and grabbed his shoulders.

"I need to find Zach. Where is he? I heard you and Drew saying he was injured. I need to get to him."

"He can't be far. Let's go that way." Sam pulled away and began to dodge through the fighting around us.

I ran beside him, punching and kicking anyone who got in our way. When he screamed in an incredibly unmanly way I leaped to his side, lifting my right leg into a high kick, booting a vampire in the chest. He sailed through the air into a demon that then began to pummel it.

"Come on!" I yelled.

I grabbed his hand and we ran, sprinting and ducking through the melee until we were blocked by Drew, or more . . . by his body.

He rolled towards us, having been kicked. He spun around and bared his teeth, snarling and snapping. He launched himself at the fallen angel roaring at him. He hit him full in the chest, knocking him off his feet. I rushed forward to help, finding myself utterly distracted when I spotted Zach.

He was kneeling, the chain still around his neck, with no Asmodeus attached to the other end. I dropped to my knees, my hands on his face. I couldn't stop touching him. He was bruised, cut on his jaw and eyebrow, his cheeks purple, and a lump protruding from his forehead. His lips were red and swollen.

"Zach." I leaned close and kissed him softly, oblivious to the fight going on around us.

I cupped his face between my hands and stroked his cheeks softly with my thumbs. I ran my hands down his neck to his shoulders and leaned closer. I breathed in deeply, sweat and blood mixing with Zach's spicy aroma.

I kissed him again, harder this time, and pulled away to gaze into his eyes. The blackness swallowed me whole. He looked so sad and hurt.

I couldn't breathe. Something constricted my throat and I was pulled up away from Zach and thrown on the floor. Asmodeus knelt on my chest, punched my face.

My head fell to the side, my neck throbbing. I screamed and bucked, trying to knock him off of me. He punched me again and again until my vision rolled and the blackness of the sky took on a gray haze. I gulped and swallowed the saliva and blood that filled my mouth, coughing and spluttering.

"Get off me!" I rasped.

Asmodeus fisted my hair and leaned close, the sweat from his body dripping onto my face. His eyes sank into mine as he opened his mouth to bare his teeth.

"Never. You're mine."

My hair was yanked, my head pulled awkwardly as Asmodeus sailed over me. Zach dragged me across the ground, pushing me behind him.

"Zach!" I screamed, when Asmodeus loomed over him.

Zach fell to his knees, clutching his chest. I froze, staring up in horror as Asmodeus held his curved sword out towards Zach.

As he pulled it away and started to swing the sword a flash of colour passed by, knocking Asmodeus to the ground. I threw myself over Zach, covering him, protecting him. I pressed my hands to his chest, letting my power rush through him.

"Come on, baby. I need you healed," I whispered.

I looked up nervously. Asmodeus roared and knocked Drew off him, dropping him to the floor. He backed away.

"This isn't over," he bellowed.

I glared up at him, watching him turn and sprint off through the battle.

"Drew?" I called, staring at where he lay.

He rolled onto his back and sat up stiffly, clutching his side. Blood seeped through his clothes, gushing down his abdomen.

"Oh my God." I sat up straight, pulling my energy back within. I wanted to get to him. I *needed* to get to him. I couldn't reach his side to heal him and protect Zach though, and he wasn't even nearly healed enough to defend himself.

Drew sensed my anxiety. "I'm okay, I swear."

"You're bleeding."

He looked down. "Yeah."

"Come to me. I can heal you."

He grimaced and shuffled across the ground, gingerly sitting next to me where Zach lay half-conscious beside me.

I placed my hands on his ribs and I sent my healing strength into him, knitting together the flesh from the gash.

He gave me a weary smile. "Are we winning?"

I looked over my shoulder. The battle seemed to be simmering down. With the absence of their leader, the army of fallen angels and demons seemed to have taken that as a cue to flee into the forest.

"I think so," I said.

I bit my lip hard, tasting blood. "You saved him. You saved Zach."

He met my eyes with surprise. I nodded. "I saw you. Asmodeus would have cut his throat but you threw yourself in front of him and saved his life."

He raised his eyebrows and gave me a small smile. "Then I did what I was supposed to do."

"What do you mean? Why did you save him?"

His smile faded.

"Why did you save him? Why are you doing any of this? You appeared from nowhere and said you were here to save me, to protect me. You didn't think I knew about any of this; you said you'd been sent to tell me about the fallen and demons and vampires. Who sent you?"

He stood up and began to turn away. I jumped to my feet and grabbed his arm to swing him back around to face me. "Answer me!"

He shrugged stiffly. "I can't."

"You mean you won't," I said grimly, pressing my lips together in a tight line.

"He means he can't." Machidiel appeared behind Zach.

I narrowed my eyes at him. "What do *you* want?"

He sighed. "You can't ask questions when you're not ready for the answers."

"I'm ready and I'm asking."

He shook his head. "You're only ready when you already know the answers."

"Ugh!" I groaned. "Shut up with your stupid prophecies and riddles. I'm so over it already! I'm so sick of you all and the way you withhold information from me. You know something about me and seeing as it's about *me*, I should be allowed to know it."

"What's going on?" Trev skidded to a halt beside me. He was panting, and smiling. Covered in blood, he'd obviously been enjoying himself.

"People keep telling me I need to remember something, that I need to know who I am . . . it doesn't make any sense, and I'm sick of it. I want to know who sent Drew to protect me. I want to know if Machidiel isn't evil, why he wouldn't catch me when I was falling and what the hell he means when he says he I need to remember who I am. Even the grammar is wrong! It doesn't make sense. I don't have the answers you're all looking for."

Trev raised his eyebrows and turned to fix Machidiel with a glare. "And what, we're keeping secrets now?"

"Machidiel, what are you hiding?" Zach rasped.

I dropped to my knees beside him and pulled him close, kissing his lips softly, urgently.

"Machidiel?" he insisted.

Zach tried to stand. I ducked under his shoulder and pulled his arm over my shoulder, supporting his weight.

"I can't say."

"What the hell does that mean?" Zach growled.

Somehow we had formed our battle lines. Zach, Sam, Trev and I stood in a huddle, while Drew and Machidiel stood side by side.

"You want me to say it again?" Machidiel asked, calmly smiling at us.

Zach took a threatening step forward. At least, it would have been threatening if I hadn't been holding him up.

"We're not *allowed* to answer your questions," Drew said, trying to appease me with a sad look.

"So someone *is* giving you orders," Sam said.

Machidiel scowled at Drew, then turned back to me. "There are secrets everywhere. There are people you don't yet know making decisions for you, trying to help you. This is bigger than you know; you just need to concentrate on being yourself and this will work out."

I shook my head. "You're not getting it. You have no right to tell me what to do with my life—none of you do. I am in control here. I am the one who gets to say who knows what, and who is involved. No one gets to make decisions but me."

"If we tell you the answer to those questions before you work out the answers yourself, it will change everything," Machidiel said.

"Is that why Haamiah is acting so weird?" I asked.

Sam hissed in a breath. "Oh my God."

I faced him, concerned. "What?"

"Before this all happened I was about to tell you—Haamiah *isn't* Haamiah."

I rolled my eyes. "Yeah I vaguely remember you saying that. It still doesn't make sense, by the way."

"I can hear thoughts and the person on the inside of Haamiah isn't *him*."

"Who is it?" Zach asked with a growl.

"I don't know." He shrugged.

"So he's been possessed?" Trev asked.

"Maybe possessed, or maybe it's someone who just looks like him; I don't know. It just isn't him."

"Wait. He said he's been hanging around with Mnemo . . . someone."

"Mnemosyne? The Goddess of Memory? What was he hanging around with her for?" Machidiel gasped, his eyes widening in horror.

I frowned. "Weren't they like . . . lovers?" I flushed with embarrassment.

"No. She's evil! She's done horrific things; she can never be forgiven, never. Haamiah wouldn't touch her," Zach swore.

I stilled. My heart slowed, becoming so loud in my ears that the noise of the ending battle faded into insignificance. Zach knew Haamiah was with Mnemosyne. He was with them in the garden of the safe house . . .

"You knew," I said, stepping away from him.

He shook his head adamantly. "I didn't. I swear."

"But you were there. When I had the vision, we went and we spoke to him and he told us about her. He said there had been humans watching the safe house and she had worked her mojo on them to make them forget about us."

"What?" He gasped. "That never happened." He stepped closer to me, pulled me to him. "Baby, what are you taking about?"

"You don't remember?" I asked, my voice trembling.

He shook his head. "I haven't been told anything about Mnemosyne. If I knew he was even thinking about talking to her I would have unleashed Raphael on him."

Raphael? That name sounded so peculiar. He was one of the archangels, I knew that, but there was something else.

"So somehow she's involved in this," Drew said, stating the obvious.

Machidiel scowled. "If Haamiah isn't Haamiah, and Mnemosyne is involved, then . . .?"

"Haamiah is actually Mnemosyne."

32

"*There is a special place in hell for women who do not help other women.*"

Madeleine Albright.

The sound of clapping perforated the bizarre, confused haze I was in. I slowly turned my head to see Haamiah walking towards us. One moment he was Haamiah, his black dreadlocks hanging down his back, his body clothed in his usual beige trousers and white, billowy shirt, and the next, he was a woman, a tall, muscly woman with bands of steel wrapped around her body and a metal ring around her forehead.

"Who are you?" I hissed. "Are you Mnemosyne?"

She frowned at me intently, her brow furrowing while her eyes narrowed. "I've met you before. Well, Haamiah does like to keep his secrets close."

I scowled. "Who are you?"

She smiled and lifted her shoulders in a shrug. "Mnemosyne. It's *lovely* to meet you, now that I finally see beneath that exterior. They hid you well; no one would have guessed. Even I didn't see it until just now."

"What do you mean?"

She lifted her arms up in a shrug. "Well, I've been pretending to be your beloved Haamiah while you were walking around right before my eyes. It's actually a little embarrassing." She giggled.

"How can you do that? How can you look like him?"

"She didn't," Zach said quietly. "We saw her as she is but she altered our memories so we remembered her as him."

My jaw dropped open. Was that possible? Had we been seeing Mnemosyne this whole time, not Haamiah? And of course that bred the question: where was Haamiah?

Machidiel seemed to feel the same way. "Where is Haamiah?"

Mnemosyne ran her fingertips across the band at her forehead and grinned. "Are you sure he's on your side? I can undoubtedly assure you he's working for us now."

"And who is 'us'?" Zach asked, stepping forward threateningly. I shuffled with him. "Asmodeus? The horsemen?"

"It has to be Asmodeus," I hissed.

Mnemosyne flicked her eyes over me slyly. "I couldn't possibly say."

"Why are we even asking her questions? Why isn't she a pile of body parts yet?" Drew snarled.

He began to crouch, lowering his body and baring his teeth at the goddess standing before us. I tensed, clutching Zach a little too hard. I wanted to kick this evil bitch's arse but at the same time, I wanted to wrap up Zach and my friends in a bubble where they couldn't be harmed.

Suspicion crept up my spine. "Why are you here? Why are you even talking to us?"

She smiled and shrugged. "I was curious."

I glanced up to see Zach narrowing his eyes at her, flicking my eyes back to the predator so as not to lose sight of her. "Curious about what?" he asked.

She closed in, seeming to almost float near me. "I wanted to see you."

"Me?" Zach asked skeptically.

Jealousy instantly flared.

She slowly shook her head, chuckling. "I've seen you at the safe house when you thought I was Haamiah, of course, only I didn't realize it was *you*. I thought you were just another simpering nephilim child."

"You wanted to see *me*," I repeated. It could have been a bit self-involved of me to even think she was talking about me, not Sam, but it seemed too much of a coincidence. "You know something about me. What do you know?"

Mnemosyne didn't answer; she simply stalked closer. When her hand reached out slowly to touch Zach, I slid in front of him and knocked it out of the way. A jolt of electricity tingled my hand when our flesh collided.

"Jasmine!" Zach gripped my shoulders and tried to push me behind him.

I held my arms out away from my body, refusing to be moved and refusing to let Zach step past me.

"It's true. This is what you look like now," she said, running her eyes up and down my body.

"Now?" Sam echoed. He sidled closer to me, Trev closing in on the other side. "I don't like this, Jas."

"What do you mean *now*?" I hissed. My eyes were fixed on her face.

She flashed a smile at me. "You were a lot scarier before."

"Before what?" I demanded.

She stepped back, turning to catch Drew and Machidiel circling her from behind. She tipped her head back and started to laugh.

She vanished on the spot. I stepped away from Zach, spinning around to see where she'd gone. She was nowhere to be seen.

"I'll catch up with you later," her voice reached us from behind. We spun to face her. Somehow she had slipped past all of us and now stood a few meters away, smirking.

"How can you even consider catching me when you don't remember seeing me?"

She was gone again.

"Come on we need to get out of here," Drew said.

"What about Mnemosyne?" I asked.

What were we supposed to do now? If she could make us forget we were seeing her in order to escape, how would I ever catch her and kill her? Also, she hadn't answered the question about where Haamiah was. I couldn't think of a better time for him to pop up magically. We needed his futuristic insight and impeccable advice *now*.

Drew turned back to me. "Who?"

Zach scowled down at me. "What's Mnemosyne got to do with this?"

33

"When someone is going through a storm, your silent presence is more powerful than a million empty words."

Thelma Davis.

I turned to look up at him. "What? You just saw her."

He scowled. "What are you talking about?"

"Do you know something about Mnemosyne?" Machidiel asked. "This isn't the time to hold anything back from us."

I gasped, my mouth hanging open. I didn't know what to say, or what to do. I looked at each of them in turn. They looked confused, bewildered, or annoyed, in Zach's case.

"Sam, help me out here," I pleaded.

"I don't get it. What do you want me to do?" he asked, weakly. He met my eyes. "Oh."

He stepped closer and concentrated. I could feel the delicate touch of his mind in mine. I felt utter relief when his face changed into a mask of shock and horror.

"What the hell?" he exclaimed.

"What is it?" Zach asked, impatiently.

I shrugged, shaking my head, letting Sam explain.

"She was here! She was right in front of us, talking to us . . . we all saw her," he said. He pointed to Zach. "She's been pretending to be Haamiah. You were the one who said she's been altering our memories every millisecond so we remembered her as him. She said Haamiah is working for them, and you asked who 'they' are."

He turned to me. "She said she let us see her because she was curious about what Jasmine looked like. She said Jasmine was scarier before."

"Before what?" Zach snapped.

I shrugged. "That's what I want to know."

Machidiel and Drew shifted uneasily.

"Let me guess; even after this, you're still not going to tell me your secrets."

Drew huffed out a breath. "We can't. I'm sorry."

I shook my head, letting my hair fall around my face in a mess. "No, you're not."

"You're right. We don't want to tell you," Machidiel said grimly. He fixed me with a stare and turned away.

"Why?"

"If you can't work out who you are and what you can do and we tell you, you'll not only be completely freaked out, your awareness will attract those hunting you."

"Someone's hunting her?" Zach growled.

"Someone's always hunting me," I reminded him. "So, somehow by my knowing what I can do, I'll trigger a homing beacon?"

Machidiel flashed a smile. "Exactly."

"And these people are so dangerous she needs to be at full strength before they come after her," Trev guessed.

"So beside telepathy, healing, fighting, fire and portals, you must be able to do something else," Sam said.

Zach wrapped his arms around my shoulders. I slipped my hands passed his waist and held onto his back, pulling him close. I rested my cheek on his chest.

"I won't let anyone hurt you," he swore.

I nodded absently. The question playing on *my* mind was could I protect *him* from whatever was coming after me? Apparently Drew and Machidiel were involved in this up to their necks. I couldn't help the guilt that was eroding my insides. Had my friendship with Sam and Trev dragged the nephilim and vampire into even more danger? Was I going to get them killed?

"What are we going to do?" Sam asked.

I was stumped. I had absolutely no clue where to begin to try to clear this mess.

"We start by getting out of here," Drew said.

"Then we need to find Haamiah," Trev said.

Machidiel ran his hand down his face. He looked exhausted, as did we all. "We also need to find out who she's working with."

"It has to be Asmodeus," Drew said.

"Maybe." I shrugged. "I'm not sure, though; she gave me this weird look." I groaned. "There's too much going on. What about my vision? Do I just forget about it now?"

Zach stroked my hair. "It's not related to Mnemosyne, so as much as you're not going to want to hear it, I think we need to push it to one side for a little while and sort this out first. Asmodeus and Mnemosyne are major threats that need to be dealt with before they come at us again." I grimaced. I knew he was right but it felt wrong to leave it.

"It's in the future, remember? It was a vision, so we can still prevent it from happening." He dropped a kiss into my hair. "Who knows, maybe fighting Asmodeus and Mnemosyne will help us prevent the vision."

"Yeah, maybe it's a warning about what might happen," Sam suggested.

I wanted to stay in the safety of Zach's arms forever. I wanted to feel his heart beating beneath my cheek and smell his scent as I inhaled him. It couldn't last though.

I pulled away and turned to Drew. "First thing's first then; let's get out of here."

Drew nodded, sighing in relief. He glared at the retreating figures and began to lope off with stealth. We followed closely. I held Zach up, taking most of his weight, and we staggered together, trying to keep up with Drew, Machidiel, Sam and Trev.

I looked over my shoulder warily as lycan appeared between the trees, some watching, while others joined our group as we ran. I huffed out my breath, trying to keep up with everyone, but still ended up falling behind. If only I could stop and heal Zach properly, but with Asmodeus out there somewhere and Mnemosyne behind us, as well as surviving vampires and demons in the forest somewhere just waiting for a chance to snap our necks.

Wherever Drew was taking us, it was too far. Zach groaned and stumbled. I leaned him against a thick tree trunk and let him slide to his knees. I crouched beside him, kissing his cheek tenderly.

"I'm just going to have to heal you," I whispered.

I flinched as a movement to my right caused the faintest of shadows in the blackness. A tall, lanky lycan stood beside me, looking around cautiously. I jumped to my feet and lifted my fists up, unsure if he was going to attack.

"I'll keep watch while you do your thing," he said, taking a few steps away.

I bit my lip. Did I chance it? Did I trust him not to attack when I was on concentrating on Zach?

No.

I held out my hand to Zach and pulled him to his feet, to the surprise of the lycan.

"We're fine," I said coldly.

I slipped under Zach's arm and tried my best to ignore his groan as I pulled him in the direction the others had gone. I shrieked when a dark figure loomed over me.

"Jesus! Give me a heart attack, why don't you?" I hissed at Sam.

He smiled apologetically. "You can talk. I turned around and you were gone." He frowned at Zach then met my eyes. "He doesn't look good."

"State the obvious much?"

He grimaced and pulled Zach's arm over his shoulder, hanging on to his wrist and wrapping his closest arm around his torso. He pulled and I joined him in half-carrying, half-supporting Zach.

Within a few seconds, the others had also realized we had fallen behind. Drew growled something undecipherable and gestured for us to follow him.

The next hour was painfully slow. We had to stop often and I was able to administer some of my healing power to Zach each time, but this wasn't just a bump on the head or a small wound. His body was covered in cuts and deep, penetrating lacerations, he kept losing consciousness, and his internal organs were almost damaged beyond repair. Each time I attempted a healing, I felt the pain running through him and was able to understand his injuries a little more. To say I was amazed he was still alive was an understatement. He didn't look quite as bad as he had last time Asmodeus had had hold of us, but the fallen angel had clearly had fun torturing him.

"How much longer?" I asked Drew.

He sniffed the air. "We're almost there. Can he make it a bit further?"

I crouched beside Zach where he lay on the ground, supported by Machidiel and Trev. I ran my hand across his sweaty forehead, noting the glassiness of his eyes.

"As long as it's not too much further. Just give me a moment."

I held my palm against the skin on his abdomen, trying to heal the rupture I could feel there. Something had perforated his pancreas, and blood and fluid were seeping through into his abdominal cavity. I pulled on my power, letting my angel magic sooth and knit the fibers together, dissolving the fluid that had leaked.

I fell back, gasping for breath.

"No more," Sam said, anxiously pulling me away. He knelt before me and cradled me against his chest. "You can't help him if you burn yourself out."

I nodded, panting. I could barely breathe; I certainly couldn't answer him. Machidiel stood, draping Zach's body up and over his shoulder. Drew hovered over me, pulling me up.

"I've got her," Sam protested. He turned me into his arms and slipped an arm under my knees, sweeping me up off my feet. I leaned my head against his shoulder, turning my face so I could still see Zach as he dangled upside down over Machidiel's back. I sucked in my breath and clutched at Sam as he started to jog after Drew.

Thankfully he had been telling us the truth, and five minutes later we had descended a steep hill and hit the outskirts of a small town. Drew shimmied down an alleyway, keeping close to the edge of building. He turned into a wider street and led the way around boxes and crates. He stopped beside a huge iron shutter which looked like a rollaway door to a warehouse, and leaned down to grip the bottom of it.

He heaved on it, pulling it up to chest height. He stepped closer and lifted it up over his head.

"Get inside," he said.

Sam ducked and we slipped under the shutter door. Machidiel and Trev slid under with us and Drew dropped the door closed, grimacing at the whine it gave as the metal grated from age and lack of use.

Machidiel dropped Zach to the floor and helped Drew stack up wooden crates against the shutter. Sam put me down beside Zach and gave me a forbidding look when I reached over to touch him.

"There's a window back there, but no doorway," Trev announced after his foray further into the warehouse.

Drew nodded. "We use this as a safety compound when we need to."

"Why would lycan ever need to be over in this part of the world?" Trev asked.

Drew flashed a ghost of a smile as Machidiel rolled his eyes. "The lycan have areas of safety near every nephilim safe house, every valkyrie home, and every vampire lair."

"Why?" Sam asked. He lifted me up to cushion my head. He ran his fingers across my forehead and through my hair, smoothing the knots with his fingers.

Machidiel coughed, seeming to send a warning to the lycan. He glanced over at him and began to pace, turning in a circle as he measured his words.

"We've been waiting for Jasmine. We knew she would come; we . . . we just didn't know in which form," he stuttered.

Machidiel roared in anger. Drew flinched and backed away, holding his hands up.

Machidiel pointed a blade at Sam. "Stop asking questions."

Sam looked down at me. *You think you've been reincarnated? That you were something else in a past life?*

I get the feeling that's what he means. Of course, the fact that it seems to make sense to us might mean we're crazy, I thought to him.

So you were something else, and you've been reincarnated. The lycan were sent by something in your past life to keep you safe but they weren't told who or what you would come back as, so they set up camp all over the world, anywhere you might reappear.

I guess they didn't consider I would come back as a half valkyrie, half fallen angel being, abandoned by my parents and raised in the human world. I smiled at the ridiculousness of my life. Just thinking like this was exhausting.

There was a small pause. *What do you think you were? You must have been something or someone pretty important to have an entire pack of lycan searching the planet for you.*

I can open portals. Maybe . . . maybe I'm a fallen angel like Lamia?

Sam gulped. I could feel the revulsion running through him.

I struggled to sit up. Everyone turned to look at me. I took a deep breath and fixed Drew with my sternest glare. I didn't trust Machidiel not to lie to me, but Drew I could read. Nephilim were easiest to understand, probably because they were half-human, but I was picking up feelings and one or two words from Drew. He wasn't a closed book; I could only hope that my telepathic ability wouldn't fail me now.

I sent my power out around me, opening my mind up wide, ready to absorb any information he threw my way. "Drew, did I used to be Lamia?"

Nausea and revulsion slithered into my head. It wasn't exactly what I was hoping for, and certainly didn't answer any questions.

He shook his head slowly, looking to Machidiel for help.

"I'm not Lilith?" I clarified.

He shook his head firmly, his mouth clamped closed in a grim line.

"But I *was* something?"

Though he didn't answer, I felt the positive energy flowing from him. Sam and I were right. I had been something in a past life; someone important. Who or what was I? Had I been evil or good? Had I been a leader, a fighter, or someone to be scared of? A political prisoner? No, the wouldn't have been sent to protect me if I was.

"Was I a lycan?" I asked, frowning. I could be on board with that. Lycan were cool, mysterious, and a little scary, but then so was I.

"Enough," Machidiel roared. He glared at me. "No more."

He pushed Drew away from me, ordering him further into the warehouse.

I didn't get the feeling you were a lycan. Sam thought.

I bit my lip. *Me neither, but what else could I have been? Why would the lycan be ordered to find and protect me if I wasn't someone important to them? And why would I have been born a bizarre mixture of species?*

Isn't that a clue in itself? Sam thought with excitement. His eyes seemed to flash at me. *You're half valkyrie, half fallen angel, a mixture of good and evil. Sorry.* He winced. *You have a , you fought alongside werewolves, you're friends with nephilim and are protected by lycan. You're allies with the harpies and possibly the witches if we can find them.*

The my dad knows have asked to be my ally, I added.

Then if we want to know who you used to be, we need to find out who is loved by all creatures. At least, most of them; demons and the fallen still seem to want to kill you.

I scowled at him as I caught the thought that flashed across his mind. *I'm not God. That's the daftest thing I've ever heard.*

Why not?

Valkyrie don't believe in the angelic God—they have their own, for starters. The also have their own goddesses they pray to.

Oh. He frowned at me. *Who do witches pray to?*

They believe in supreme energy in the universe: they call it Divine energy. It's divided up into gods and goddesses. There are loads of them: Dianna, Hecate, Pan, Astarte, Isis . . . there are hundreds and they all channel different aspects of power.

Huh. How do you know that?

I shrugged awkwardly. *I'm not the illiterate dropout you all think I am. I have layers.*

Sam huffed out his breath in a chuckle.

I smirked. *I found out when I was with the valkyrie.*

He nodded. *We need to work this out. Machidiel and Drew won't tell us, even though they keep telling you to remember who you are. I can't think of anything else to do.*

Meditate?

He rolled his eyes.

What are we going to do, Sam?

"Jasmine," Zach whispered.

I turned to him, pulling out of Sam's arms to lean across my love. "Are you okay?"

He nodded, coughing. "I'm okay. Are you?"

I smiled. "I'm fine, I promise."

"You want to include me on that very in-depth conversation you two have just had?" Trev muttered.

I glanced around, seeing that Machidiel and Drew were nowhere to be seen. "We figured that as I have a significant amount of allies—none of whom actually mesh—in a past life I must have been someone linked to them all."

"Someone they were all friends with? Or maybe each species owed a debt to you?"

I shrugged. "I've no idea."

"We're also wondering what we're going to do. We're here, in the middle of nowhere, surrounded by demons, yet somehow we need to find Haamiah, find our way back to civilization, and kill both Asmodeus and the Goddess of Memory," Sam whispered.

I closed my eyes. "Easy as pie, right?"

Laura Prior

34

"Detachment is not that you should own nothing, but that nothing should own you."

Ali ibn abi Talib.

Gabriel

Twenty-five years ago

In the heavenly hall, Jophiel and Gabriel whispered, still arguing over the best way to unite the species, when Raphael suddenly appeared before them . . . surrounded by warriors.

Jophiel tensed and took a step back.

"What is this?" Gabriel demanded.

"Treason," he answered with a grim smile.

"You think we . . .?"

"I know you are. Don't try to lie your way out of this, Gabriel, I know you're planning on going to the human realm and ally yourself with the beasts."

She shook her head. "They're not beasts; they're potential friends, they can help us."

"No. It's forbidden." He signaled to the warriors. "Apprehend her and put her in the dungeons. You'll be there a long time for this. It has been decided to wipe the human plane of the disease that is nephilim, vampires, fallen, witches and the rest, yet you take it upon yourself to defy us, to actively work against your own people? You're no angel."

"You don't understand what will happen if you do this," she said, nervously turning her head as the warriors approached her. "Don't do this, Raph."

"You've left me no choice."

He turned away and sauntered through the warriors, letting them close in on Gabriel and Jophiel.

"Stop! This isn't right," Jophiel shouted.

As she tried to reach for Gabriel, she found herself hurtling through the air towards a pillar. She hit it hard, a gold leash wrapping around her body dozens of times, holding her pinned. She bucked and wriggled, trying to gain an inch, a single centimeter to help free herself, while she watched the warriors surround Gabriel and place her in chains, despite her struggles.

"Stop!" Jophiel screamed.

Gabriel wasn't a criminal; she was trying to defend the heavenly realm in her own way. How could Raphael send her to the dungeons? How could the warriors obey him instead of Gabriel or herself?

"Michael," she screamed.

A blow to the face forced her into silence. Her head spun, gray fuzz blinding her to the sight of Gabriel being carried away.

She opened her eyes to see Zacharael grinning down at her with malice.

"Free me! Let me help her. Why are you doing this?" She gasped.

"Gabriel is the reason my sister is dead."

"How?"

"She gave Zanaria the mission to defend that , and she's the one who continues to advocate protecting them. She'd sacrifice us all for that scum if she could," he snarled.

"And me? Why are you doing this to me?" She sobbed.

"You're nothing. You're just another sheep, following Michael and Gabriel around. You don't make any difference; you don't help us or save us. You don't have any purpose. You're a waste of space."

"You're saying that because you're hurting."

A dagger flashed by her face as he embedded it in the pillar beside her head. "You know nothing about life, about love, or loss. Don't think to presume anything about me."

He stepped back as the warriors began to disappear. He looked up once and let his wings carry him away.

The gold leash vanished and Jophiel slid to the floor. She kneeled, looking up to where they had disappeared. What in the Heavens should she do now?

35

"Tough times don't last; tough people do."

Unknown.

I woke up to the sound of raised voices. There seemed to be arguing and shouting all around me. I opened my eyes and furtively peered up at the figures now lit by dawn's light.

My stomach sank as I immediately recognized Zanaria and Maion. I felt a little appeased at the number of lycan now crowding around us, taking shelter in the warehouse; at least I knew they were on my side.

Zach was still unconscious beside me, and Sam and Trev stood a few meters away, shielding us from the others.

I called on my power and let it churn up through my stomach and out through the palm of my hand to flow into Zach. I felt the instant relief as his pain lifted, allowing him to surface. I caught his eyes as he flicked his eyelids open.

"Hey," I whispered.

"Zacharael!" Zanaria's voice pierced my happy bubble.

Her hand briefly touched my shoulder as she wrenched me away from her brother, causing me to fall backwards. I glared at her as she threw herself over him, gushing over his wounds, kissing his cheeks.

Zach groaned as she pulled him up so he was sitting. He looked past her and held his hand out to me. Zanaria brushed his arm aside and she and Maion pulled him to his feet.

I scowled and collected my legs under me, forcing my body to rise, albeit unsteadily. Sam arrived at my side, supporting me.

"We need to get you home," Zanaria said.

"You're not taking him anywhere."

Maion glanced at me then back at Zach. "Friend, you need to return to the heavenly realm to be healed."

He shook his head. "Where is Elijah? He can heal me here."

Zanaria sighed. "He's busy elsewhere. You have *us*. We're your family."

Zach gently took her shoulders and pushed her aside. He stumbled to me, wrapping his arm around my waist. "Jasmine is also my family."

A glow of warmth and love spread through me at his words.

"And these *lycan*?" she sneered. "Are they your family too? What has she done to you? Look at yourself; friends with lycan, injured by fallen angels, the guardian of a valkyrie, looking after a vampire? What's wrong with you?"

"Don't speak to him like that," I hissed.

"And you . . . I told you to leave my brother alone. You're ruining his life."

I stepped in front of Zach, fury pouring through me. "You can hate me all you like. You can be as big a bitch as you can be and it won't make any difference. Zach is my soul mate and by hating me you're just hurting him. I'm not like you and I'm clearly not like anyone else you've clashed with before, because you know what? I'm not going to lie down and take it. You can throw me to the wolves and I'll just come back leading the pack."

A murmur ran through the lycan as they grinned, collectively shifting their power to me. They pushed closer, narrowing their eyes on Zanaria.

Maion immediately pushed her behind him and pulled his sword free from the sheath at his hip.

"Back off," he growled.

The lycan seemed to flow around me, backing me up. They surrounded Trev, Sam and Zach, offering their support and muscle. The way my rage was flowing, I wouldn't need any help to take down these fuckers.

"Enough," Machidiel said, stepping forward between our two factions.

"She started it," Zanaria whined.

"She didn't, and you know that. You have issues with others and those issues have no place here. Work with us or go," Machidiel said calmly.

I lifted my chin and glared at her. What would she choose? Would she stay and act meek to appease Machidiel while continuing to plot behind my back, trying to turn Zach against me? I hated to admit it, but if Asmodeus and his demons came back, we could use Maion's muscle, but if she left, he would go with her.

Zanaria gritted her teeth. "I'm not leaving my brother here alone. I'm obviously the only one who can see something wrong with this picture."

"What picture? The fact the species are coming together? Lycan, valkyrie, vampires and angels working side by side to fight evil? I thought you were different. You were one of few who believed angels could coexist with another species," Machidiel shouted. He seemed utterly exasperated and I was incredibly surprised. Who would have guessed this irritating angel who I had previously accused of being fallen, would be on my side?

"I meant nephilim. Nephilim are part angel; they have angelic traits and should be protected." Zanaria blinked back tears. "The fallen used them against us and since I've been back, I've wanted to see them all dead. Maion made me realize that was wrong. They should still be protected."

I inhaled deeply. That was a huge admission on her part. After she had actively campaigned to have us all murdered, this was definitely unexpected. Throw in the part about Maion being the one to change her mind . . . was my world turning upside down?

"That doesn't mean that angels should trust the lycan with their lives," she added.

The lycan began to growl and snarl.

"I trust them," I said quietly, silencing the masses. "I trust them and Zach trusts me, so I guess the question is, do you trust Zach's judgment or not?"

She bit her lip and looked past me to where Zach stood silently. Slowly, she began to nod. "Fine. I'm staying, but only to make sure my brother is safe. Don't get in my way."

I shrugged and stepped back, almost falling over Sam to escape the tense huddle we had formed. I reached a dejected-looking Zach and helped him sit down on top of a crate.

"I need to finish healing you."

He caught my hand between his. "You can't. You're not healed fully yourself."

"What if we're attacked again?"

He smirked. "I'll be able to kick some ass; don't worry about me."

I smiled. "I can't help it."

"I can help with that," a deep voice called.

We turned towards the entrance where two lycan were escorting Elijah in. My heart leaped for joy; he would heal Zach.

I was right; he immediately got to work, pouring his strength into him, healing him from the inside out. Within ten minutes Zach was stronger, no longer weak and pale, but was standing, helping Elijah to sit on the floor.

"You gave me too much," he chastised.

Elijah smiled wanly. "It sounds like you're going to need your strength."

I kneeled by Elijah and touched his shoulder. "Thank you."

He gave me an absent nod in return.

I sat beside him and rubbed at my forehead. It was beginning to throb, sparks shooting behind my eyes. I was exhausted and hurt; it was no surprise I was now going to be plagued with a headache.

"Are you okay, babe?" Zach pulled me closer, letting me lean the side of my head on his shoulder.

I breathed deeply, ignoring the smell of blood and sweat, reaching for his wild and spicy scent.

"Jasmine? What are you doing here?"

I spun in a circle facing Haamiah. He looked guilty, as though he'd been caught doing something he shouldn't.

"I was . . . looking for you," I frowned.

I reached for my forehead again, stroking the pounding pulse there. Where was I? I was in a room with wooden walls and beams holding up the ceiling. It was dark and musty, boxes and trunks piled up on all sides.

Haamiah held a curved sword in his hand. The handle was glittering, jeweled, encrusted with emeralds and sapphires. He clenched it tightly, and glared at me. He seemed to be frozen in place, as though my finding him here were horrifying.

He cursed, looking over his shoulder, before plunging the Falchion into the wooden beam in the middle of the room beside him.

I froze, my surprise giving way to complete confusion. The blade disappeared. It should have still been visible, the tip protruding through the wood and the handle from this side, but it was gone— completely invisible.

I took a step forward. "What-?"

The air in the room began to shimmer: a telltale sign of a portal. A tall, beautiful woman stepped out from pure air and closed in on Haamiah, running her hand down his arm. She leaned close, licking his cheek from jaw to eyelid. She turned her eyes on me, focusing intently.

"Who do we have here?" she whispered softly, beguiling.

Haamiah's eyes opened wide, scared. "No one of any importance. Do what you came to do and go."

She turned to face him fully and leaned in, sucking on his lower lip. "Where is it, lover?"

Haamiah gulped. "Where is what?"

She laughed. "You've been playing these games for so long, you forget there are others who have been playing similar games for much longer." She leaned in closely and stuck out her tongue, licking up his cheek again. "Where is the Falchion?"

"What do you want with it?" he hissed.

"You know what I want with it. You're a Principality, remember? You can see the future." She twirled her fingers beside her head in the air. She looked insane. Her eyes were huge and fixed, staring at her prey as she twirled her body around him.

"You want to open the gates to Heaven," he said.

She clapped her hands. "Well done, gold star for you."

"Who are you working for? This isn't you; someone's making you do this."

She smirked. "Oh baby, this is me." She tilted her head and ran her hand down to his pants. "There may be other interested parties, but this is me."

"I won't believe it. You weren't like this before."

She shrugged. "It's been a millennium since you last cared enough to search for me; a girl can change in that time."

"Can you turn evil in that time?"

She scowled and pushed away from him. "I've always been bad. The only thing different here is that you used to like it. Are you going to tell me where it is or not?"

Haamiah shook his head stiffly. "Are you really going to torture me to find it, with a witness?"

She turned to me and smiled, her long hair swinging over her shoulder. Her eyes met mine and grew hard. "They don't call me the Goddess of Memory for nothing. I want the Falchion and I have friends capable of performing the best kind of torture. I'm going to take you there and you're going to tell me where it is."

"Where? Who do you trust with your secrets?" Haamiah bit out angrily.

She turned back to him, beaming her white smile at him. "The four horsemen."

I gasped for air, sitting up away from Zach. He caught me just before I fell off the crate to the floor.

"What is it?" he asked.

I clutched at my chest as Sam dropped to my feet. He looked up at me intently, his jaw dropping open.

Horror ripped through me, agony spreading from my pounding head down to my toes.

"Oh my God." I gasped, tears pouring from my eyes.

Zach pulled me close, angrily confronting Sam. "What is it? What's wrong?"

Sam paled and stepped away from me. "Oh my God."

"What is it?" Zach growled.

"She just had a vision," he said quickly.

Machidiel, Trev and Drew pushed the Lycan out of the way to hover over me. Machidiel dropped to the floor and clapped his hands on my knees, ignoring Zach's warning growl.

"What happened?" Machidiel asked.

I covered my mouth with my hands, every inch of me trembling, screaming. "The vision I just had was a memory. It was the memory that Mnemosyne had wiped from my mind. It was the same . . ." A sob tore through my throat.

Sam continued for me. "It was the same style as the vision she had before. It means it wasn't a vision at all. It wasn't something that was going to happen in the future; it's a memory. If she was just having a memory flash, then that means she was there when the horsemen were torturing someone but her memory was wiped and she only remembered it when she was sleeping. Mnemosyne gave Haamiah to the horsemen to torture and the horsemen are torturing Haamiah to find the Falchion."

36

"I may appear harmless but inside I'm completely badass."

Unknown.

I stared up at my friends in utter misery. How could I have left him there? How could I have abandoned Haamiah? The same thought seemed to be going through everyone else's heads too.

My heart broke when Sam and Trev turned away from me. Machidiel fell silent and Drew turned his head, running his hands through his hair. At least Zach pulled me close and kissed my hair.

"It's okay. It's not your fault," he whispered.

"It's absolutely her fault," Zanaria snapped. She stepped away from Maion and narrowed her eyes at me, curling her lip up in disgust. "You left him there to be tortured. The horsemen are some of the most evil of creatures in existence. They are sadistic, ritual and won't stop until they get what they want from him. In your cowardice you've doomed him to pain and terror."

"Fuck you," I snarled. I jumped to my feet, my eyes still steaming with hot tears.

"Zanaria, enough," Zach said, glaring at her.

I should have felt comforted that he was defending me against her—in fact, I'm sure I would when this died down—but still, she was right. I shouldn't have left him. All I remember about the decision was being frightened and confused and . . . *that boy.*

I turned to Zach. "There was a guy, remember? He told me they were the horsemen. He's the one who made me leave."

"Yeah, blame it on someone else," Zanaria sneered.

Machidiel stepped closer, lycan parting to let him through. "Who was he? What did he look like?"

I shook my head and shrugged. There was nothing I could think of that stood out, nothing that would be particularly helpful. "He had brown eyes, brown hair. Oh! There was a scar running through his eyebrow and down to his cheek."

"Did he tell you his name?"

"No, but . . ."

"But?"

I sighed and looked up to Zac, clutching at his waist. "He seemed nice, normal. He was worried I was going to run straight up to them and get hurt."

"He knew who you were?" Machidiel asked with suspicion in his voice.

I thought back to the memory. "No, I don't think so; I think he was just sad and frightened."

"Or, he was working for the horsemen and you did exactly what he wanted you to do," Zanaria said.

That bitch was seriously getting on my nerves. At least my tears had dried up and my eyes were now just stinging in anger.

"He was hiding from them. He was scared."

"He had every right to be. What could a kid do against the horsemen? He was right to send you back. You would have been killed," Zach said, tension running through his body making the muscle in his jaw twitch.

"Wait, how did he send you back?" Sam asked suddenly, reappearing by my side.

I pursed my lips. "I don't know."

"He must have had powers, some ability to send you back to the safe house."

"Are we missing the most important part in all of this? It was a memory which had clearly been wiped and then resurfaced while you were sleeping, right?" Trev said. "So Mnemosyne had to have been there."

I froze. "Why would she wipe my memory if she let us see her now?"

Trev bit his lip, wincing as his fang split the flesh.

Sam sucked in his breath. "It's all starting to make sense now."

"It is?" I asked, rolling my eyes.

Sam nodded. "Maybe they thought they could get what they wanted from Haamiah and when he wouldn't tell them what they wanted to know, she came to find out herself."

"Okay, that does make since," I agreed.

"It still doesn't explain how he was able to send you back here or how Mnemosyne was able to wipe your memory before you could tell anyone when you didn't even see her there."

I racked my memory, trying to remember what happened clearly. "He *did* have powers. He was telepathic and he was able to control me somehow."

"How?" Zach demanded

"Um, he silenced my voice."

Everyone stared at me, confused.

"I don't know how, but when I tried to scream, even when I tried to talk to him, my lips were moving but no sound came out."

"A nephilim?" Machidiel asked.

"Maybe," Zach said.

"Wait, it still doesn't make sense to me. He said the weirdest thing," I frowned in concentration.

"Think, Jasmine, it could be important," Machidiel urged.

Zach growled at him. "Back off."

I rubbed my forehead, feeling the headache pounding away. "We were arguing because I wanted to go and rescue Haamiah, and he was just hiding behind the trees, watching. He said I wasn't really there but that the horsemen would still sense and trap me like him; that's why I thought it was a vision.

"He said he was trapped there?" Sam asked.

I nodded. "That's what he said."

Machidiel began to pace. "He didn't know you can open portals, so what if his essence is trapped there so he presumed that your soul had found its way there and that's why he didn't think you could rescue him?"

"But you had actually opened a portal. You *were* there," Sam added.

"Then you can find your way back and save Haamiah," Zanaria said, curling into Maion's side.

"And Mnemosyne?" I asked, still not really understanding her part in this.

"If she's working against us, which seems to be most likely, then maybe she saw you just before you left that plane and wiped your memory, or caught you here before you could tell anyone," Machidiel suggested.

"What if she's not working against us?" Sam asked.

"Highly unlikely," Maion grunted.

"What if she withheld the memory, knowing you would go after him, until the moment when everything fell into place?" he suggested.

"That sounds like something Haamiah would do." I smiled.

Sam shrugged. "What if it is? What if they're working together?"

"That's ridiculous. After everything we know about her and from what she's said, we need to assume she's working against us," Machidiel said

Sam met my eyes. *There's something more to this. You know there is.*

I think you're right. I'm not sure about her working with Haamiah though; why would he willingly give himself up to the horsemen to be tortured?

He's a principality; maybe he has a plan.

Maybe. Just maybe. I leaned my forehead on Zach, while keeping my eyes on Sam.

An explosion had Zach knocking me to the floor. He leaned over me, protecting me from the debris that flew over us. Crates, boxes and pieces of iron and steel were blasted through the warehouse.

An object was thrown through the gap in the wall and smoke began to fill the room. All around me lycan began to drop like flies as fallen angels poured through the hole.

Drew appeared over Zach's shoulder. "Run!" he hollered.

Zach dragged me to my feet and pulled me away from where Drew lay, twitching on the ground.

We ran through the warehouse, jumping over boxes to find an exit. Everywhere we turned, fallen angels and vampires blocked our way. Zach pushed me behind him towards the wall and stood in front of me, guarding me. Sam and Trev were thrown into the wall beside me while Machidiel stood beside Zach. Zanaria and Maion had apparently escaped. Good for them.

Asmodeus sauntered through the fallen angels surrounding us and stood tall before me.

"You know what I want. Let's not play games."

"You're not having her. I will not let you have her," Zach growled.

Asmodeus grinned. "You and what army?" He gestured around him to the piles of lycan. "You seem to have lost yours."

I sucked in my breath. I didn't have the energy to fight him, and though Zach was healed, he would still be exhausted. Machidiel and Trev couldn't take them all—there had to be at least twenty fallen angels and vampires backing Asmodeus up. We didn't have a chance.

I eyed Asmodeus. "Let them go and I'll come with you."

"Jasmine, be quiet!" Zach roared.

I flinched, jerking into Sam.

We're not letting him have you. There has to be some way out of this.

I looked up, searching the room for an idea, some kind of solution to this. I could hear Asmodeus talking, I could hear the argument between him and Zach, but all I could see were pipes running above our heads and below us through the rotten floorboards.

Pipes. Gas pipes and electrical wires I would imagine . . .

I glanced across at Asmodeus. He stepped closer. If I could douse him with gas fumes and light him up . . . we could be home free.

Praying Sam was listening to me, I inched to the side, beginning to slide down the wall slowly. I reached down and gripped the pipe running by my feet.

One, two . . .

Sam flew at Zach, knocking him to the floor and out of my way. I pulled the pipe by my feet, bending the metal and aiming it for Asmodeus.

Trev flicked a match at him, and the flames rippled over Asmodeus's body from head to toe.

Roaring, he bolted, sprinting out of the warehouse, his fallen angels in tow. Zach shook Sam off and ripped the pipe from me, tossing it to the floor. He grabbed me, covering my mouth either because he was mad or to stop me from inhaling the fumes. He picked me up and ran with me towards the back of the warehouse.

Machidiel kicked a hole in the wall and we poured out into the street, fleeing in the opposite direction to where Asmodeus was heading.

As soon as Zach took his hand away from my mouth I yelled. "What about Drew and Elijah? They're still in there!"

"They're not; their pack was already pulling them out as we left. You just couldn't see them because you were fighting me."

"Or because your giant man hands were covering my eyes," I hissed.

As Zach dragged me down an alleyway I could see flames licking at the sky in the distance. Asmodeus had taken to the air.

It was pointless being quiet so we sprinted, our feet slapping the ground as we grunted and panted. We bolted through the town, finding a secluded courtyard.

A figure I hadn't expected to see slipped out of the shadows. She looked as beautiful as always; her blonde hair flowing down her back, her figure encased in a fitted, black cat-suit.

Lilith.

She flashed an angry look at me. "If you've finished playing games with Asmodeus, I want what's mine."

"And that would be?" Zach spat.

"I want the Dagger of Lex. It belongs to me and I want it now!" she snarled.

"I don't know where it is," I said.

"You're lying."

I gulped. I wasn't. I wish I did know where it was. The Dagger of Lex had to be somehow linked to Zanaria, as it was her I brought back from the Pool of Souls, but she would never tell me where it was, though she might tell Zach.

"You have twenty-four hours to give me what I want or I'm going to eat your friend's eyeballs and entrails," she hissed.

"Haamiah? Where is he?" Sam demanded.

She whipped her head around to fix her eyes on him. "Somewhere safe. Somewhere you'll never find him unless you give me what I want."

"I'm going to kill you," I said coldly.

She grinned. "You can try." She turned away. "Twenty-four hours."

37

"I'm not like most girls . . . that's where you made your first mistake."

Unknown.

The moment she vanished through her portal, we turned to face each other. I imagined that each of us was hoping someone would come up with a solution. We seemed to be all out of them.

"She wants the Dagger, so we need to find it and give it to her. This is Haamiah we're talking about," Zach said angrily, his black eyes seeming to swallow me up.

"So how do we find it?" Sam asked.

Machidiel groaned. "It needs to stay hidden. Its very presence will put the entire planet in danger. Used correctly and with the Falchion, it'll open the gates to the other realms. You think they just want to get into the Heavens and kill everyone there? Don't be so blind! They're going to open Hell's gates first and let them straight into Heaven."

"But this is Haamiah," Sam said, heartbroken.

"We won't let them kill him. We'll get him back, I promise," I swore. I turned to Machidiel. "Can't we give her the dagger of Lex and free Haamiah and come up with another plan to stop them from opening the gates?"

"The Dagger is dangerous on its own. We might put off the opening of the gates, but the dagger was designed to start the apocalypse. Whether it's used as a weapon to kill something or someone, its energy harvested, or to open a freeway linking hell, earth and heaven: if Lilith has it, she'll destroy us all. The only thing we can do is keep her away from it."

"Can't we at least find it and then come up with something to free Haamiah and keep the dagger safe? Maybe the witches can disarm it or something," I said.

Machidiel frowned at me. "That's not a bad idea. However, that still gives us twenty-four hours to find an object that has been missing for centuries."

"It's a shame she doesn't want the Falchion," I muttered.

Zanaria and Maion stepped out of an alley leading into the courtyard where they had obviously been spying on us.

"You are all so infuriating! You don't even see it, do you? The Dagger of Lex is right in front of you, and you don't even see it," Zanaria cried. She took a step forward and glared around at us.

"What do you mean?" Maion asked, protectively pulling her back under his arm.

Zanaria's eyes flashed at him, intense and wide. "The Dagger is in this room. *The Dagger,* is breathing, talking, and living right under your noses, and none of you have realized."

I tensed as six pairs of eyes turned to look at me. Zach stiffened and put his arm around me protectively, mirroring Maion's stance across the yard. Nervously I tilted my head to look up at Zach. He stared down, his eyes black and deep, warm and melting. I could look into his eyes forever. Even now, when everyone was staring at me, I felt safe with him.

His teeth flashed at me, and I belatedly realized I had been staring at his lips. I copied his smile, relaxing.

"You're looking at the wrong person." Zanaria's smooth voice had taken on an irritated edge.

I pulled my gaze away from Zach's and faced her.

Her cold eyes caught mine. "The boy is the Dagger. That's why he has been with Haamiah for so long, you idiots!"

I gasped and stepped forward so I could see Sam. It had to be him. Sam had never known either of his parents. He had been with Haamiah for as long as he could remember.

He looked equally shocked, frozen in place. His face lost all colour and he swayed on his feet, quickly supported by Trev.

"Oh my God," I whispered. I couldn't tear my eyes from him.

"I'm a weapon?" he said.

Zanaria quirked an eyebrow. "Why else would he keep you around for so long?"

Maion looked troubled. He worried at his lip as he held Zanaria close. "You want to give them the boy?"

I scowled. "We're not giving him up," I said firmly.

"We need to do anything possible to get Haamiah back. We need to give her the Dagger of Lex—you said so yourself," Zanaria insisted.

I turned away, taking a few steps, breathing deeply. We weren't giving Sam up; no way were we giving him up.

Maybe you should. His voice reached me. He sounded weak and dazed.

"We're not giving you up," I said, steel running through my words.

"So you want to sacrifice Haamiah?" Zanaria asked.

"Shut up!" I shouted. "Just shut up. We're going to get Haamiah back and were going to keep Sam safe."

"Here, here," Trev agreed.

I caught his gaze and attempted a smile.

"No one is giving Sam up. If anything, Haamiah clearly wants him protected. We need to honor that," Zach added.

"How do you know that?" Maion asked Zach.

"If he wanted to tell them where he was, Sam would have been already been taken."

I watched Sam as he backed away from us. He placed his hands against the wall surrounding the courtyard and leaned closer, resting his head against the stone. My heart ached for him as he closed his eyes. I could feel the horror and despair emanating from him.

His whole world had been completely turned upside-down. For Zanaria to just spit life changing information out like that . . . I couldn't have hated her more.

"Aren't we forgetting something incredibly important?" I hissed. I stepped towards Sam, putting my hand on his back, wanting to comfort him. "What about Sam? How is it possible for him to be the Dagger of Lex?"

Zanaria crossed her arms and stubbornly looked away.

"I'm being serious, Zanaria. Start talking."

"*Zanaria* . . ." Zach rumbled.

She tutted angrily, "It's a long story and it isn't really mine to tell."

I spun around and glared at her. "Spill."

She sighed in annoyance, flicking her hair over her shoulder. "About twenty-five years ago, Lucifer tried to overthrow Malik and escape Hell."

"Malik is the Guardian of Hell?" I clarified, thinking back to the many dull lessons Haamiah had made me sit through.

She rolled her eyebrows, obviously not in teaching mode. "He didn't succeed but it was close. He had planned a revolt on the human plane at the same time as a diversion while he targeted Lex, planning to use him to escape. He almost did. A lot of angels were killed in the process . . . including Lex."

Sam's face paled further. He was definitely on information overload.

"Lex was a good and one of the strongest telepaths in the angel realm," she said, a little softer, seeing Sam's distress. "He was Malik's twin and the only one who was able to read his mind."

"So Lex would have been able to open the gates?" Trev asked.

Zach stirred. "He would have access to the angelic magic used to keep the gates closed. To open them, he'd only need to read Malik's mind and pass the information over to Lucifer."

"And then Hell would be unleashed on earth," Zanaria said.

"So where does Sam fit in?"

"Lex was dying when Malik found him in Lucifer's clutches. Lex already knew he had a human child—Sam. Being impulsive and rash, in his last moments he transferred more of his angelic essence to the boy, ensuring an even stronger telepathic ability. This telepathy combined with his bloodline, ensures he is the only one who, beside Malik himself, is able to open Hell's gates. Sam is the only one able to read Malik's mind and learn what magic, spell or device will allow the beasts to escape. That is why he is a weapon created by Lex to be used for good or evil; he is the Dagger of Lex."

"Why did he do it?" Sam asked.

Zanaria glanced at Maion, and fiddled with a strand of hair, twisting it round and round before pushing it behind her ear as she measured her words.

"I guess—"

"You guess or you know?" Sam interrupted.

She flinched. "I know that he was worried you'd be left on your own, unprotected. Your mother was . . . flighty, and he didn't trust her to look after you. He thought if he gave you more of himself that Malik would look after you."

Sam clenched his jaw. "But he didn't."

She shook her head. "No, he didn't. He was too distraught. He couldn't even look at you. A call went out among the guardians for someone to care for a young nephilim boy, but at the time there was an uproar in the heavens; the angels wanted to rid the earth of nephilim and all other supernatural creatures. No one wanted to take the job on."

"Gabriel asked me," Zach said, stonily.

I spun around to look up at him in shock. "She did? She asked you to be Sam's guardian angel?"

"Not exactly; she had been hounding me to protect the nephilim for years. She told me I'd never see my soul mate if I didn't do what she asked." He shrugged, "I don't like being threatened so I decapitated every messenger she sent."

I grimaced. "You killed angels?"

"She didn't send angels. Gabriel was unique among the archangels in that she used other beings to do her dirty work."

"She's insane, actually," Zanaria added, spitefully.

Zach frowned at her. "Until you, she was the only angel to ever have other species as allies. Gabriel has the traits of a principality; manipulating situations to suit her own game. She wanted to unite all supernatural creatures to form one super army to fight the apocalypse."

"Only, everyone else already knew the only way to fight the apocalypse was to preemptively strike and eradicate our enemies," Zanaria said.

"And that is still the current plan, by the way," Maion added.

"Yeah? How's that plan working for you?" I cocked my head to one side and narrowed my eyes at them.

"Not well," Zach answered.

"So, you refused to be Sam's guardian? Why did you take on me?" I asked.

"Someone had a good argument," he said.

"We're digressing," Zanaria snapped.

"The call went out to the angels and Haamiah took me in?" Sam asked.

Zanaria shrugged. "At that point I was decapitated, so I can't help you from there."

"Your mother kept you for the first few years of your life. Haamiah took you when the second call came. Another archangel was going to take you, had actively petitioned for you, but something happened before she could."

"Who?" Sam asked.

"Gabriel's sister, Jophiel," Zach said.

"Ugh, Michael's lapdog." Zanaria rolled her eyes.

"Why is she his lapdog?" I asked.

"If she ever had an original thought I think her brain would explode," Zach said.

"You don't like her," I said, jealousy rippling through me at the passion in his voice. They obviously had a history together and being a self-confessed psycho girlfriend I couldn't help feeling angry about it.

Zach gave me a small smile. "We've had numerous run-ins. Anyway, back to your question," he said to Sam. "Haamiah took you in when Jophiel couldn't."

Trev glanced at Sam, voicing the question he was unable to. "What happened to his mother?"

Zach grimaced apologetically. "I honestly don't know. I'm sorry."

Sam nodded absently.

I want to ask if you're okay, but I know it's a stupid question, I thought to him.

I don't know what to do. I owe Haamiah my life.

If he wanted to save himself, he would. He doesn't want to give you up. Believe in him; he's a Principality. This is going to work out somehow; we just can't see it at the moment.

My dad is dead and my mother might be out there somewhere, but didn't look after me; I think it was better not knowing about them.

I'm so sorry.

38

"I think my Guardian Angel drinks."

Unknown.

"So what is the plan?" Trev asked.

"We hide Sam and I open a portal to wherever Haamiah is and rescue him," I suggested.

"Pfft!" Zach hissed. "Like that's happening."

"We give Sam to them and get Haamiah back. Haamiah can then come up with a plan to get us out of this mess," Zanaria fixed a sneer at me.

"We need to nullify Sam's powers first, if we're going to give him to them," Maion added.

"Are you crazy? We're not giving Sam to *anyone*," I blasted.

"Listen, little girl, Haamiah is a thousand-year-old angel. You're a child, and a stupid one at that. We make the plans and you follow," Zanaria snarled.

"Enough," Zach exploded, furiously clenching his fists. "I'm sick of the bickering, so shut the fuck up."

We fell silent, Sam, Trev and I huddling closer. Zach stalked towards his sister and Maion.

"If you're not on board with saving the halfling then get lost," he spat. "We're not giving him up; we'll find another way."

"If you're planning on taking on the horsemen you can count me out," Zanaria said, holding her hands up in defeat. "I'm not dying for another nephilim. No way."

"Then leave. It's best if you go while you have the chance," Drew said.

I looked at him, surprised. I actually agreed with him, but still . . .

Before anyone could recover from the surprise, Machidiel cleared his throat.

"If you don't want to die for another nephilim, I'd take the opportunity to get out while you still can," he said, adding his weight to Drew's advice.

"I'll take you home," Maion said.

"Take care of her," Zach said gruffly. He clapped Maion on the back and dropped a kiss into Zanaria's hair.

"You know I will," he replied. Maion wrapped his arms around Zanaria and spread his wings, taking them into the sky.

I shuffled my feet on the spot, feeling confused and awkward. Zanaria had no faith in me; what about the others?

I tilted my head to look across at Machidiel. "And you? Are you taking off too?"

He gave me a lazy smile. "Out of everyone here, I believe in you the most. I'm going nowhere."

Not knowing what to make of that, I shrugged. "Good. We can't take on the horsemen, Mnemosyne and Lilith as we are. We need more fighters," I said.

"The lycan pack is with us."

"Then I just need to find my way back there. We can take them on," I said.

"Jas, these are the horsemen of the apocalypse," Sam said, biting at his lip. "We need a proper plan."

"I have a plan: we go, we kill them, we get Haamiah back."

Zach wrapped his arm around me. "If you can get the portal open then let's do it."

I ignored the concerned faces of Sam, Trev and Elijah and reached for my power. I felt it churning through me, seeking an escape. I gave it one.

It poured through my body, twisting and forming, trying to shape the direction I wanted to go, but the portal was never produced. My shimmering mist continued to swirl and turn, enveloping me in silk, but we remained standing in the courtyard.

Exerted, my strength began to wane and I let it drop. I frowned up at Zach, a little embarrassed and very confused.

"It wouldn't form," I said, struggling to come up with an explanation.

"Why?" Trev asked.

I shrugged. "My power was there but the portal itself seemed to be prevented from opening."

"You need the Falchion," Elijah said.

I looked him, propped up against the wall. "Why? What will it do?"

His gaze met mine before skittering away. "The Falchion will open any locked realm, not just the heavenly realm. That's why Mnemosyne wants it."

"You knew this all along?" Zach scowled at him. "What else do you know that you haven't been telling us?"

"Nothing, that's it," he said.

As I stared at Elijah, his thoughts came at me wrapped up in a feeling of guilt and desperation.

I just need to get it to them and they'll free him.

I bit the inside of my cheek. Get *what* to them? Was he talking about the horsemen? Was he planning on trading the Falchion for Haamiah? Seeing as that's what my original idea was I wasn't about to out him, but I didn't like knowing he was lying. If he had ulterior plans of his own, what else was he plotting?

He's a good angel, Sam thought, joining me in my silent deliberation.

I know, I replied. *I trust him to do the right thing. After all, why would he heal Zach just to send us to our deaths?*

"Okay," I said to Elijah. "Then we need to get the Falchion and try again."

"Easier said than done; the Falchion is missing," Machidiel said softly, narrowing his eyes at me.

I sucked my lip into my mouth, not looking forward to confessing. Sam met my eyes. "I know where it is," I said, after taking a deep breath.

Everyone's eyes fell on me like a ton of bricks.

"How do you know where it is?" Zach asked, incredulously.

I winced. "The memory I had of Haamiah and Mnemosyne. I was looking for Haamiah in the safe house and I went into the attic. I saw him hiding it there before Mnemosyne appeared."

"You didn't tell me," a flash of hurt appeared in Zach's eyes before being hidden away.

I groaned, my heart twisting. "I'm sorry, I only remembered it about five minutes ago."

He stepped back away from me, only one or two steps, but I felt his absence, his withdrawal, like a hole in my chest.

"So we head to the safe house," Machidiel said, capturing my attention again.

I turned to look at him, taken aback when I realized he was grinning from ear to ear. What was he so happy about? I presumed it was because he had been proven right; I was keeping secrets. There was more to me than there appeared to be.

I nodded slowly. "Okay, we go to the safe house, get the Falchion then rescue Haamiah."

"Don't forget the rest of our allies," Trev reminded me.

Machidiel chuckled. "Thanks to you, we're not alone in this. This is a first for the angels."

I smiled, hope spreading through me as I realized he was right. The witches, harpies, human rebellion and valkyrie were our allies. We stood a chance; a *good* chance."

"So contact them," Zach said eagerly. "The sooner we meet them the better."

"Where?"

"Tell them to meet us at the safe house," he said.

Sam handed me his phone. "I'm surprised this thing isn't broken."

I grinned. "Me too. You reckon I can get a signal?"

I dialed my dad's phone number, silently praying that he would answer. He did.

"Caleb, I need your help," I began.

He listened, I explained; the result being the valkyrie were onboard and would meet us at the safe house fully armed and ready to kill, and would send word to the witches. By the end of the conversation, the lycan pack had regained consciousness and Drew promised that they would be there in force. Zach sent his own message through the grigori, who promised to inform the harpies and warrior angels, and have them meet us there.

I looked around at our group; I would fly with Zach, but who would go with Machidiel and who would be left behind?

When I voiced my question, I was met with scowls.

"I'm not being left behind; this is *my* fight," Sam said, standing his ground.

"Trev is a better fighter. If you're walking into an ambush at the safe house, you need another fighter, not someone to protect," Drew said. "In any case, we'll be taking Elijah with us."

I frowned at him. Could he be any ruder? I nudged Zach's arm with my elbow.

He glanced at me and shrugged. "The lycan's right. Sam will be safer with the pack. We won't do anything without them, so he'll not miss out, but four of us are going to be there before anyone, so it makes sense for the four best fighters to go."

Oh, my God. Yes he was hundreds of years old, but did he have to lose his compassion in his old age?

He sighed when I glared at him.

Drew jumped to his defense. "It's true. You can sugarcoat it anyway you like, but it still stands."

I bit my lip and looked at Sam, guiltily. Zach and Drew were right and I couldn't help the thought winging its way through my mind.

Sam turned away sullenly, kicking at a stone on the ground.

"Maybe there's a way he can come with us," I pleaded with Zach.

"The lycan will take care of him," Drew said. "We'll travel with Sam to the safe house. Don't approach the horsemen until we get there."

I frowned at Drew. "Why are you pushing this? What interest do the lycan have in him?"

He took a deep breath. I was waiting for him to repeat his true but hurtful words about Sam not being a good-enough fighter. Instead, he surprised me.

"Do you really want to hear more about prophecies?" he asked, raising his brow in question.

Machidiel hissed in a breath and let out a low rumble of a growl at him. I jumped back, bumping into Zach. What was going on with those two? They knew something; they were sharing a secret. I rubbed at my forehead. If this was somehow mixed in with prophecies and myths, did I really want to know what was going on?

"We don't have time for this," Zach said. "Sam, you're going with the lycan."

In a whirlwind of a moment, Zach had picked me up and launched us into the air.

39

"I think she's caught between who she is and who she wants to be."

Unknown.

My stomach dropped away as we rose higher and higher. As the gravity sucked at my body I clutched at Zach, burying my head in his neck. After a while when we slowed in our ascent, sailing forwards rather than upwards. I bent my knees and slithered up his waist to wrap my legs around him, locking my ankles behind his ass.

Despite having never flown first-class, I could still say that flying by angel was definitely the comfiest way to travel. I felt safe and warm, and the thrill of flying zoomed through me, lighting up my nerve-endings and sent my stomach spinning. While cuddling into him, if I angled my body slightly I could see the forests pass below, small towns and larger ones, and eventually the sea. As far as I could see, blue and white ripples covered my world. It was magical. Breathing in Zach's scent mixed with the saltiness of the ocean, the sounds of sea birds, and blue and white sparkles shimmering both up and down at me.

I might not know Zach's past, or even a lot about the angelic realm, but I knew *him*. I knew the instant his focus shifted from the battle ahead to me, my hair and my body. Connected to him as I was, I felt the instant the adrenaline rippled through him, stiffening and hardening every muscle in his body.

I grinned, hiding my face in his neck. I felt his teeth nip my neck, his hot breath on my shoulder. He bit harder, licking my flesh afterwards, warming and freezing me at the same time. Excited nerves zipped down my chest as he moved across, gently nipping my throat. He tilted me backwards. I let my hair slip back over my shoulder and I dropped my head back, arching into him.

He lowered his hands, running them down my back to cup my arse tightly, grinding my core to his stiffness. I grasped hold of his shoulders, pulling my body back up and close to him, opening my mouth to his. He licked his tongue across my lips and bit at the corner of my mouth.

I licked back, needing to feel the smoothness of his lips and the pressure of his tongue on mine.

We dropped suddenly, as though his wings had given up. We spiraled down towards the ground. I clenched my teeth and squeezed my eyes shut, trying not to squeal, somewhat unsuccessfully when I moaned breathlessly.

Zach pressed my head into his neck, holding me close with his hand at the back of my nape, laughing.

Before I had chance to hit him for laughing, water splashed up and over us. The shock of the cold water had me panicked and I fought for air

Strong arms wrapped around my waist and the water rushed past me as we broke the surface. I wiped the salt water from my face, staring at Zach in shock, pausing when I realized he was laughing. His teeth flashed at me, his lips pulled wide with hilarity.

"You did that on purpose?" I asked, frowning.

My frown was momentary; who could stay mad at a guardian angel with a playful streak? I brought my hand down in the water and splashed him, grinning. He dunked me again, pulling me under the water. I wriggled, forcing him to bring me to the surface again.

Wrapping my legs around his waist, I smiled when he lifted me higher, out of the water. He ran his hand between us and slipped into my now very wet clothes. Nipping at my breasts, he sunk one finger into me.

I arched my back as ripples ran through me. I groaned, relaxing into him. Zach laid me back in the water. I lifted my torso, floating on the surface, my arms spread out. Small waves washed under me, water spray lapping up at my skin.

I felt his hands run down my breasts to my hips and he peeled my pants down my thighs, dragging them to my knees. He ducked under the water, his hands clamping on my buttocks. He tilted my pelvis, biting at my lower lips, his tongue circling around my entrance. His tongue delved, teasing and tasting.

He made a meal out of me, sucking on my clit and biting softly. I felt pressure between my buttocks and groaned when he slipped a finger in, stroking me from front and behind. I could feel the weight begin, swirling through me, sparks shooting up inside.

I yelped as Zach spun me around. I tensed my body, remaining upright as Zach bent my legs to accommodate his muscular body. He moved in behind me, his cock sliding straight in, filling me up. He kept us afloat while sinking into me again and again. He reached around, placing pressure on my clit as he spread my lips wide, so wide, to allow easy access for his body. His balls hit my buttocks over and over as splashes of water slapped at my breasts. I held onto his arms, keeping my back pressed against his chest. The icy water pricked my nipples hard but there was no free hand, mine nor his, to squeeze and stroke them.

The tempo picked up, his throbbing cock ramming into me with the force of a train as my body clenched and spun, on overload from the sensations. I grunted, my breath coming in pants and moans as I gripped tightly to his arms, needing something to hold on to, something to anchor me.

I exploded, my body jerking, relaxing, and completely out of control. I arched my back, falling back into him. He laughed and slid his hands up my body, letting me ride on his cock for the moment. His hands reached my breasts and he cupped them, squeezing them in his big palms. I dropped my head on his shoulder and turned my face to his, nibbling at his earlobe.

"I love you," he said over the sound of the waves. I stopped my play and waited for him to look down at me. When he did, I was blown away by the intense look in his eyes.

"I love you too," I whispered.

He kissed me fully on the mouth; slowly, softly, and with meaning, with lust and life.

"We shouldn't do this. We should have kept going. Haamiah is waiting for us," I said, reluctantly pulling my mind back to the task we had set out on.

"I needed to see your smile," Zach said. "I can't stand seeing you so tense. After everything that's happened I needed to say thank you."

"What for?"

"For being you. When I agreed to be your guardian I never realized how special you were or how important you would become to me. You're a mystery."

"Not to you." I shook my head. "You know me better than anyone."

He smiled slowly and sighed. "Everyone sees what you appear to be but few experience what you really are. You are my universe, and I feel as though the universe is in you."

I laughed, happy tears welling. "I don't know about that. Your sister thinks I'm an evil, sadistic demon bitch."

He shook his head. "She's wrong. I adore your fiery side just as much as every other part of you. As for Zanaria . . . everyone is fighting their own demons, their own battle. Just let her get on with it and she'll come around when she's done."

"I think she thinks I'm taking you away from her."

"That would be impossible. She's just getting a more complete me."

I bit my lip. "What do you mean?"

"We're soul mates; I was only half a soul before, now I'm complete." He smiled. "Do you want to know something interesting?"

"Always," I replied.

"Now, I don't know this for certain, it's just hearsay, but when He creates creatures in the Heavens, they are power embodied, strong, fearless and magical. He splits them apart and sends them as two separate entities."

"Why?"

"Because then they must trust, love, cherish and honor those around them if they are to find their other half."

"Does it work?"

He shrugged, kissing my throat. "Sometimes."

"It seems like a mean thing to do. Why create whole, happy creatures and then break them apart?"

"I don't know. Maybe it's not true."

I closed my eyes and leaned back, groaning when Zach began to wiggle up my trousers, covering up my body. It felt weird now. After being naked in the water, free and cool, wearing wet clothes seemed constricting and too tight.

Zach's power exploded behind and below us, and water shot out from all sides. His wings blasted out and we soared into the sky, each beat of his wings sending air beating. And the race was on again.

40

"Keep some room in your heart for the unimaginable."

Mary Oliver.

A few hours later we had landed in the garden of the safe house. When Zach let me shimmy down his body, I couldn't help but stare in shock at what used to be our home. The mansion looked as though a bomb had hit it. The roof had caved in, black scorch-marks covering the walls of the house and the exterior buildings. The glass windows on the side of the house we were facing had blown out, sparkling shards of glass glinting at us from the ground.

Trev stepped close to me. Reading his mind, I knew that he and Machidiel had arrived before us and had already searched the area.

I rubbed at my eyes, fighting the overwhelming urge to scream.

"I can't believe this," I said, sounding forlorn even to my own ears.

Trev nodded, remaining silent.

"We should be living here in peace, going to classes, developing our skills . . . living like normal people." I looked down as Zach linked his fingers through mine. "Instead, we're part of some mythical battle that I don't even understand. Lilith wants the

Dagger of Lex to open Hell's Gates, Asmodeus wants me; his own personal key to open up a portal into Heaven to escape the apocalypse, and Mnemosyne and the horsemen want the Falchion for some unknown reason. Our leader is in the hands of our enemies being tortured, our healer is tapped out, and who knows if what we know is even what we know—having someone alter our memories at her every whim certainly isn't helping."

"Breathe," Zach urged, his black eyes swallowing me whole.

"Zach, there's too much going on." I struggled to catch my breath. My heart was racing, my body taking on a panicked edge.

His lips met mine, his tongue sweeping inside as he thoroughly distracted me by ravishing my mouth. A moment later, I was breathless for another reason.

"Better?" he asked, licking his lips.

I took a deep breath and nodded. "Much."

"Let's get Haamiah back and he can sort all of that crap out," he said.

"Okay. That sounds good," I agreed, trying to smile.

"It's in the attic?" he asked.

I grimaced and looked up at the house dubiously. Judging by the missing roof and scorched wall, I could safely presume that the inside was worse.

Zach and Machidiel headed up the garden, jumping the stone steps to the verandah. Trev and I followed slowly. Listening sneakily, I knew that Trev was eager for a fight. His adrenaline was rushing through him, his engine was revving and his eyes continually searched for anyone approaching.

I trailed at the back, dreading what I would find inside for a multitude of reasons; the loss of my home, the only place I had ever belonged, worried I would renew the horror of the demonic attack or see any of the dead, and worse than any of that, terrified I wouldn't find what I was looking for.

Trev looked back and noticed I had fallen behind. He took my hand. I gripped his fingers tightly and stepped into him, sliding under his arm.

The glass crunched under our feet as we entered the kitchen, the door hanging off its hinges. The kitchen was a mess; furniture was ripped up and scattered across the room, and the television was lying on its side, beyond repair. Even the walls had been torn apart as though a beast had clawed its way out of them—which we knew had actually happened.

Leaving the kitchen we entered the dark hallway, walking past the charred and broken doors leading to our study rooms and the offices. I followed the angel's example and crept slowly and quietly so as not to awaken any sleeping monsters.

Reaching the staircase, I grimaced. It was completely unusable. The steps were completely gone; the banister snapped and in pieces on what was left of the floor. I turned and looked up at where the staircase should have reached; it was pretty high up, too high for me to jump.

Machidiel grabbed hold of me and thrust me up above him, letting go.

I shrieked as I flew through the air, quickly remembering to reach out and catch hold of the upstairs railing and pull myself onto the floor of the corridor leading to the bedrooms. So much for being quiet. Zach landed next to me a second later, pulling me to my feet, hugging the wall where the floor was less likely to cave in. He snarled at Machidiel as he and Trev landed beside us.

Zach took my hand and pulled me along behind him, throwing one more glare at Machidiel. We jumped over holes and broken floorboards, climbed unsteadily over walls that had collapsed until we passed my bedroom. The door lay broken where it had been smashed in, my belongings scorched. I felt Zach's eyes on me for a moment before he gently tugged me onwards, leaping over a huge hole with me in his arms.

We reached what should have been the narrow, winding staircase leading the way into the attic, only there were piles of rubble in place and an opening up above us. Before Machidiel could repeat his assistance Zach crowded me, placing his hand on my waist and lifted me up. He sat me on his shoulder and I wriggled until I was able to get my knee up and pull myself through the gap. Zach pushed on my foot, letting me use him as leverage to power through.

I crawled into the room, kneeling on the wooden beams—the only part of the floor remaining intact. Zach heaved his body through the hole after me and sat on the edge, watching.

I crawled towards the middle of the room where the beam I knew the Falchion was in still remained, despite being incredibly charred. I tucked my feet under me and rose up, my legs trembling. I reached to where I thought the Falchion would be, moving my hand across the wood in search of the blade.

When my fingertips brushed the metal, my whole body almost melted with relief. I closed my hand around the handle and pulled slowly, praying I wouldn't dislodge the beam and bring the entire house crashing down on us.

It slid out with ease and I drew it back, weighing it in my hands. I gasped as heat spread through my palm, shooting up my arm. I couldn't help but smile at my ridiculous thoughts but it felt invigorating and enthralling; holding this angelic weapon in my hands felt like touching a piece of Heaven. This had been created in the Heavens, and now I was holding it.

It was heavy, much heavier than I'd thought it would be. The Falchion had a curved edge and glittering handle. It was so beautiful it deserved to be displayed on a wall in a museum somewhere, not here in this mess, with evil beings fighting over it in their attempt to destroy the world. No, something this beautiful could never fall into their hands; I would find a way to keep it safe.

I turned around and smiled as Zach stared wide-eyed at me, and the beautiful weapon I held. I bit my lip and stepped carefully and slowly in a line toward him, letting him take the handle from me. I crouched down and sat next to him, holding onto his arm as he lowered me down to Trev.

Once he had jumped down beside me, we headed back the way we had come. The whole time I prayed that we wouldn't run into anyone, terrified that now I had the Falchion in my grasp it would be taken from me.

We managed to climb through the upstairs corridor before we heard the first noise. A bang, like the smacking of a door against a wall, echoed through the house. That was all, but it was more than enough to send shivers running up my spine. The creak of floorboards from down beneath us was the next noise to reach us.

Zach grabbed my arm and roughly threw me into my bedroom which we were conveniently standing outside of. Trev and Machidiel pushed in and lifted the dressing table, turning it on its side to cover the gap.

"If you're going to do something with that thing, now would be the ideal time," Machidiel said, stepping back from the blockade.

Zach put it back in my hands, closing my fingers around the hilt. I stared up at him, ripples of anxiety making me shake as I took in the three men facing me expectantly.

"How do I make it work?" I asked.

A crash had Zach backing me into a corner protectively.

"I don't know, just hold it and try to open a portal," he suggested.

"Jas, you'd better do something now!" Trev hissed, leaping away from the doorway.

Zach wrapped his arms around me. "Open a portal anywhere, babe, we can try this later."

Machidiel backed away from our blockade and turned to face me. "Think of Haamiah. Use the Falchion to open the gate. Do it now."

I scowled at the arrogant angel and clenched my fingers tightly around the hilt, my knuckles blanching white with tension.

I reached for the coil of power within me, letting it unravel, pouring out of me as if it could sense the urgency. Mist floated out and sparks flashed, light then dark, black shadows blinking slithering towards me. I sensed a barrier, something viscous preventing me from entering. I tightened my grip on the Falchion of Tabbris, and ran my thumb over the sapphires. I fell forward, landing quite unexpectedly flat on my face, Zach, Trev and Machidiel, landing beside and partially on top of me, still linking hands.

I groaned and rolled over onto my back, shoving Zach off. He quickly scooped me up in his arms.

"Are you okay?"

I groaned again for emphasis. "I'm fine, I think."

I touched my hand to my forehead, wiping away the beads of sweat. I sat up on my own, looking up at Zach as he stood. I held my hand out, smiling when he pulled me up to my feet and tucked me under his arm.

Trev and Machidiel were already standing, checking out their surroundings. Though I had been here before I empathized with them, already feeling short of breath due to the oppressive heat and humid air. My clothes were sticking to me already and I plucked at them, grimacing.

"Which way?" Trev asked.

I turned slowly in a circle. I felt my instinct pulling me towards the left, deeper through the trees into a compact area that didn't look particularly easy to get through. I took a deep breath and headed off, stepping lightly, pushing through the closely-weaved branches.

Zach followed me, hovering protectively over my shoulder. Trev and Machidiel trod silently behind us. We only made it a few meters before a low groan reached my ears. I sprinted forward, not caring about the noise I made as the branches whipped at my skin and ripped at my clothes.

I neared a clearing, the one where I knew I would find the horsemen and I skidded to a halt, hiding behind a thick tree trunk.

"Don't ever do that again," Zach hissed in my ear.

I ignored his warning and peered around, searching in the darkness for figures, shapes or bodies.

"They're there," I hissed.

"Where?"

I turned and frowned at him. "What do you mean? They're right there."

I turned my head back and rested my cheek against the tree, biting my lip as I narrowed my eyes on the four horsemen.

They stood side by side, their backs to us. Haamiah, or at least the outline of his shape, remained covered in shadow, hanging up on the sheer rock face. I could see the metal poles; swords, sticking out of his body, holding him pinned. I listened for his thoughts, hearing nothing in reply. Unconscious or dead, I didn't know.

"Jasmine?"

I pulled my attention away from the horsemen and up at Zach, hearing the annoyance in his voice.

"What?" I scowled.

"I don't see anything."

41

"I have come to believe that caring for myself is not self-indulgent. Caring for myself is an act of survival."'

Audre Lorde.

"What do you mean?" I hissed. "They're right there."

Zach crowded close, his body pressing mine into the bark. He looked down at me.

"There's nothing there."

"They're there; we just can't see them," Machidiel whispered.

I turned my whole body, gasping at him. "What?"

He shrugged. "You're hearing their thoughts, feeling the vibrations of their souls and the mini-portals they surround themselves with. You're the only one who can see them."

"You knew about this?" Zach growled.

Machidiel gave a serene smile. "What are you really asking me? I know the only chance in Hell of getting Haamiah back is to be here, now. I know the only chance of defeating the horsemen is with her."

“You didn't think to mention this before?” I said, turning back to the horsemen.

“She's not doing it. We can't help her.”

“Of course I am,” I hissed. “We haven't come this far just to back down now. Haamiah is *right there*.”

“I can't help you,” Zach said angrily, his eyes flashing. “And I wouldn't know if Haamiah was there or not because I can't see him. We're getting out of here.”

“No.” I wrenched my arm away from him, noting the anxious look on Machidiel's face. “You want to know what I can see? Haamiah is stuck to a wall in the dark, swords stuck through his arms and legs, holding him pinned to a rock behind him. The horsemen are just standing there looking at him.”

My breath froze in my lungs, my heart painfully contracting as another figure moved out of the shadows.

“No!” I gasped at what I saw. I stepped out from behind the tree, only to be pulled back by Zach.

“Are you crazy? What the fuck do you think you're doing?”

I couldn't speak, couldn't explain—couldn't tell him what I had just seen. My body shook in horror with the desperate need to vomit.

“What is it?” Trev hissed as I gagged, bending over to heave.

Zach and Machidiel pushed me into Trev and risked exposure trying to spot what had sent me over the edge.

I dropped to my knees, letting Trev pull me into his chest, offering his comfort and support. Over his shoulder I saw movement. I jumped to my feet and knocked Trev to the floor as I skidded into the bushes, tackling the intruder.

The boy was here. The same one I had met last time. I pinned him to the floor, straddling him. His brown eyes stared up in pain and anguish. His brown hair was matted with blood. I followed the scar down through his eyebrow and cheek.

"What do you want? Why are you spying on us?"

Zach forcibly lifted me off him and he and Machidiel held him on the ground.

"What *she* said," Zach growled.

The boy flinched. "I know why you're here; you're here to get your friends back."

I nodded.

"*Friends*?" Machidiel echoed, the only one to catch the all-important word.

I stood tall, pushing my shoulders down, my chin wobbling. "They have Sam."

Zach and Machidiel turned in slow motion, their eyes widening as they took me in.

Trev looked ill. "No. No way. They can't."

Machidiel stood, backing away from the boy in shock. "No, that's not possible. He was with the lycan; they wouldn't go back on their promise."

"The lycan?" I asked.

Machidiel nodded, looking guilty.

I narrowed my eyes. "You had prior arrangements. You're not talking about Drew promising to keep him safe. Why? When?"

He nodded. "A very long time ago. The lycan have been allies of the angels for decades." He brushed aside Zach's attempt to argue. "A select few angels know of this and had negotiated an agreement with them. Sam shouldn't be here; something's gone wrong."

"I'll say," I said. "Still, it makes no difference; it just means we have two people to save."

"It makes a lot of difference," he snapped. "It means someone has betrayed us."

"Why? Who?" Zach snapped, leaving the boy on the floor to push Machidiel backwards, threatening him.

"I don't know."

"It has to be either the lycan or Elijah, right?" Trev guessed.

I stepped back to the tree trunk I had used as coverage. I reached out with my mind.

Sam? Can you hear me?

I tensed as the horsemen turned to look at each other then, one at a time, turned to look into the trees surrounding them.

Jas? His voice came to me.

I watched as one of the horsemen took two steps towards him and let his fist fly, connecting with Sam's face. He dropped to the ground at their feet.

His consciousness drifted in and out, pain shooting through his face and down his neck.

Traitor.

I heard the words as clearly as if he had spoken them out loud.

I'm coming, I promised.

I turned back to the angels, Trev and the boy, who still reminded me of someone; I just didn't know whom.

"What's the plan?" I asked.

"We get the hell out of here," Zach answered immediately.

"We can't leave Sam." Trev backed away until he stood side by side with me.

"I'm with him," I said, challenging Zach.

Machidiel nodded and pursed his lips to hide a smile. Was he the traitor?

"I'm going to get Haamiah back and I'm going to use my bare hands to rip apart whoever sold us out," I said slowly, carefully enunciating each word.

Machidiel tilted his head slightly, still smiling.

"How do you plan on doing that when we can't see them?" Zach loomed over me, baring his teeth. "You're an idiot if you think you can do this alone."

"What's your plan? I presume you have one." Machidiel crooked his eyebrow.

"She not even twenty-seven human years. Of course she doesn't have a plan to defeat the horsemen," Zach snarled. "The angels have been trying to produce a viable plan for centuries and haven't yet found one which will work."

I bit my lip. "I can connect with each of you telepathically, so I can direct you. Trev will run for Haamiah and free him. He'll get hold of Haamiah and Sam and protect them and I'll open a portal to send them back."

"Not to the safe house, please," Trev cut in. "I don't want to be killed the moment we land."

"Right." I nodded, thinking quickly. "I'll send you to the valkyrie's home. They'll have left someone there to protect the house. Machidiel, Zach and I will take on the horsemen; distract them until Haamiah and Sam are out of here."

"At least you're not fool enough to think you can kill them," Zach muttered.

"It will be easier to direct us if you stay out of the fight," Machidiel added. "It'll split your concentration too much if you're trying to fight as well as give out instructions; you'll only get one or more of us killed."

I nodded, agreeing. "Fine I'll stay where I can see you, but out of range of any immediate danger."

Zach threw me the Falchion. "You'd best hang onto this then." He stepped close and pulled me into him, his lips reaching mine, sucking and biting.

I took a deep breath and watched them creep towards the horsemen, the boy remaining by my side.

Okay, Zach, head left, and Machidiel go right; split their focus.

I watched Zach creep to the left and I made him wait, crouched in the darkness until one of the horsemen stepped out of reach of the others.

One, two . . .

The angels exploded into action. Zach missed the first punch but caught him on the second; he slid to the right and whipped his sword around to slice at another that swooped in joining the fight. He kicked at the horseman, sending him flying onto his back through the trees. Machidiel jumped over the hooded figure as he flew past, his sword clashing with another horseman's a thousand times a minute.

I couldn't keep up; Zach seemed to have developed a sense of where they were, knowing instinctively when they were narrowing in on him, while Machidiel was just fighting for his life.

I directed Trev around the edge of the battle, relieved when he reached Haamiah. He stepped up, using the cracks to rise up and reach the swords pinning Haamiah to the wall. With my heart in my mouth, I watched him heave, struggling to release our leader.

I'll help him. Just don't attack me again.

I spun around, facing the boy. He held his hands up to me submissively. I nodded and let him rush past into the trees, along the line of fighting. He reached Trev and pulled with him, letting the fall to the floor in a mass of blood.

I concentrated on Zach.

Coming in from the left. Move!

I shivered as Zach narrowly missed being skewered.

Get Sam and Haamiah away from the fight, I ordered Trev.

I screamed as Zach was hit in the chest and was thrown against the rock wall. Unconscious, he dropped to the floor.

I didn't think, only reacted.

I ran, lighting myself up and jumped. I hurtled through the air, clutching the rock wall and dropped down to land between Zach and the horsemen. I lifted the Falchion in front of me, letting my fire engulf it.

"Now it's my turn," I hissed.

The first horseman rushed at me, a thick blade aimed at my head. I ducked, letting it sink into the rock. I waited and spun at the last minute, letting a second blade glance off the Falchion. I hit it blow for blow, smiling as lightning erupted in the sky above us, crackling with the intensity of my emotions. I kept moving, spinning and ducking, trading one horseman for another.

"Switch," Machidiel shouted.

He jumped close and bent over, letting me roll over his back to face the horsemen on his side.

"Stop! I delivered the Dagger of Lex to you: I want my son."

A familiar voice screamed out over the battle. The horsemen paused, turning their heads in unison to take in the person who had shouted.

Elijah.

Traitor.

My mouth dropped open as I took in the angel as he stood at the edge of the clearing.

"Where is my son? We had a deal," he shouted.

One of the horsemen pointed to the boy standing beside Trev, the boy who was helping Sam to stand.

That was Elijah's son? The healer had betrayed us, made a deal with these soulless creatures for him?

"That's right, darling. The Dagger and now the Falchion are mine," a strong, feminine voice whispered behind me.

I spun around, bringing up the Falchion to meet Lilith's sword. We pressed them tightly together, matched for strength. I stepped to the side, bringing the Falchion down to slice her fingers. She shrieked and hit at my sword, knocking me aside, then punched me in the face.

I spun away and jumped, throwing a kick at her. I kicked high enough to land it her in the face, grinning angrily. I would have my vengeance.

I spotted the horsemen narrowing in on Machidiel.

They're both on your left, sword coming at you . . . now! I screamed in my mind.

I ducked and dived onto the floor as one horseman and the Queen of the Damned attacked me at the same time. I rolled over and flipped up to my feet, lunging at Lilith with my Falchion. I was knocked to my knees, and when I looked up my heart plunged. Demons rolled out of the trees, snapping and clicking their teeth, eager to kill.

There were too many. Everywhere I looked they stood ready, leaning forward to scent the blood being spilled. One, too excited to refrain, jumped into the fight, roaring at me as it hit me in the face with one giant, clawed paw.

I rolled on the floor, spitting blood out of my mouth. I looked up just as it reached for me, screaming as it was knocked aside by someone else jumping into the fray; a murderous flash of tattoos and blond hair . . . Caleb.

I grinned and hit out with the Falchion, trying not to let my relief and glee distract me. All around, flashes of purple and green and red, gorgeous valkyrie joined the fight, flinging knives at the horsemen. Howls began to ring around us, loud and terrifying to anyone but me. The lycan leaped out of the trees and poured into the clearing, snapping their teeth. I took a second to beam at the fighting going on around me. The witches had to have found a way to send them here, as there weren't any other angelic portal users on the human plane

I was caught by one of the horsemen; it was my fault for losing concentration. He belted me in the stomach and threw me up in the air, bringing me down hard against his leg. My body groaned as bones cracked, pain flooding my senses.

My vision blurred, gray sparkles appearing as my eyes seemed to explode. I gasped, completely unaware of anything but pain. There was nothing else.

42

"To be nobody but yourself in a world that's doing its best to make you somebody else, is to fight the hardest battle you are ever going to fight. Never stop fighting."

E. E. Cummings.

Gabriel

Twenty-six years ago

Jophiel peered down the dark stairs into the blackness of the dungeons. She listened carefully for voices or footsteps. Hearing none, she descended the hundred steps into the darkness, feeling her way with her hands, following the wall downwards.

After what seemed like an hour, she reached the bottom. Having never been here before, her heart froze with fear. Give her an army of fallen angels, dragons or demons and she would confront them with glee, but this . . . this was terrifying.

The dungeon was vast, with metal cages running down both sides and a small opening on both sides leading to more cells. Lit torches were held on sconces on the walls, out of reach of anyone in the cages. Eyes sparkled out from the darkness, silent prisoners held for centuries, angels accused of treason, murder and deceit, and some proven of it.

Jophiel moved into the room, careful not to make any noise as she swept past the cages, peering into them though not getting too close. She searched those closest to the steps and tiptoed down the opening on the left to view more cages.

She followed the path to the very end, not seeing her.

"Jophiel?" a weak voice called out.

Jophiel spun around. "Where are you?" she hissed.

She followed Gabriel's directions to the furthermost cage: the darkest and coldest.

"Oh my God, I have to get you out of here," she cried as she saw the bare cage with only a pile of blankets on the floor for comfort.

"If you're planning on breaking her free, any chance you can bust me out too?" a lazy voice said.

Jophiel peered into the cage next to her sister's. Machidiel, a friend of Zacharael's, was also incarcerated.

"Why are you in here?" she whispered.

"Running with the wrong crowd, as usual." He laughed.

He was so weird. Jophiel shook her head and turned to Gabriel. "How can I get you out?"

"Whoa, I wasn't finished. Aren't you interested in who I've been running with?" Machidiel wrapped his hands around the bars of the cage, peering through at Jophiel.

"Not especially, no," she replied.

"I've been running with lycan," he said, ignoring her.

Laura Prior

"And? What's your point?"

"Don't you think it's odd, an angel friends with a lycan?"

She scowled and shook her head. "No, not really."

He paused, and that slight shift in his arrogant persona was just enough to capture her attention.

He glanced slyly at Gabriel, cocking his eyebrow. "You might just have a chance of pulling this off, Gabe."

Jophiel looked shocked. "Since when have you two been friends?"

She bit her lip. "I wouldn't necessarily say friends, more colleagues."

"You're working together? On what?"

Gabriel made a noise of irritation low in her throat. "There's no time for this: listen to me. You need to find Lady Vista. You need to find her and tell her what has happened. Ask her to show you the way."

"The way to what?"

"To unite the armies."

Jophiel shook her head, afraid. "No, that's your job. Don't lose hope; I'll free you."

"Make sure you find the oracle first," Gabriel hissed. "Go! Before they find you here."

"I can't leave you here," Jophiel trembled, clutching Gabriel's hands through the bars.

"You have to. You can't help me yet. You need to go, now."

"*Gabriel*," Jophiel whispered desperately, tears flooding her eyes.

"Be brave, Jophie. I know you're strong. This is your time. I know you'll make me proud. Gabriel leaned close, kissing Jophiel's forehead through the bars.

Jophiel stepped away from the edge of the cage and turned away, fleeing into the darkness.

Machidiel stepped back, turning to the cage beside him. "Well?"

The lycan there shifted slightly, a glimmer of movement in the darkness. "It sounds promising. Are you sure she will honor an alliance?"

Machidiel moved, letting Gabriel peer through the bars at their fellow prisoner. "If your pack do as you promise, she will honor an alliance," she said. "Are you sure the lycan you have in mind will do it? If he backs out or changes his mind at the last minute, we'll all be doomed."

The lycan scowled. "The lycan we are talking about is my son, and he will never go back on his word. Our souls will rest safe once again."

Gabriel nodded sadly, one lonely tear rolling slowly down her cheek. "I can only hope she forgives us for what we're going to do. I'd be very surprised if we get out of this alive, never mind with our souls intact."

***

Hours later, Jophiel had entered another realm known as a playground for immortals. Here, vampires, fallen angels, witches, elves and every other species converged together in relative safety, drinking, cavorting, and sharing secrets.

One place in particular was a draw for the otherworldly: a gothic mansion, a stone's throw from the sea, was home to the beginning of many a coup, and to one of the most powerful and unshakable oracles in all of existence.

Jophiel subtly worked her way through the room until she spotted the woman she was looking for: Lady Vista, one of the most accurate seers in all the realms, and one used by all manner of creatures. Typically she was shunned by the angels – being *other*—but right now, she was Jophiel's last option.

Lady Vista was walking through the crowd of immortals, not speaking to anyone, but observing them as though she were in a zoo. She was a typical immortal beauty, wearing a completely see-through gown. Everything was on show from nipples to ass; another reason the angels generally shunned her and her hangers-on.

Jophiel took a deep breath and pushed her way through the crowd until she reached the oracle's side. The oracle stopped and turned to face her, looking down at Jophiel with a curved smile.

"I've been waiting for you."

Jophiel rolled her eyes. *Duh, otherwise she would be a pretty rubbish oracle.*

"I need to know something," she said hesitantly.

The oracle crooked her eyebrow.

"You know why I'm here, so get on with it," Jophiel said angrily, crossing her arms.

It took a while, but eventually the oracle smiled, and gestured for the angel to follow her. She led the way through the hall, the crowds parting for them without a word or a look, and she made her way up the staircase at the back of the room, trailing her hand along the bannister.

Checking to make sure Jophiel was following, she walked down a dark corridor, lit only by one candle, and she pushed a door open at the very end.

Jophiel cautiously followed, closing the door behind her as she looked around the room. It was small, decorated with materials of every sort: velvet and silk drapes hanging from the ceiling, marble floors, woolen cushions on sequined chairs. In the middle of the room there was a very low table set only inches up from the floor, with a blue ball balanced in the middle; a crystal seeing-ball, of course.

Lady Vista sauntered to the ball and pulled up her dress slightly, kneeling beside it. Jophiel paused, thinking through her options. There really weren't any. With Gabriel locked up, she owed it to her to find out what was going on. The reason Gabriel couldn't just confide in her and spill her secrets would be revealed to her one way or another.

"Fine," she muttered, kneeling on the opposite side of the ball.

"Put your hand over the ball. Don't touch it; let it touch you," Lady Vista said softly.

Jophiel rolled her eyes and quickly put her hand over the ball. Within seconds she felt a sucking sensation at the palm of her hand. She grimaced and tried to keep her hand still, gasping when it was forcibly sucked down onto the ball.

Mist covered her eyes, a gray cloud covering her entire vision until she wasn't looking at the oracle or the ball any longer. She couldn't even feel the ball touching her skin.

She seemed to materialize in a forest. The only telltale sign of it being a vision was the shiny glimmer of the trees. She jumped, goose bumps rolling up and down her flesh when huge black eyes blinked at her. Of course Lady Vista was there too; it was her vision after all.

Jophiel waited and waited, but nothing else appeared. She was running out of time; every second she wasted here, her sister was rotting in that dungeon.

"I need to see what happens. Show me," she cried. "I demand it. You will obey."

The outline of a figure flashed on the floor. Jophiel frowned and narrowed her eyes. It was a boy; unremarkable really, just a boy the same as millions of others, only this one . . . was dead. She stiffened as she took in his chest wound. She turned, another image flickering at her, demanding attention. This one was alive and very familiar.

Zacharael swung his sword across his body in desperation, warding off the demons attacking him. He roared in anger as a wound appeared across his arm, blood spraying out.

In the vision, Jophiel clapped her hand to her mouth, her heart pounding in terror. What was happening? She searched for others; where were the other angels? Where were the warriors helping him?

There was no one; he was alone.

"Why is he alone? Where are the others?" Jophiel hissed.

As a sword penetrated his chest and he fell to the ground. Jophiel was ejected from the vision, *violently*. She flew across the room, hitting the wall with a crash, smashing the tiles beneath her, and slid to the floor.

She lifted her trembling hand to her mouth and lightly touched her lips, the vibrations of her terror running through her body.

"Jophiel . . ." the oracle said gently. She knelt beside her, took her hand and squeezed.

She shook her head, slowly at first, then the denial exploded from her. "No! No, that can't happen. Make it stop!"

She leaped to her feet and began to pace, the oracle quickly moving out of her way.

"You've seen the future. I have no say in it."

Jophiel pushed the oracle with both hands, slamming her against the wall. "There has to be a way to stop it."

"There might be a way," the oracle said hesitantly, a crease forming between her eyes.

Jophiel spun and dropped to her knees before her. Pleading, she took the other woman's large hands in her own small ones and gripped them tightly while gazing up into her eyes.

"Please. Tell me what to do. What was Gabriel going to do? I know she had a plan."

"What did she tell you?"

Jophiel bit her lip. "She wanted me to take in a nephilim, look after him until he could take care of himself and to cover for her while she went to the human plane to . . ." she glanced around suspiciously. Gritting her teeth, she continued, ". . . form *one* army."

"As in, unite the species? Say, isn't that against everything the angels stand for?" Lady Vista asked with a grin, flashing her white teeth.

Jophiel sniffed. "Tell me what to do. Gabriel's no longer in on this. She's going to be *detained* for a while."

The oracle bit her lip and took a deep breath. Focusing on Jophiel's beautiful face, on the trembling of her lips, the flush of her cheeks and the tears in her eyes, she sighed. "It's about the angel isn't it? You were shocked about the boy, but you didn't really care about *him*."

"Tell me what to do. Tell me how to save him." Jophiel demanded.

"Would you give up everything you know? Would you give up *everyone* you know, to save that angel?"

Jophiel met her eye for eye, lifting her chin and stiffening her spine in resolve. "Without a second thought."

Lady Vista bit her lip and nervously stared at Jophiel. "If you do this, he will never appreciate you for who you are. He will never know you. You'd really give up everything for someone who doesn't know you?"

Jophiel nodded. "I would."

The oracle cast her eyes downward in defeat. "Then there is a way. But, the odds will be stacked against you, you will face the worst of humanity, and you may never find yourself again or recover what you will have lost."

Jophiel's chin wobbled as she tried to smile, trying to hold on to the hope that she could save Zacharael. "I accept that."

"Very well." She stepped back and began to turn away from her. "May I ask why? When all he has done is show you disdain, why would you sacrifice yourself for him?"

Jophiel took a deep breath and forced a smile. "He's my soul mate."

***

Back in the heavenly realm, Gabriel's allies had soon accosted Jophiel. Haamiah had promised to take care of the nephilim boy Jophiel had been planning on raising, and he had made her memorize the names of their allies on the human plane. Jophiel had been shocked and more than a little disturbed to realize Gabriel had *colleagues* among even the most unsavory of species. With names and places stored in her head, despite warnings that she might not remember them, she headed off for a terrifying future which would likely end up in death. . . . *hers*.

With promises made to Gabriel and secret goodbyes said to her friends, Jophiel crouched behind a pillar in the heavenly reception hall, watching as Zacharael stormed through on his way back from a battle on the human plane.

Her eyes drawn to him, she sighed, her heart breaking. "Why am I so afraid to lose you when you're not even mine?" she whispered.

When he was gone and the hall was once more empty, she stepped out from behind the pillar and ran towards the gate.

"Jophiel, stop!"

She spun around, alarmed at the sound of Raphael's voice. "I know what you're doing; Gabriel told me. Trust me when I say she'll pay for putting this nonsense in your head," he shouted from the top of the hall.

"Leave her out of this. You can't stop me from going." Jophiel continued to walk backwards, looking behind her to see how close she was to the gate in case Raphael tried to forcibly stop her.

"You don't know what you're doing. You can't do this. Your past, present and future remains here in the heavenly realm. Your duty is here with us," Raphael argued, beginning to run towards her.

"I'm going and you can't stop me, Raph," Jophiel shouted, leaping away to put a distance between them.

"Don't do this! You'll condemn yourself to hell; you'll never come back here. You're going to die," he threatened, his eyes wide with anxiety.

Jophiel sprinted to the gate, wrenching it open. She turned back as Raphael neared, resolution and anger in his expression. Her heart was torn in two. She felt ill, as though she were drowning. "I love you, brother, but you know my name, not my story," she said. She looked at him one last time as he sprinted for her in desperation and panic, and she leaped through the gates.

Laura Prior

43

"Be who you were created to be, and you will set the world on fire."

St. Catherine of Sienna.

I lay panting on the ground, my legs spread out, one arm twisted beneath me. My breath was shallow and light, though it sounded loud in my ears.

I needed to save him. *Zach.* My angel. And now I knew what everyone had been telling me to remember: I was Jophiel, an archangel who had given up everything and everyone in her life to save her soul mate. And I wasn't about to fail now.

I twisted the ring around my finger. It was still subduing my powers, but now I knew what I could do, now I remembered who I was, now I knew my secrets and the secrets the lycan and Machidiel had been keeping from me, I didn't need it anymore. I let it slide down my finger, giving it a little push with my thumb. Pure power roared through me.

I opened my eyes as a shining line of metal came down directly to my face. I lifted the Falchion and stopped it. I kicked out with my leg, knocking Lilith down beside me.

She glared at me, pausing slightly to appraise me . . . *seeing* who I was, or at the very least, seeing that there was something different about me.

My body shook with the force of magic that flowed through it freely, literally sizzled with heat, and my eyes rolled back in my head, almost orgasming over the strength pouring from deep within. The air shimmered around me, vibrating off my skin.

I grinned. "That's right. I've remembered who I am, and you *should* be afraid."

She rolled away, knocking the Falchion out of my hands, and we came at each other in a flurry of fists, punching and beating at each other. All around, savage roars and shrieks echoed and I could see the animosity of it all combined, the horror it protracted, reflected in Lilith's worried eyes.

I let my rage explode around me, my fire heating until blue ripples covered my skin. I shrieked and leaped on top of her, pounding my fists into her face. I shrieked with euphoria as blood spurted from her mouth and eye. I leaned close and breathed my flames into her mouth, relishing the way she screamed.

She threw me off her, and I rolled to the side. I found my feet first and swung the Falchion at her, slicing cleanly through her neck, watching dispassionately as her head rolled on the floor.

The horsemen turned to face me, shrieking together in one terrifying squeal before disappearing, dissolving into their own portals.

I dropped to my knees and then onto my chest, lying on the ground, panting. I let the flames subside, feeling completely depleted of all strength. I could see the fight subsiding rapidly; with Lilith dead and the horsemen gone, the demons quickly fled or were killed by the valkyrie and the lycan.

I closed my eyes and let my body rest for a moment. What did I do now? What would Zach do, now that it was over? We had the Falchion and the Dagger, and I had killed Lilith. There were still the horsemen, Mnemosyne and Asmodeus to bring down, but hopefully that would be the end of it.

My mind ticked over and I felt a sliver of doubt slicing through me. I hoped the horsemen wouldn't attempt the apocalypse on their own. I had been sure Lilith was the ringleader, but what if she wasn't? Of course, there were other more immediate problems to be dealt with, too. Elijah was a traitor, and the boy was his son. No matter what his reasons were, no matter that he clearly would do and had done anything to keep his family safe, I would never be able to forgive him for trading Sam to the horsemen and Lilith. I would never trust him again.

However, Haamiah needed to be healed, as did Zach; would he heal them? I could attempt it myself . . . only I was a little tapped out.

Another thing to be discussed . . . I was Jophiel, an archangel. Or at least, I had been, in a past life. I wasn't fool enough to think it meant anything would change in terms of my acceptance or my *cool* factor; it was a past life, after all. Also, it wasn't as if I felt like I were her, more that I was watching a movie. I knew the story and I knew I was actually there, but it wasn't really me. Not *me* me. Though Zach had hated me—no, *her*—in that life, it shouldn't change anything in this one. He was still my soul mate.

I turned my head to look for him, frowning when I saw Sam nearing me in a state of panic.

"God, Jasmine, are you okay?" he cried.

Laura Prior

"I'm okay," I reassured him. "Where's Zach? I need to see him."

Sam's face paled, sweat beading on his forehead. His eyes looked at me in horror.

I groaned, forcing myself to sit up. "What? What's wrong?"

It didn't even occur to me that something could be wrong with Zach until I read it in his mind.

I was up on my feet, broken bones and torn muscles but silent memories as I ran as fast as I could possibly run towards the dark shape lying on the ground beside Machidiel and Trev.

I skidded on the floor beside him. I cradled his head in my lap and leaned across his chest, placing one palm over his heart where a gaping wound split his flesh open. I drew on my power, feeling it sizzle and tingle as it poured through my fingertips into his body. I knew it was circulating, connected to it and him as I was, but there was no reaction. My emotions froze, disappearing. I could see and feel nothing, could only focus on healing him.

His wounds continued to ooze. His chest remained still, his lips unmoving.

"Breathe!" I screamed. I pressed both hands to his body and strained, pushing my mist into him.

"It's not working," I shrieked at Haamiah. "Elijah, help me! Heal him!"

He dropped to his knees beside me. "I can't," he whispered, his face ashen.

"Heal him now, or I swear to the Gods I will rip you apart," I swore, my eyes flashing hot with anger.

"He's gone. His soul is already gone. There's nothing to heal; he's gone," he said.

Denied.

I shook my head and focused, concentrating on the familiar feeling of my power swirling around inside me. He wasn't dead; he wasn't. Just a few minutes more and he would be fine. I just needed some help. Out of everyone here, someone could do something. Why wouldn't anyone help me? Even if they hated me, Zach was one of *them*.

I felt the presence of someone too close to me, brushing against my arm, and was about to let my rage loose when I felt Sam's calming presence in my mind. I needed air, I needed space. Zach *needed* to open his eyes.

Zach's body began to shake. I hissed in a breath, hope springing to life, burning with acidity through my gut before my head caught up with my eyes. I stilled, watching as Sam began CPR, pounding on Zach's chest.

I carefully slid Zach's head down my thighs and rested him on the grass. Sam leaned over and blew air into his mouth once, twice, then continued compressions.

It went on and on with no change.

There was something else. I turned to Trev. "Do it," I growled, rage living and breathing inside of me. I held his eyes with mine, still, uncompromising, forcing my will into his. He wouldn't deny me this.

He didn't ask for confirmation or clarification, only knelt beside me and leaned close.

The lycan and valkyrie pushed the angels that protested back, blocking their view and protecting us. I was vaguely aware of my army of beings keeping me in the center of their protective bubble, but it meant nothing to me at the moment. Trev sank his teeth into Zach's arm, drawing deeply. He swallowed again and again. He pulled up and met my gaze only once before sinking his teeth into Zach's neck to speed up the process. He needed to consume more blood and it needed to be quick. Zach was fading, I could feel his essence slipping away, his soul pulling away from mine.

Trev took the blade I held out and slit his wrist deeply, severing veins and arteries. He gasped as he did so but leaned over, holding his cut arm aloft, dripping the blood into Zach's mouth.

It was such a slow process. I could almost feel each bloody drop hit his mouth, trailing down his face onto the grass. I took his jaw in my hands and opened his mouth; it wasn't difficult. His jaw was slack and fell open with ease. I watched with satisfaction as Trev's vampire blood poured into Zach's mouth until his cut began to heal itself, the trail of blood slowing and eventually stopping. Trev swayed and sat back in the grass.

We waited and waited and waited. There were no more protests from the angels who were disgusted by what we had just done. They waited just as the rest of us did for Zach to open his eyes. The silence was deafening. There were no birds chirping, no trees swaying, no bellowing of monsters in the forest.

I stared at the love of my life, all of my hope teetering on the brink of collapse. He would wake up; any moment now he would wake up and take me in his arms and tell me he loved me. Or, more likely, he would make some sarcastic comment about me forcing vampire blood down his throat, but he would be alive. His black eyes would look into my mine and I would feel his soul connecting with mine.

Just one more minute . . . and another one.

Nothing happened. He was gone. Even when I win, I still lose.

Zach . . . was gone.

To be continued . . .

ABOUT THE AUTHOR

Laura Prior grew up in the north-east of England, and has travelled the world while working as a nurse. She is currently living and working in Melbourne, Australia, with her partner. She enjoys snowboarding, long walks, shoe-shopping and cocktails. She loves reading passionate novels with strong female characters.

Find me:

www.facebook.com/fallingforanangel

Twitter @falling4anangel

www.laurapriorbooks.com

Made in the USA
Charleston, SC
09 June 2014